JADED Hearts

HARPER SLOAN

Cover Design by Sommer Stein with Perfect Pear Creative Covers
Cover Photography by Perrywinkle Photography
Editing by Jenny Sims with Editing4Indies
Formatting by Champagne Formats

Loaded Replay PLAYLIST

"Speakers" by Sam Hunt
"Wake Me Up" by Avicii
"Addicted" by Saving Abel
"Trumpets" by Jason Derulo
"Jealous" by Nick Jonas
"Free Bird" by Lynyrd Skynyrd
"In Your Arms" by Nico & Vinz
"Steal My Girl" by One Direction
"First in Line" by Matthew Mayfield
"Done" by The Band Perry
"Love Me Like You Do" by Ellie Goulding

Listen to the *Jaded Hearts* playlist on Spotify

Dedication

TO THE READERS.
This is for you.
For your patience and understanding.
Your love for my work and unwavering support fuel my dreams.
Thank you for believing in me and making each new world we
journey through together even more memorable than the last.

To Contact Harper

Email: Authorharpersloan@gmail.com
Website: www.authorharpersloan.com
Facebook: www.facebook.com/harpersloanbooks

Other Books by Harper Sloan:

Corps Security Series:
Axel
Cage
Beck
Uncaged
Cooper
Locke

Hope Town Series:
Unexpected Fate
Bleeding Love
When I'm with You

Standalone Novel:
Perfectly Imperfect

Coming Home Series:
Lost Rider – Coming April 25, 2017
Kiss My Boots – Coming August 29, 2017

Disclaimer:

This book is not suitable for younger readers due to strong language
and adult situations.

Prologue

Signing with the record company of our dreams should have been the best thing that ever happened to us.

And it was ... for a short while anyway.

While the glitz and glamour of fame's promise was shining as brightly as our stage lights, we could forget where we came from and live in the glory. The money bought us every happiness we ever craved. Those false securities that you think will make your life better. The instant friends, lovers—you name it—would do whatever we asked just to spend a second in our presence.

We had it all.

The only problem was those quiet moments between the insanity. When reality slapped us in the face that all we really had—all we could count on—were each other.

My brother, Weston, is the only constant I've ever had in my life. I know he will never let me down and will always be my biggest supporter. We grew up with parents who hated us. Really … it sounds ridiculous; the notion that parents could hate their children, but ours did … no, do. They made no secret of it when we were younger, and they continue to attempt to pick at our very souls like the vultures they are.

My earliest memory of them is somewhere around third or fourth grade. That was the year that they seemed hell-bent on reminding us that we had ruined it all for them. Constant screams and verbal lashings.

According to them, *they* were on the edge of fame. Then we came along, and it all went downhill. Even now, I still don't understand how they came up with that logic. How *we* were to blame for *their* reckless behavior. The same reckless behavior that, in reality, had ruined whatever path they might have traveled. It had nothing to do with us, but to them, we were essentially their bad luck.

When we hit middle school, it got worse, but only because they knew that they could leave us for long periods and we wouldn't die.

Our parents, like us, were born to be stars … or at least, they assumed they were, and they had no qualms about reminding us of that fact daily. Unfortunately, they lacked the drive and ambition needed to strive for everything they ever wanted. At the first challenge thrown in their path, they decided to take the low road full of scavengers and sinners.

Like I said, vultures through and through.

Our dad knocked up Mom in the early eighties when big hair rock bands were all the rage, and *theirs* was seconds away from signing the record deal that would make their careers.

Then they found out about *us*.

The twins who ruined it all.

And all those long nights, performing in whatever local hole they could find and bouncing from town to town, just waiting for their big break, were washed away.

Mom was no longer the singer who men lusted over. Not when we ruined her body. And our dad was so deep in the bottle I'm sure he didn't realize he was swimming in it. Again, something else blamed on us.

When their band fell apart, they decided hating us was almost easier than hating each other. They had a common goal in their blame, and right or wrong, we would never be anything other than a reminder of why they weren't living their dream.

Their bandmates obviously didn't share the same bond that Weston and I have with Jamison and Luke. God forbid I ever found myself in a position like my parents had been in, but I know my boys would band together, and the show would go on.

Because for us, this is it.

This is our future's promise of a better life, and even if it's starting to look like more of a curse than a promise to me, we will die before we give it up.

Unfortunately for me, I'm pretty sure there are a few people who would love to make that happen.

I'm getting ahead of myself. You're probably wondering, who

am I?

I'm no stranger to you. I'm on every magazine cover. You open social media, and I guarantee you a sponsored post exists about my group. Turn on the radio, and boom—there we are.

I'm everywhere.

I'm Wrenlee Davenport, lead singer of Loaded Replay. I've learned the hard way that plenty of people in the world would love to have a piece of me, but they don't give one shit about the person behind the voice.

They see the persona. The record label loves to market the *fake* me as the sexy singer with the body of a sinner and the voice of a saint. But for me—I'm probably always going to be that stupid little girl who believes my prince charming will come riding in on his black horse—because really, black horses are so much more badass than white ones—and prove to me that every little jaded piece of my heart is worth loving.

And *he* will love me for me.

For *Wren*.

Not the *Wrenlee* who, more times than I care to admit, has had to drink myself stupid just to face my fucking life.

Yeah … fame and fortune are nowhere near anything I ever dreamed it would be like.

It's my own personal hell, and I pray that something or someone is out there who can prove to me that the world isn't screwed because the majority of humanity is too busy licking the windows on the outside to see the beauty behind it. All they care about is what's at face value when what matters is skin-deep.

I should feel bad for Prince Charming. My knight in tarnished armor. Because he'll have one giant battle on his hands to make me believe that someone might be left out there who doesn't just want a piece of me.

Chapter 1

Wrenlee

"**G**ood morning, LA! This is Alice—you know, the better half of Brice and Alice in the morning—and today, we have a special treat for you all." The overly chipper voice of the female radio personality coming through my laptop's speakers instantly causes me to cringe. That could be more from the hangover I'm struggling with than the fact that she's all happy and preppy, but it's more likely because I've always suspected deliriously happy people hid something evil under all that pep.

"That's right, Alice; this morning, we finally get to share the much-anticipated single from Loaded Replay's new album, *Black Lace*. For months now, we've been waiting for this one, and I have to say it doesn't disappoint."

"Of course, fans are still going nuts over their last single when guitarist Weston Davenport stepped out of the shadows to perform. Who knew that man could seduce a woman with just his voice!" I look over at Wes and roll my eyes. He just shakes his head as his shoulders move with silent laughter.

"I think you're getting a little carried away there." Her partner in crime chuckles through the speakers. "Maybe wipe some of that drool? Let's get back to the big news, and that is all about their new album."

Yes … let us get back to that. I just barely resist the urge to roll my eyes. I'm sure this is when they'll start their normal gushing bullshit session. Just like every other radio show. It's almost as if they follow some sort of manual when it comes to this PR bullshit.

"For the listeners who have been living under a rock, Loaded Replay is arguably the first band of its time that has successfully created a new genre of music. Sure, many have tried, but they lacked the staying power and raw talent that these four have in spades. They managed to marry sounds that are eerie to the late seventies classic rock and eighties rock and roll, while at the same time adding their own unique twist. Of course, a lot of that is attributed to the unique sound of the one and only Wrenlee Davenport, lead singer of Loaded Replay. That voice of hers has a gritty rasp that will give you chills. Of course, she's so hot I'm sure she could get away with sounding terrible outside of the recording studio, and people would still flock to them. And just in case you're wondering, she doesn't sound terrible. I've seen them live five times now, and I'm still blown away each time at the pure perfection of that girl."

And cue the eye roll. I'm pretty sure if they roll any more than they are right now, they might just pop right out of my damn head and out of the room. It's the same old song and dance. They talk more about how I look and pair that with our success than they do about the fact we really are just that talented.

"I don't think just having her pretty face at the forefront is the reason that they've won numerous Grammys, AMAs, and so on, though, Brice."

Point one for the annoying tool.

"Yeah, well, with a face like that, do you really think it isn't part of their charm, Alice?"

A tan, thickly muscled forearm reaches forward and snaps my laptop shut, cutting off the morning show banter before they can piss me off even more. I close my eyes and count to ten, so I don't give Weston a bitchy attitude he doesn't need, deserve, or want.

I've been on edge for the past few weeks—something that my bandmates have unfortunately been on the receiving end of. I can't pinpoint exactly what feels off, other than the fact we're prisoners in our own life. Things I once found beautiful about our life are now just dull and lifeless. I crave normalcy, even though realistically, I know I will never feel that again. I just want a break. A break from it all where I can lock myself away at home and try to find what I lost in the last few years—the reason I eat, sleep, and breath. My love of the music.

"How long are you going to have a giant stick up your ass, Wren?" His lips curl up, and I can't help but smile back at his handsome face.

Weston and I have always been close, and honestly, he's probably the only one who could call me on my shit without getting a boot up his ass. It doesn't hurt that, as my twin brother, he's older by twelve minutes, and he never lets me forget it. Even if we didn't have the twin bond, what we share is unbreakable and unconditional.

Only two other people could get away with that kind of crap with me.

"I'm just tired, Wes," I lie, hoping he doesn't press for more.

"Yeah, you've been tired for a while now, Wren. I get it; we all are. Just say the word. If you need a break, I'll talk to Dix and make it happen."

"You know just as well as I do that we don't have a break coming for a while. Not with *Black Lace* about to release, the tour almost through, and the label negotiations to re-sign falling all at the same time. Not to mention, they're already beginning to hound us to start recording the next album, assuming it's a done deal that we'll stay with them." I stop talking because if anyone understands how crazy things have been lately, it's Wes.

"Think you forgot one important item for that to-do list,

little sister." He leans back and pulls his neck from side to side; the disgusting sounds of his bones cracking fill the living room.

"Yeah? And what's that?"

Once again, his lips tip up, but this time, I know it's not in humor. It's because he knows he has something hanging over my head. "Don't think you're getting out of it this time. Even Jamison agrees that it's time to step up our security team. Getting his cocky ass to see how serious things are should be sign enough for you. That last asshole almost got you killed, Wren. No way am I playing games when it comes to your life. It's time to get some security that's worth a shit." He's silent for a beat, and then he whispers, low enough that I almost miss it, "You're all I have left."

He's right, but he's wrong too. We're all we have left as far as blood family goes. Our parents might still be alive, but they lost the right to be called family a long time ago. The guys, Jamison and Luke, are our family, but no matter how close the four of us are, the bond that Wes and I have will always be the most solid— and most valuable.

"How about this ... how about you and whoever else you feel is going to need to approve this next round of silent, broody, old men parading as security just sit down and pick someone? We both know that whoever the label sends over is never going to be worth a shit. I think the last group was just out of high school, Wes. Plus, it's not like they even talk to me anyway, so what's the difference if I'm there or not? They know the deal and what they're up against. That's all that matters, right?"

Wes sighs deeply, stands from the couch, and walks over to

the floor-to-ceiling windows of our hotel suite overlooking the busy streets of New York City. I reopen my laptop just in time to hear the end of our new single dance through the air. God, I'm so proud of that song. Finally, freaking finally, I talked Wes into stepping into the spotlight he never wanted to be in the middle of to sing with me. After he had got over his initial resistance to sing, and his first solo single was such a huge hit, added by how much our fans loved hearing him, our new single "Black Lace" was born. It's a song that hits close to home for us—one about mourning the past you never had and a future you will never see.

"It worries me that you don't take this seriously, Wren. After the last—"

"Enough." He looks at me with a frustrated stare when I stop him. "You want me there? To pick out some men who I will never speak to, fine. Just tell me when and I'll be there."

I should have known. When he turned and gave me that crooked smile, one thick dimple flashing and his eyes looking guilty as hell.

Yeah. That's when I should have known.

"Uh ..." His smile deepens.

"Just tell me, you fool." I smile back, kicking myself for never being able to stay mad at him for long.

"The guys will be here in an hour. Things are a little different this time. We all agree that the label's number one concern is saving a buck with wanna-be, mall security style rent-a-cops, so we took the liberty of reaching out to a few reputable security firms. Ones with experience handling high-profile clients. The men we're interviewing will all stagger in thirty-minute blocks …" He trails off when he notices the look of horror I'm wearing.

"I'm sorry, did you just say the men—as in you have a vast number of them that requires you to say anything other than 'the company' or 'the man'?"

"There's, uh, twenty-seven of them this time."

"Twenty-seven men? Or twenty-seven companies? All of them here to do what? Put on some one-trick pony shit show to prove they can protect one little bitty female? How do you even know these guys are really who they say they are?"

His blue eyes, so much like my own, heat with frustration when I'm not taking this as seriously as he feels I should. The truth is I'm not really sure if I care that some invisible threat out there is focused on me. It's the price we pay for fame. There will always be a threat. This circus we live has taken a toll on me mentally, and I know it's not too far off before my depression and jaded outlook on life gets the best of me. I just want to be normal.

"I'm serious, Wrenlee."

"I know you are. I just don't get why you keep trying. It's obvious that, regardless of which apes you have standing around me at all times, it will never end. There is always going to be someone—somewhere—who wants a piece of me. Pretty soon, the novelty of it will wear off, and the focus will move on to you or one of the guys. We've been dealing with the same damn thing for years, Wes. I don't see you interviewing private security for yourself or one of the guys!"

He jumps from the seat he had just taken on the couch and

rounds on the lamp sitting on the end table. When he lifts it and tosses it against the far wall with enough force that the little pieces of glass and porcelain come flying toward me, I know I've pushed him too far.

"Why do I keep trying? Jesus! I keep trying because no matter what you say, stalkers and threats against your life aren't just something I can sweep under the rug of reality. Wake up, Wren. Death threats in Atlanta? Pictures of you *inside* our last hotel suite in Tennessee? What will it take for you to finally take it seriously? None of this shit has ever focused on the rest of us. It's always you, and I'm not going to sit by and laugh about it or sweep it under the rug like you keep doing. Not when your life could be at stake."

I sigh and feel my lip quirk, not in humor—no, far from that—but in frustration. "It's just some overzealous fans, Wes."

"Damn, you can be stupid," I hear rumbled from behind me and turn to see Jamison, our drummer, stroll into the living room area, scratching his dark blond hair and shaking his head. "Stop being a stubborn brat," he grunts with a smile.

"It's not anything new, you guys. We've had this crap for years. You guys have had the same type of shit, and I don't see you sporting a trail of testosterone-driven, egotistical goons." I know I'm grasping at straws now. They aren't wrong, and I know it. The gravity of the recent events has me worried too. I'm just not sure if I can muster up enough fucks to give. They might have some overexcited fans, but it's nothing like what I have to put up with. I used to think it was because I was the face of the band or the woman, but now, a little part of me does think Wes has a point.

"Please, Wren. Just take it a little more seriously. For me."

And just like that … Wes plays his trump card.

Chapter 2

Wrenlee

Predictably, the morning we interviewed security firms was a hot mess. It seemed like the boys had not done their homework; the majority of men representing their companies only had lust-filled eyes for what having clients like us could do for their business. Not to mention the few who very clearly just wanted to take the job to be closer to me. That's not my ego talking—it's the fact that they showed up, interviewed, and left with erections. When you spend more time talking to my tits than you do breathing, there's an issue.

We only got through half of them before we had to cut it

short, finding not one promising one out of the bunch. Not that I'm kissing a gift horse in the mouth for the unexpected interruption, but I would have rather it been for something else. My phone calendar alert went off halfway through our morning list of hopefuls, reminding me about an interview I had for *Modern Rock* magazine at noon. Dix, our manager from hell, conveniently forgot to remind us he had booked the interview. I hate when he does this crap. Singles me out from the guys to make it less about the band and more about me—the sex symbol men crave and women want to become.

Don't get me wrong; he works the guys just as hard as he does me—cashing in on the fact that they're three of the hottest bachelors in the music industry. Let me talk about my music, my band, any day. Let me pretend that the world doesn't see right through *that* and just craves *us*—our images with no care to anything that makes us tick. What happened to the good old days when the music industry was about the feelings a song could evoke and less about the sex symbol who was singing it?

The guys, though, eat up the attention. I'm apparently the only one who hates it. Then again, they're guys, and pretty much every guy I've ever known has always wanted one thing from a woman, and that damn sure wasn't a relationship. It's because of that sex god status we have pinned to our foreheads that women flock to lay at their feet. Or under them. Same thing.

I stopped trying. Stopped entertaining even one night of fun with a man between my legs. I want someone to want me, *not* all that other crap. I want someone who can't stand to be away from me, not because of the fame he might gain, but because just being near me brings him happiness. Until I find a man who cares more about me as a person than the celebrity, I'm happy to lock myself away.

Part of me thinks that if we didn't have a manager like Dix, maybe we could get back to the important things—like our music. You would think that with as popular as we are, we could get some decent help, but our label doesn't give one shit about Dix being a terrible manager. To them, he gets shit done—or at least, it appears that way—and we continue to produce chart-topping hits. As long as we continue to reign in the music industry, they will continue to believe it is because of them and Dix. Of course, it couldn't be because we work our asses off to make sure we produce and perform music that is as addicting to the world's ears as drugs are to a junky.

And one of the things they—the fans and the label both—love is crap like this type of shit they have set up for me. The lifestyle pieces that give our fans a window into our lives or, in this case, me. It makes them delirious with jealousy to have what we have. Painting the picture that the grass is greener on our side.

What a pile of shit.

The grass hardened and browned a long damn time ago. Weeds sprung from the ground, and insects started to eat away at anything that used to make me love this.

I miss the green grass. The lush feel of it against your skin, the appealing sight of it glowing in the sun, and the smell that makes you wish for a cold beer and a cold pool.

I know I probably would sound like an ungrateful brat—if I were even able to voice this freely without worrying that our PR reps would have to clean up my mouth's mess. People never realize what might look perfect from the outside could really be a prison without bars. We have no freedom to live our lives. The press constantly hounds us, cameras are in our faces day in and day out, and we have to field rumors emerging from the smallest grain of truth. I can't even go buy my own tampons without someone chasing me.

Even with all of that, though, my little black jaded heart keeps searching.

Searching for what I'm beginning to think is impossible to find.

Someone who isn't trying to gain something just by knowing us.

Someone who can be *my* gain in life … the tangible thing that can anchor me to the ground and prove that everything we've overcome hasn't been for nothing.

Someone who reminds me I'm more than just a pretty face.

Someone who makes me want to believe the lyrics we write.

Until then, we're just little fish circling the fishbowl, praying to see the ocean again.

Round and round.

Until we're so dizzy that we can't tell the shit from the stars.

I sigh, leaning back and picking at the leftover nail polish on my fingernails, and think back to before all of this. Back to when we were just happy to perform anywhere. As long as we had each other and our music, we didn't need anything else.

When Wes and I met Jamison and Luke, we were just little kids who would bang on old storage bins and dream of performing for thousands. We never imagined our lives would end up like this. We just wanted an escape and to play the music we loved. Music brought us together, creating a safe haven from our personal hells. At least, that was true until we were signed. Then the friends we thought we had quickly turned on us when the money rolled in. Everyone wanting something. Their greed made them hungry for the fame we quickly gained, and they couldn't see past it. But despite it all, we remained humble, and each of us still just wanted to live our dream and make the music we love.

"Casey Brookes will be here in five, Wren; the front desk just called and said she was on her way up."

I smile at Jamison, letting him know without words that I heard him, and get up to head over to what I hope is a clean pile of laundry in the middle of the living room area. I rifle through a few tops before settling on one. I take off the oversized hoodie I had been lounging in and pull a tank over my head. The gray material falls lightly against my thin frame, tight around my chest, and flowing down over my flat stomach. I might be short, just over five-foot-two and thin, but at least I was blessed with great boobs.

Brushing out the wrinkles over my chest, I call out through the hotel suite. "Jamison! Do you know where that red flannel shirt that Luke had on the other night is?"

"Probably somewhere in his room rolled into a dirty ball." He walks by the doorway, stuffing a Pop-Tart in his mouth. "That would be my guess, at least. You know he won't do laundry until you do it for him, and you only do it for him because you like to steal his shit," he says around his mouthful of food.

"You eat like a pig," I grumble when large chunks of his snack fall from his mouth and onto the floor. Stepping over them, I walk toward Luke's room.

He's right; I'm guilty of coddling them. I don't just do it because I love to steal their clothes. I do it because I feel like I owe them for always being there for me. If doing their laundry helps make their lives a little easier, then so be it; it isn't like I don't have to wash my own anyway.

I know, logically, I don't owe them anything, but they're my family—regardless of only being blood-related to Weston—and without them, I know our lives would be a lot different than they are now. Even if we hadn't hit it big in the music industry, we would have each other, and that's all that matters.

Moving to the middle of the large suite, I look around, hoping that the shirt might jump out and bite me. My time before the reporter gets up here is slowly ticking down. I hear the guys tinkering around; none of them are willing to stop working on the new songs we've been writing to help, not that I blame them.

It's always like this when we travel. If we aren't on our tour bus, we always request a hotel large enough to have a suite with four bedrooms, a large living space, and a kitchen. It helps us have some sort of normalcy. We've only been here for two days and it already looks like a tornado blew through. I guess when you live on a bus, and all of your personal space is basically one small bunk for the majority of your years, it makes sense that when you can spread out, you really go for broke. And we sure do.

"Where is that damn shirt," I grumble to myself, bending over to check another pile of laundry near the kitchen.

"Nice ass, Wren." Luke laughs from behind me, causing me to jump up and lose my balance before I fall ass first into a pile of his dirty laundry. "You know, you could put pants on before you start wagging that ass around in the air. Not that I'm complaining." He ducks when I toss some jeans at his head.

"I'm not naked, you pervert."

"Close enough," yells Jamison from the living room. "She's been parading around in just a hoodie with her little bows out all morning. I just let her think that bag she calls a hoodie was covering them up so that I could enjoy the show. It's been way too long since I've gotten some, Wren. You're killing me here."

I look over just in time to see him grab his crotch and thrust his hips toward a laughing Luke.

"You guys are gross."

"But those bows," Jamison says, walking further into the room and wagging his eyebrows suggestively at me. "Those. Damn. Bows."

Ever since I got two delicate black and gray bows tattooed on the back of my thighs, Jamison has been going on and on about them. I'll admit they're hot as hell, which is part of the reason I got them. Plus, they look freaking awesome when I'm wearing a short miniskirt on stage. Each of the bows hit my just under my ass and take up almost the whole width of the back of my thigh.

The guy who tattooed them had used his hand to measure the size, so they weren't too big for my leg. They're beautiful. The tattoo artist did a kickass job making each of them looking like real black lace. It was my way of celebrating the new album, and now that they're finally healing, I've started showing them off more. But—that also means my going pantless around the guys is going to end soon, thank God. Those two animals never miss a chance to comment on them, and even though it would have been easier just to cover them up, I hated the feeling of the healing tattoo against the fabric. It's already itchy enough when it's in that peeling stage without the added aggravation of clothing, so I just went pantless as much as possible.

"Stop looking at them!" I laugh when Jamison goes to nip at my leg with his fingers. "Pinch me again, and I'll kick you in the nuts."

He draws back and with a dramatic sigh puts his hand over his heart. "How could you talk about hurting my manhood, Wrenlee Davenport!? I'll have you know that my nuts would be deeply saddened if you were to hurt them. They're sensitive and need lots of loving. If you want to come over and pet them, I won't stop you. Just in case you were wondering."

Ugh! I roll my eyes, flip him off, and turn back to look for Luke's red flannel shirt.

"It's in there," Weston says, pointing through Luke's open bedroom door toward his bed, before smacking Jamison on the head and moving into the room.

I follow his direction, ignoring the three men who follow

behind me.

"Since when is my room party central," Luke asks, flopping down on his unmade bed.

"Since you keep stealing my clothes," I joke with a wink.

"That," he says, pointing at the shirt I'm slipping my arms in, "is most definitely not your shirt. You stole it and keep trying to keep it. I like that shirt."

"I didn't steal it from you!" I laugh. "It was mine first!"

Really, it *was* mine. The stylist from our last music video originally bought it for me, but Luke's a clothing whore and likes to steal the shit I grab first. It doesn't help that I have a small obsession with men's flannel shirts. I could give you a ton of reasons why, but it probably boils down to daddy issues. Craving a stupid safety blanket is a need I can't seem to shake.

"Oly brings those for me, and your sticky fingers grab them every time!" he exclaims. "Why would she buy dude's shit for you? You swim in them."

He isn't wrong. Oliver, one of the record label's stylists in charge of outfitting us for all video shoots, has a small crush on him and always loads up Luke's options. Maybe if I started letting Oliver dress me, I could get my own shit like Luke gets.

"But Wren looks hot while she's doing it, so you probably should just let her." Jamison laughs and grabs my hips now that I'm standing and thrusts his body toward me. Given that his six-foot-one puts him almost a foot taller than I am, the lump of his junk grinds against the middle of my back.

"Get off me, you brute!" I playfully shove him, laughing right along with him. I hear the suite's bell chime right when I get free, making me scramble to look for my leggings—the last thing I need is for this chick and whatever crew she has with her showing up when I'm half-naked.

I hear her enter, greeting whoever answered the door, as I pull my leggings up. Taking one last check in the mirror to make sure I look decent; I duck as Jamison and Luke almost plow me over in a mad dash to the living room—each shoving the other and trying to be the first to leave the back hallway where my and Weston's rooms are. I'm sure they're both hoping that this Casey Brookes chick is willing to stick around later for a little off-the-record fun with them. I don't even want to think about the last time I walked in on those two sharing their fun. No, thank you.

I give the gray shirt a tug, so the black tank under it shows, adjust the flannel so it hangs off me in an effortless messy-yet-put-together look, and then check my makeup in the mirror. It gives me a few much-needed seconds to put aside the Wren that the public doesn't get and slip on the Wrenlee mask on that everyone outside our close-knit group knows. After all, she's who the public cares to see. The side of me that I always hide … the side that wishes she could just enjoy the peace and quiet and let the public persona that wears sex and sin like a second skin come out and play when it's time and enjoy it. I used to be like that, but lately, I can't seem to get back to that. The disconnect I feel inside grows bigger and bigger with each day. I can't find the *something* I'm looking for. If only I knew what that something was.

Chapter 3

Wrenlee

I want to kill her.

Casey Brookes is as ambitious as it comes. I wouldn't be surprised if you looked the word up and right there next to it was her face. All perfectly put together, she doesn't have a single blond hair out of place, and her makeup is impeccable. She's nauseatingly beautiful, but what makes her the ugliest person I've met in a while is the greed in her eyes. She's thirsty to make it to the top. You can practically feel her pulsing with the knowledge of what this interview will bring to her career. That, you can tell, is all she cares about—not actually getting to know me or giving me a platform to talk about our music. She doesn't want to ensure we're seen as real people … nope, she wants to use us while feeding the masses something juicy, even if that juice is drained from just a fraction of the truth.

The second she walked in the room, I could tell she was going to be trouble. She took in every inch of the room in seconds and the four of us in lightning speed, her mind ticking and spinning away with each angle she could attempt to draw. Even though she shot Jamison down with a good-natured laugh, I could see behind the fake smile. She was going to get a story here if it killed her, and if my interview didn't garner that for her, she would use Jamison's offer to get it. Luke lost interest easily, retreating to his room where you can hear him and Weston plucking away at their guitars. Luckily, I don't have to worry about it, but I make a mental note to pull all three of them aside to warn them before she can sink her claws in.

"So Wrenlee … it's okay that I call you Wrenlee, right?"

Seriously, she's been here for the past fifteen minutes, asking question after question to Jamison, and she's just now focused on me—the person she's supposed to be interviewing. I open my mouth to respond, but she cuts me off instantly.

"I know you're aware that we're looking for a day in the life piece, but I was wondering if you wouldn't mind giving me a little of the history of Loaded Replay before we get started. I was thinking a little rags-to-riches type of thing, so to speak, would be amazing for your fans. Our readers absolutely love that kind of stuff, and it will give them, along with your loyal fans, a level of reality that would help them relate to you—feel closer—and in turn, they get a taste of what it's like to go from nothing to everything. What everyone dreams of, I'm sure." She looks up from her huge purse—or maybe it's really a suitcase—after pulling out a recording device. She gives me just a brief glance before returning to her bag and digging again.

"Uh, yeah …" If she wants me to repeat the same story that we've always given all of our fans, then that's fine by me. Anyone who's followed us from the beginning knows this story, so it's not going to be my problem when she realizes she should have done her homework. Maybe it will speed up this process and get her the hell out of here.

"So what do you want to know? Do you want some story about how hard Weston and I struggled growing up? Maybe we can add in some fake juicy sexual abuse story that happened later in life?" I smart sarcastically. I have this chick pegged. She wants a story—any story. Lifestyle piece, my ass.

"Oh, yes. Tell me all about that." She's practically salivating with dreams of a story of a lifetime and completely misses the sarcasm.

"Sorry, sweetheart," I hiss. "If you're here thinking you're about to dig up some shit no one knows that will take you from the basement to the penthouse, you're sorely mistaken. Weston's and my history is just that … history. The guys and I, we've always been very open with the media when it comes to our lives, but those details are ours, and you damn well know we've never entertained discussing them."

She narrows her eyes. "But you admit that you had a poverty-stricken childhood and you were mistreated by your parents?"

Do what? "Did you just grab that out of thin air and decide to roll with it? Sorry honey, you're going to have to try harder than that. I was being a smartass, and if you even think about printing some bullshit that isn't true, I'll make sure our lawyers tie you up in legal shit for years. Our parents are off the table. Always have been and always will be."

She blushes but doesn't speak to defend herself.

"Right. I'm sorry. How about more of the history to how Loaded Replay was formed? Where you all met and how you came up with your name?"

"Honey, did you even research us before showing up? We keep our personal lives private. What's already out there about our pasts is all you're ever going to get. You could just Google it and save me the breath, but since it's not that easy, I'll help you out. We grew up in a trailer park in the middle of nowhere, Tennessee. Weston and I met Jamison and Luke when we were six, and our parents moved us into their park. Our trailer was in the middle of theirs. We've been best friends since. We started performing at local places in high school for extra cash, and as soon as we graduated, we hit the road. We played wherever we could until we were discovered. As for our name, well"—I smirk—"life was just one loaded pile of shit on repeat for us—until we found each other, that is—and the rest, as they say, is history. We decided to take that loaded pile of shit on repeat and make our own version of it. One that feels and smells a whole lot better than the last one."

She opens her mouth, I'm assuming to ask another stupid question, but I hold my hand up. "I'm assuming you have a photographer here to take some pictures?" I ask, picking at the polish that I had been picking at earlier, determined to get the last of it off.

"Y-yes," she stammers.

"Right. How about you call him up and tell him he can stop sulking down in the lobby where you left him. We can grab some pictures while we finish up your questions, and you can try to get some shit written down that you can print—truthful shit—and then you can get the hell out of here?" I stand up, officially dismissing her, and move to the bar to pour myself a shot of whiskey.

It's going to be a long afternoon.

Her photographer is a short, fat, balding man who won't stop looking at my ass with his beady, creepy ass eyes. The guys instantly stopped what they were doing when he came up and have stuck close since. They've always been a little overprotective when it comes to me. Especially when strangers are in our space. And when strangers wear their creepiness like a badly tailored coat, well … something animalistic in their protective ways takes over.

With every pose that Casey asks of me, you can see the photographer's breathing speed up. My guess is if I looked at his crotch, he would be working hard on a chubby, but no way in hell were my eyes going to wander down south. Thankfully, she stopped asking interview questions because every time he had to pause for me to answer, I could see him adjust his crotch. Talk about disgusting.

"So, Casey, tell me what you need after these pictures?" Weston asks, coming to lean against the couch opposite me with his hip resting against the armrest.

The stylist who came up with the photographer keeps moving my hair, straightening my top, and all-around fussing with just about anything. Wes's eyes never leave mine as I continue to pose next to the hotel room's window, and I can tell with one glance that he isn't happy with the fact that some stranger—equally as creepy as the photographer—keeps touching his baby sister.

He isn't alone in his feelings. I'm used to Dyllan, *my* stylist, but most importantly, my best friend. She isn't creepy, and she doesn't try to touch my boobs at any given opportunity. Had I known this little impromptu interview was going to happen, I wouldn't have sent her back to LA early.

"Oh, just a little of this and that," Casey answers his question, interrupting my thoughts. "Say, want to have a seat and chat while they finish up Wrenlee's pictures?" she asks him with a hopeful tone.

"Yeah, that won't be happening." He crosses his arms and continues to look on unhappily. I snort out a laugh when Casey gives a look that screams that his dismissal just crushed her every single dream.

Could she be any more transparent?

At the sound of my choked hilarity, her head snaps over in my direction quickly. "Wrenlee, would you mind if we pause for an outfit change? The magazine likes to have a few options. I'm sure you understand." She waves her hand, dismissing any objections I might have had in favor of my brother, preening like a cat in heat just hoping for some lovin'.

"Sure thing, Casey," I say with a sugary sweet voice.

"Maybe we could go for something a little more … girly and wholesome this time?" she suggests, looking back at my flannel with distaste. I'm sure she—Miss Pearl and Silk—would have an issue with what I'm wearing.

"Girly …" I pause, pretending to ponder her request. I give Wes a smile, and his eyes crinkle, knowing I'm about to give her more than she asked for. "And wholesome, got it. Sure thing, Casey. Anything I can do to help you out, after all."

She doesn't look up. Instead, she continues to try desperately to get my brother to notice her, pissing me off even further.

Jamison saddles up to me on my way to my bedroom, throwing one beefy arm over my shoulders. He walks over to my closet and gives me one of his trademark killer smiles with his hand on the doorknob.

Yeah, it looks like Jamison's ready to have some fun at Casey's expense too.

"Strip, killer," he says over his shoulder.

"Oh, Jami, you just want to see my underwear, don't you? You perv."

I make quick work of pulling my flannel off, ripping the two tanks over my head, and pulling my leggings down my legs. By the time he tosses the gray and black striped long-sleeved crop top in my face, I was already standing there in my black lace thong and bra.

"Nice, Wren." He nods his head and licks his lips. "Maybe do a little spin for me?" he asks hopefully, twirling his finger in the air.

"Shut up, Jami." I giggle and yank the shirt over my head. Pulling my bright red hair to the side, I make sure the shaved part on the side next to my temple and just above my ear shows. "Give me those shorts." I point behind him at the shorts I had on top of my suitcase and wait for him to throw them over. I laugh at his groan of disappointment when I'm all covered up. The black shorts fit me like a second skin, looking more like sexy boy short underwear than an actual item of clothing one would wear out of the house.

"Turn now; let me see those sexy ass bows."

"Shut up, Jami, you horn dog." I laugh and slap him playfully when he tries to turn me forcibly by my shoulders. "I don't know why you waste your time. We've known each other for what? Over twenty years now? Have I ever once given you the impression that I would ever let you touch this?" I ask, waving my hand down my body.

"You wound me. Oh, how you wound me."

"Yeah, yeah. Seriously, though, be honest … will this get that bitch to stop her shit and hurry this crap up?"

"Pull them down some in the front, let those sexy little

hipbones play peekaboo, sweetheart."

I start pulling down the waist of the shorts and laugh to myself when Jamison starts to groan again.

"You need to get some. Some that comes from anyone but me."

"I know. Oh, I know." I give him another shake of my head when he reaches down to adjust himself again.

"Seriously, Jami. We really have known each other for so long that it's beyond creepy that you still get a chubby for me."

Opening the door to my room, I step into the hallway and walk toward the living area where I hear my brother talking to Casey.

"Almost forgot these," Luke says from the doorway to Weston's room and hands me my red Doc Martens.

"Thanks, babe," I say with a smile and lean up on my toes to give him a kiss on the cheek.

After making sure my boots are on, and my shorts are still riding low on my waist and high on my ass, I step into the living room and smile when I see Casey's cocky ass attitude falter.

"Wholesome enough for you, darling?" I question, doing a little twirl.

Creepy photo dude almost drops his camera when I go and stand by the windows again, this time with my legs braced apart and my arms hanging loosely at my sides. *He* doesn't waste a second, pulling his camera up to his eye and snapping away. However, Casey doesn't have such luck because she's making some weird gagging noise. Wes starts laughing full out when Casey starts to fumble with her paperwork and stands up so quickly she almost trips face first.

"Well, that's not exactly what I had in mind," she stumbles.

"It's what you're getting, though. Start thinking about any more questions you might have, Casey. I've had enough for the day."

She doesn't respond, but then again, I wasn't waiting for her to. I spend the next fifteen minutes posing for the camera and making sure these pictures are the best I've ever taken.

"I'm going to go change, if you don't mind. I hope we can have this little interview wrapped up shortly?"

"Of course," she seethes through clamped teeth.

Chapter 4

Wrenlee

I rip off my shirt then pull some sweats over my shorts and a large tee shirt over my head—another stolen from Luke's stash—and mentally pep myself up to go back out and deal with Casey.

Casey, who I am sure is pissed that I took control of her day.

I should have known better than to let my attitude get the better of me. Lord knows she's probably going to print that I'm the biggest raging bitch ever. It wasn't until we were almost done with the pictures that I remembered the email from the label higher-ups, telling me they wanted to get some 'wholesome' images soon; something different—but also something that isn't me. They thought that new images would dissuade my 'crazy fans' by painting me in a less desirable picture. Of course, with my bitch fest and going all sexy badass, they're not getting wholesome.

What a joke. This whole day is a joke.

Honestly, the more I think about it, I'm glad I didn't bend to what they wanted. They can't backpedal now because they made this beast. They can't change what they've worked their asses off to capitalize on, and honestly, anything different from what I actually did wear would make me someone that I'm not. So, I might as well feed it. I give everyone what they want; at the same time, I keep a part of *me* without stripping another piece of my sanity away in the process.

On the way to the door, I look into the vertical mirror that hangs on the wall. If Dyllan saw me dressed like a hobo, she would kill me. Not just because she's my stylist and it's her job to make sure I always look good, but because she's my best friend. She personally makes it her mission always to be on the top of her game; therefore, she makes sure those connected to her don't make her look bad. After all, her image and those she styles might as well be a walking, talking business card.

Turning back, I grab my phone and take a picture of myself in the mirror, flipping off my reflection in the process. I fire off a quick text to her, knowing that she's busy spending time with her sister to help her plan her upcoming wedding. I get a little kick out of knowing she will be fuming in her seat and can't do anything about it with bridezilla around.

With a smile, I open the door and duck just in time to miss my brother's fist poised to knock.

"What the hell, Wes?" I gasp, standing up and facing his ire.

"Get out here and finish this interview. That bitch just tried to grab my dick!"

Rolling my eyes, I walk around him and down the hall into the living room where I left everyone. Casey is doing her best to play the uninterested party, but I can tell by the slight blush on her face that she's either embarrassed or planning to make a move again.

"Okay, let's finish this interview," I droll, not even having to fake my annoyance.

She looks up, around me, and searches the room. Even if I couldn't hear my brother enter behind me, I would be able to tell by the slight flare in her eyes that she is tracking his movements.

Snapping my fingers in her face, I finally get her attention. "If you could stop and focus on me, that would be fantastic. My brother isn't interested, and even if he was, he isn't stupid enough to sleep with someone who's a part of the media. If you don't have any questions, I have better things to do with myself."

Her eyes narrow. Her nostrils flare. But damn, she's good at holding back because after she visibly pulls in the sides of her cheeks and bites down, she seems to collect herself.

The next hour passes by with her asking a million questions about the past four months we've been on tour, my relationship with the guys, and any romantic relationships I have. She tries her hardest to get some gossip, but I know how to play the game. By the time I tell her for the tenth time that I'm—happily—single, I'm not only bored but also fed up with her.

"Right. Please, Wrenlee, can you tell me a little more about the last leg of Loaded Replay's tour? Now that the new album is about to drop, do you guys plan to add anything extra to the shows?"

"We have plans to add a few extra things to our set, but it will still be a good mix of the old stuff as well as our new songs. The guys have been working their asses off to get the next album done, so you never know, fans might even get some stuff that no one has even heard before."

"How awesome! I bet the fans will love that. Will you be adding any more surprise venues like you guys did for the first leg?"

"They wouldn't be surprises if I answered that, now would they?" I laugh, lacking humor.

"They were more of a spontaneous thing anyway," Luke adds, relaxing on the couch next to me where he had been sitting since we started the questions again.

I hear a knock on the door but ignore it. I continue to focus on Casey and her creepy photographer.

"From everything we've been hearing, the fans loved the intimacy of those spontaneous shows. I know, as a fan myself, I would love to attend one."

"We love doing that kind of stuff, to be honest," Jamison says. "It reminds us of where we started."

"We're hoping that when this tour ends, we might be able to do something smaller, a bar hop tour of sorts," I tell Casey. "We still have a lot of details to iron out, but I'm sure your readers would love to hear that smaller, intimate shows are in the works."

"Wow! That would be something else. No other performers of your popularity are leaving the big arena shows. From what I understand, that's where the money is." She doesn't look up, furiously scribbling on her notepad.

"Money doesn't mean everything. We want people to experience our music. Make new memories that are wrapped up in each beat of Jamison's drums, strum and riff that Luke and Wes's guitars create, and every word I sing. It's important to us that we are able to give others the gift of our music."

"Right, I'm sorry—I didn't mean to imply anything differently. So, in conclusion, I have one more question for you all. Rumors are going around right now that you guys have been dealing with some stalkers. Can you elaborate on that?"

"No." My answer is instant and emphatic. Not just because I don't want her to know, but also, aside from the basics, Weston has been keeping many of the details of our latest incidences from me. As much as it drives me nuts, I know he does it because he wants to protect me. To be honest, I'm still not convinced it's not just some harmless, overzealous fan.

"Oh, come on, you have to give me something." She snickers awkwardly.

"I think what Ms. Davenport is trying to tell you is that it is none of your business, and the last thing she plans to do is feed your need to break a story over her safety."

Spinning around at the deep rasp of the stranger's voice, I'm shocked but impressed that someone who doesn't even know us or the situation has effectively shut this bitch down.

"And you are?" she inquires, apparently not sensing the intimidating vibes dancing off this guy.

"None of your business."

She straightens in her seat, resting the notepad she had been taking notes on her lap before focusing her attention completely on the stranger. My eyes move back to his; the power coming from him, even in his relaxed stance, makes me wonder what he would look like if he were really trying to intimidate.

He's hot.

Like *really* hot.

Tall, he's at least six-foot-four—seeing as he stands taller than my brother—with a trim runner's body. Good God, he's beautiful. He's built, that's for sure, but without looking like he spends hours upon hours working on it. I bet I could pinch him and wouldn't be able to find an ounce of fat on him.

My gaze continues to roam over his chest, admiring how the solid black fabric of his shirt stretches across his broad shoulders. A light dusting of dark hair peppers his jaw. Clearly, he doesn't shave completely, but it's apparent he also works hard to avoid a full-on beard. It makes him look mysterious, dangerous almost, but doesn't mask the strong angles of his jaw. His nose is straight, lips are full, and his dark hair is about a week past the need for a trim.

Avoiding eye contact, I trail my eyes back down until I see the sizable thickness behind his jean zipper. You can tell the man isn't hard, but my guess is he's just … gifted.

Damn. I fight not to squirm in my seat. Whoever this guy is, I wouldn't mind unwrapping the present he promises to be. He looks like he belongs on the cover of one of those corny romance books Dyllan is always reading.

Feeling a sharp tug at my hair, I look over my shoulder at Luke. His lips are pressed tight in an obvious struggle to hold back a laugh if the crinkling at the corner of his eyes is anything to go by. He gives a nod of his chin in the direction of Hotty McBulgePants, and I reluctantly look back, this time up into his eyes and not his dick.

"I asked if you had finished your interview so that I could help escort your guests out," the stranger questions me. His features don't change in the slightest, giving me no hint of his feelings.

Ignoring him, I look back over at Casey. "Did you get enough?"

She nods, looking more uncomfortable now. "I think I can get the rest I need from your manager. Dates and information on the last few weeks of your tour so we can highlight them in the piece."

"If you'll follow me," Hotty McBulge demands of her, not moving to the side when it becomes clear he hasn't given them much room to exit the living room. "Make sure you have everything that you brought up with you, please. We will not be granting access again, regardless of what you try to conveniently forget in hopes of getting back up here."

"I … I …"

His eyes narrow, stopping her before she can finish.

"If you would walk back to the chair you were just sitting in, you can pick up your recording device as well as your personal cell phone *and* the keys that you placed on the side of the couch. Your photographer can also go back to where he was standing by the kitchen island and pick up the coat that I just saw him stuff under the chair in front of where he had been standing. Like I said, you won't be coming back up for *any* reason, so planting something here would only result in that item being placed in the trash."

Blushing profusely now, she quickly gathers up each of the items he called her out on and hurries out the door. He walks behind them, only returning after the door had clicked securely shut.

"Holy shit, man! How did you even see all of that?" Jamison asks when the man walks back into the living room area.

"Training," he answers in a bored tone. His eyes sweep over the room, alert and calculating, before settling his attention on my brother. "My employer called ahead and told you I would be a little early. I trust that isn't an issue?"

"You're with Corps Security? Out of Atlanta?"

"Correct."

"I didn't think you would be here for another hour or so, man. Sorry, I know that wasn't something you had to do just now, but thanks."

"Does the label normally schedule your interviews without

37

making sure adequate security is present with you?"

Jamison and Weston laugh, Luke grunts, and I couldn't help the snort that escapes me even if I had wanted to.

"The label only gives us security when we're going out in public, traveling, at a venue, and that's about it. Once we're inside the hotel, we get no one."

"You're telling me that they get you here and then you don't see them again until you're scheduled to leave?"

"Got it in one," I smart, gaining his delicious dark gaze. I can't tell the color of his eyes, but I wouldn't mind getting close enough to study this man and find out.

"And what happens if you want to go somewhere?"

"Then we go," Luke answers.

"You go? Without protection?"

This time, when Jamison and Wes laugh, it holds no humor at all. "They have no problem making a shit ton of money off us, but they don't exactly want to spend it in the process," Wes answers when they stop laughing.

"You're serious?" He looks around the room, his expression getting colder with each nod of our heads.

"Why don't you sit down, man? We can fill you in on the past few years with Bitchhouse Records." Jamison points at the couch, and the man moves around, ignoring the couch in the middle of the room in favor of one of the chairs against the back wall.

"It was my company's understanding that Brighthouse isn't aware that you're looking to acquire your own security detail?"

"That's right," Wes starts, sitting next to me and causing the cushion to dip.

I grab his leg to steady myself, my own legs that I had tucked under my body flying forward in an effort not to fall into his lap. I notice the man across from us zeroing in on my palm on Weston's leg, his eyes narrowing so slightly I almost miss it.

Interesting. Well, it appears that he might not be a robot, contrary to his previous actions and stoic disposition.

"They've tried, but we've sent away just about every idiot they've tried to hire for our security. It's pointless to keep them around when they're more interested in trying to get some from the groupies that hang around after the show. Not to mention the last bunch who tried to hit on Wren every chance they got. The last guy abandoned his post in our dressing room in favor of fucking one in the bathroom; that's how the last crazy dude got close to Wren."

He remains silent when Jamison stops talking, looking at me briefly before turning his attention to my brother. "And none of you—besides Wrenlee—has issues with fans taking it too far?"

"Not any issues that we care to have halted," Jamison answers. I snap my head around to glare at him, and he holds his hands up with a laugh. "What? They want some; I'm happy to help out. I don't want that shit drying up."

"You're going to get a flesh-eating disease, and your dick is going to rot off, you sicko."

He looks at me like I've just said the worst thing ever. "If you would give me some loving, I wouldn't have to turn to strangers,

39

Wren."

"Never. Going. To. Happen." I stress each word and slap away his hand when he reaches up to mess with my hair. "I'm going to go order some food. Anyone else?"

They ignore me and continue their talk with the man whose name I still haven't caught. The only thing I know about him is the air of danger he wears against the body my own is humming to discover.

Walking into the kitchen area, I can't decide if I want this man to guard me or if I need to guard myself against him.

Chapter 5

Chance

"Tell us a little about yourself?" the one I know as Weston Davenport asks. Now that Wrenlee has left the room, the odd sense of jealousy that I felt after seeing them so close together dissipates, slightly.

How fucked up is it that I'm jealous of her touching her brother?

Beyond fucked up, that's how much.

Cutting off my line of thought, I immediately push it aside and focus on my job—the reason I'm here, the one thing that will hopefully keep me here. I've made peace with the shit that happened back home before I left, but if I get this job, there won't be a chance for me to fuck up again.

"My name is Chance Nash. Thirty-one, single, no kids. I've worked for Corps Security as head of personal security after spending a handful of years in the Marines. My training as a former Marine was in special ops, specifically dealing with hostages in enemy territory. I cannot give you more details than that, but my employer can verify the training that I gained from that." I take a deep breath before continuing, feeling like an idiot. "I have a background in interrogation, as well as specialized training with various forms of combat and weapons. I did a brief stint as a negotiator for the local PD SWAT team two years ago in my hometown of Hope Town, Georgia, but after some personal issues, I decided that it was best to focus on my work with Corps Security. In all honesty, I needed a change of pace, and when your request came across our desks, I personally asked to foresee this job. Granted that one is offered, that is."

"Dude, you probably could have just said your name and position at your company, but uh ... thanks?" the blond one, Jamison, says, but I'm not one hundred percent that that is his name. You would have to live under a rock not to know who the members of Loaded Replay are, but I've never really paid much attention to them—past their lead, Wrenlee, that is.

Directing my attention to the last one who spoke, I continue. "Jamison, is it?" I wait, giving a brief nod when he confirms his name. "Right, well, you should always know all that there is to know about the person or persons in charge of your safety. I'm saving you the trouble of asking, as I'm sure that was coming next … after my name and position at Corps Security, that is."

"Right," he continues, deflating slightly. I can tell he's the type of guy who's used to people laughing at his jokes. I should save him the disappointment and let him know he won't get that from me.

"What makes you think you're the right man for the job?" Weston asks, and I almost cringe. I know I'm right for the job, but after everything that happened back home a year ago, I can't help the little seed of doubt that tries to plant itself inside me.

"Because when it comes down to it, my clients' lives are the only thing that matter, even over my own, and I'll do anything I need to in order to ensure their safety. If the issues that are of concern remain, I will continue to care for the security, but I will also get to the bottom of the responsible parties."

They're silent for a beat before the one who had been silent up until this point speaks. "Have you ever failed?"

"Luke, is it?" I inquire when he finishes speaking.

He nods.

"I'm not perfect, but when it comes to what I'm hired to do, my training, and the lives of others—I do the best to be as close to perfection as I can. No one likes to fail, but you would be hard-pressed to find someone who hasn't. Even the best of the best have a black hash mark against him. To answer your question, though, I failed once. I can't tell you how much shame I feel about it, and a lot of the reason why I need a change of pace is because being home reminds me of what was almost lost. I've been told there was no way I would have been able to prevent what happened, no one could have, but that doesn't make it any better. So, with that said, while I might not be perfect, I will do everything in my power to be."

"Honesty. Not something we've experienced with the last bastards who came up here for the job," Weston says.

"It's the only way to go into something as serious as personal safety. I'm not looking for new friends. I'm here to do what is needed of me until you no longer need or want me here. Just because I'm not here to be your next drinking buddy doesn't mean I don't care. I guarantee you won't find anyone better than myself or my team."

"How many men are on your team?" Weston asks curiously, as he leans back in his seat, relaxing slightly. Good, it seems like I've impressed the one I feel is the most important to have on my side when it comes to being hired.

"Three others. One for each of you. It's my understanding that the main concern is your sister, but I believe that it would be best to have someone for you all."

"And yourself?" Weston continues, his eyes growing from curious to condemning.

"I'm here for her and only her. The other men who will be here as well are all highly trained, but no one is as good as I am. You want her to be the main, so the main gets the best. She's the one you have stressed is in the most need of protection. While I trust my men, I don't trust anyone more than I trust myself."

In their silence, I can hear her tinkering around further in the suite, far enough away not to hear us, but close enough that we're all aware of her presence—being close. I move my gaze around the room, making sure to lock eyes with each of the three men.

Leaning forward, elbows on knees, I resume. "I'm not here to get my dick wet if that's what your silence is really asking me. I'm not sure of all the details with your past security experience, but I'm here to keep you all breathing and not for any other reason."

"Are you fans of our music?" Jamison oddly asks.

"I am." There's no sense in denying it because not many people out there aren't fans.

"So you're aware of us?" he adds.

"There isn't anyone around who isn't." Honesty drips from my words. I can tell he isn't asking to inflate his ego; instead, he's trying to ascertain if I genuinely mean what I'm saying.

"Then you're aware of Wren?" He doesn't have to say anything else for me to catch his meaning. I let the silence linger as I think of the woman in question and how the media has labeled her.

She's a goddess.

The unattainable one, according to the world that loves them.

The woman other females wish to be and the one males crave to be with.

She's rarely spotted with a man outside of these three, so she's become somewhat of the most eligible bachelorette to their fans.

She's short, petite, and delicate, like a pixie. Then she opens her mouth, and the raw power and dirty grit that has made her famous knocks you on your ass. She might look delicate, but at that moment, when she's performing, she becomes a delicate little badass. She's a contradiction wrapped up in one hell of a package. One hell of a stunning package.

"I would lack a heartbeat if I wasn't," I reply, continuing with my honesty. There would be no point in handling their questions any other way.

"And?" her brother asks, now with a sharpness to his voice.

"Just because I'm not a blind or deaf man doesn't mean I'm a stupid one. You would be hard-pressed to find someone who didn't feel the same way about her. All I can do is assure you that it won't be a problem." Even though I mean what I'm telling these men, a small part of me can't help but wonder what I would do given the chance to have her.

"Right," Jamison, the one I can tell is the carefree jokester, butts into the now tense room. Disbelief hangs in the air. "You're aware that we're about to pick up another six weeks' worth of tour dates? We'll keep you on the road with us, and you'll never go home in that time?"

"I'm aware, and it won't be an issue," I tell him, my eyes moving to Wren when she enters the room.

She has one hand holding up the ridiculously baggy sweatpants she's wearing and the other carrying a beer. She doesn't give her attention to any of us before sitting down back in the seat next to her brother. Tucking her legs under her ass again, she takes a sip of her drink.

"No family at home who would need your attention?"

I had been so busy looking at her that I missed who asked the question, but I give them all a quick glance before answering. "No one besides some close friends, and since they're all connected to Corps Security by blood or marriage, they understand and won't need my attention, as you say. In the last two years, I've been gone from home for all but a few months. They're used to not seeing me around."

I don't miss the look they give each other.

I don't miss the look they all give Wren.

I don't miss the nod of acceptance from her to the men in her life.

And I don't miss the look of relief when I accept the job they offer me two minutes later.

The only thing that slipped my attention was the one thing that I couldn't have predicted.

My life was about to change.

For the first time in almost ten years, I was about to set myself up to give someone else power over me.

And I would be powerless to stop it.

Chapter 6

Wrenlee

Nothing in the world compares to the feeling you get when twenty thousand people are screaming your name, stomping their feet, and making the air come alive with the power of their excitement. Knowing that they want nothing more than just to see you is exhilarating. That all it takes to drive them to the brink of insanity is to see your face, hear your voice, and enjoy the music you create that will rock them to their very core.

It's a feeling I don't think I'll ever get used to.

It's a feeling I hope I never have to live without, but in the same breath, one that I wish I could have just a little reprieve from.

I could feel them before my feet even left the dressing room. The sounds of pure fan-crazed madness stayed with me while I walked the long corridor that leads from all of the dressing room and storage areas to the belly of the beast, so to speak, under the stage area.

It was the biggest rush in the world. No high in the world could ever compete with this pre-show adrenaline rush.

I loved it.

I hated it.

Every second of the buildup before a show was euphoric. Every second and every minute of our almost three-hour set was even more so. The letdown, crash and burn, and sweaty, hot mess that would follow in its wake was just as beautiful as the beginning of it all.

This was our dream.

This was our life.

Our completely out-of-control, insane life.

No matter how much I loved it, though, I still have moments when I wish we were back in some no-name bar just dreaming of the big stage. Where no one knew who you were and still couldn't get enough of your music.

This has been the guys' and my lives for the last few years, though. And love it or hate it, you don't ever go back to a normal life after finding the kind of fame we have. As soon as Loaded Replay hit the music scene, we have never stopped climbing. We started out as a small house band, hitting every local bar or dive that would have us. There was no active hunt to find what we have now. I think we honestly would have been happy just creating music, no matter what, because we had each other.

Things got insane when we were first discovered. A sound like ours hadn't existed since the late seventies. Sure, we don't sound exactly like the classic southern rock bands that flooded the music scene back then with heavy guitar solos and drum beats that made your blood flow a little faster—but that's because we sound better.

I like to think of Loaded Replay as a Lynyrd Skynyrd sound with a new-school twist. Someone once compared us to a Skynyrd and Fleetwood Mac love child. Our new twists and flair are what make our sound unique from that old-school sound. We take the old-school sounds and mix them with the new-school influences of our youth.

We're pure sex in music form. An orgasm to your ears, if you will.

Even with all that, though, nights like this remind me that with every high you climb, a downfall is always to be found. The moments that make you wonder if this is something that you can live your life always doing. Those stolen moments make me question whether we could give it up and attempt to live a life as close to normal as we could find.

Something away from the madness.

On those nights, I stand on the stage, surrounded by people who love the person they think they know, and feel like the loneliest person in the world.

It makes no sense, not even to me. I should be happy, loving life and counting my blessings. Don't get me wrong; I'm not completely miserable. I know how lucky we are. No matter how I feel, it isn't just me in this either. I love these guys and would do everything for them, but is it too much to ask to find someone who will love me—Wren—at the same time as giving me a little shield of normalcy by creating a relationship that I have yet to find since we started.

I've been struggling with this for a while, and even if it wasn't for the crazy fans who have been getting too close lately, my guys can feel that something is wrong. I think that is a big part in why they're sticking close. They can sense my discord.

It's probably also a big reason why they're so dead set on hiring our own personal security. They can sense my mood, and it's set off every overprotective ape vibe that they have. They might not know *exactly* what they're sensing, but they're not going to leave anything to chance. I love my guys to pieces, but at times like this, I feel like they're smothering me.

I stop my inner pity party when the crowd's deafening screams and cries for me pound into my brain. I reach out right when one of the roadies—Kellie, I think her name is—starts to mess around with my earpieces, securing them behind me before laying each one on my shoulder for me to put in myself. The second I push them into my ears, though, the headache that had been crawling up my spine all night bursts into fireworks of pain. The swarm of unease in my belly from my migraine is making itself impossibly known.

I feel like I'm going to be sick.

Or pass out.

"Thanks, Kel," I tell her when she moves to step away, after handing my mic over to me. She looks away, something she's done since the beginning of our tour. I've tried to make her comfortable with us, but regardless of what I do, she never seems to handle being close. I don't mind, though, because she hasn't ever given me any warm and fuzzy feelings anyway.

I look over at the guys to see if they're ready. Pushing aside the pain of my headache, I give them a bright smile and a thumbs-up. You can tell by just one look at the three of them—all looking like overgrown kids on Christmas morning—that they're feeling the pre-show rush. Their smiles are wide, and their eyes are totally wild. They're ready to rock the shit out of New York City.

"Let's do this, boys," I call out to them. We take our places on the platform that will rise, bringing us from underground to smack dab front and center of the stage.

Before we even reach the stage, Wes starts to move his fingers; the deep bass that ripples through the speakers increases the intensity of the crowd's screams. When the platform locks into place, I toss my hair over my shoulder, look through the blinding lights at the mass of people before us, and give them what they want.

Myself.

And they go absolutely manic.

Two hours and fifty-nine minutes later, I'm ready to throw up because my head hurts so badly.

I take a deep pull of air through my nose and open my mouth to belt out the end of our latest hit, "Black Tears," the first single from our new album, *Black Lace*.

You broke my heart
With one black tear.
I thought from the start
It would last for years.

I hold the last word out, providing the harmonic rasp that I'm known for. I give the crowd what they came for. The power of my voice, the mask I wear that makes them think I'm having the time of my fucking life, and my boys at my back.

I make sure they aren't aware that this migraine is quickly making me feel like I'm about to die.

Don't get me wrong—I love what we do. We create pure magic with our music. The dreams we crafted in the minds of our fans while they listen to our words and the beats that my boys so masterfully play. It's because of those dreams that we are able to give them the ability to create memories, enhancing them for the years to come.

"New York City! You guys are the best! Thank you for

welcoming us tonight and coming out to party. Don't forget to pick up the new album when it drops—we hope you all love our new shit! Until next time, you sexy beasts!"

I give the crowd another huge, fake-it-till-you-make-it smile before raising my hand for a playful little wave then turning and giving them my back. My smile dies the second I feel the air from our stage fans hitting the back of my bare legs. No need for me to continue the charade when they can only see my backside, and I know they can no longer see my face. The ear-piercing screams and cheers continue as I play the part of sex god rock star, putting more sass in my step than normal—swaying my hips seductively with each stride.

I see Jamison jump down from the little platform that his kit is set up on, his face still on the crowd behind me. I'm always the first one to leave the stage after our final song. The guys leave their instruments behind to give the crowd a little extra love before joining me backstage. The noise from them amps up even louder than before, and I look over my shoulder to see Jamison and Luke paying a little extra attention to the group of twenty-something sorority girls who were in the front row all night. Wes usually joins in, but he's just giving a few lazy waves while looking out at the crowd.

Instead of leaving the stage, as I normally do, I stand back and place a small smirk back on my face, watching them flirt their asses off. Now that they know the show is over, the crowd is still thirsty for more. We've already given them two encores, so there isn't a chance we're going to do more.

My brother turns, shoving Jamison into Luke with a nod in my direction. They give the masses a final wave before heading toward me. I give Wes a small shake of my head when his concerned gaze lands on mine. He knows, just by looking at me, that I'm feeling like absolute shit. He hasn't pressed me on it yet, but I know it's only a matter of time. It's been like this for me for a while now, though, and I know I just need a break. Hell, at this point, I need a break more than I need my next breath.

"You okay?" Jamison asks. Dropping his sweat-drenched arm over my shoulders, he turns me so we can exit the stage.

"Just a little headache, Jami. Nothing that a little Advil, a shower, and a good night's sleep won't fix."

"Need me to wash your back?" he jokes with a wink, but when my elbow lands in his gut, he drops his arm, a rush of air expelling from his lips from the force of my blow. "Fuck me, Wren. I was only joking."

"Yeah, well, keep your womanizing ways to yourself or else use it on the easy sluts that fall at your feet, sicko. I'm not in the mood for your jokes today. How many times do I have to remind you you're like a brother to me?"

"Hey! They aren't sluts; I'm just irresistible. They shouldn't be at fault for my allure. And besides, isn't the fake brother trend in? Every time I hit that random button on my favorite porn site, I get some weird brother-sister fetish videos that pop up."

I stop and point at him. "You're disgusting."

"So," he says, dragging out the word, "does that mean we aren't going to make our own amateur film?"

I hand my mic off to Todd, one of the stagehands who works with our audio and visual team, before pulling my earpieces from around my neck. I don't even know why they bother fitting me for these things anymore. I get they're supposed to keep me connected, my pitch toned, and all four of us in sync, but I have never needed help making our music the best it can be. They always end up dangling around my neck anyway. Night after night. Show after show. It never changes. I look around for Kellie to hand her my earpieces, but I don't see her, so I place them—with the guys'—on the table where some of the other bullshit our roadies are in charge of is piled.

Our manager, Dix, gives me a roll of his eyes when I stomp past him and into our dressing room five minutes later. He's frustrated with my attitude, I know, but I can't seem to give a fuck at this point. No matter how frustrated he might be with me, it doesn't even hold a candle on the lack of satisfaction we all have with how he's doing his job. I've been asking him to get the label to give us a break for the last two years and nothing; so it's something I've been taking out on him since he can't seem to make it happen.

According to him, the label says that we need to keep the momentum of the wave—ride it until it breaks. It's absolute shit because there is no fucking way that wave will ever break. We're so on top of our game, and everyone else's in the industry, that not a damn thing could knock us down from the top at this point.

What is one damn break going to do to change that?

Nothing. That's what.

But to them, we're just the cash cow, and fuck us if we're burned out; they want that cash to keep rolling in. Which is just another reason that I'm sick and tired of all of them. What do they think is going to happen if they keep pushing us?

"Where are we tomorrow?" Luke asks as he, Jamison, and Wes push into the room, moving Dix forcibly out of the way with little care and a whole lot of intentional movements. I hold back my laughter when I see my brother slam the door in Dix's face, leaving him in the hallway.

"Fuck if I know," Jamison answers him and then instantly shoots a scowl at the door when Dix opens it and enters our area with a huff.

"You're all flying out to LA in a few hours. The busses and crew will make their way there as soon as they've broken down the set tonight. You have to be in the studio tomorrow afternoon to start recording the next album. You've got"—Dix pauses and looks down at his phone—"about two weeks—a little less, actually—to get as much down as you can before the West Coast leg of your tour picks up in Vegas."

"Do you think we can have some time to eat, sleep, and piss in between all that, Dix?" Jamison sarcastically says. "Fuck, man, the next album probably won't even drop until next year. Can't they let us have a little downtime?"

"I'll see if I can pencil that in." He rolls his eyes with a heavy sigh. "You know I would give you guys more time off if I could, but I have the heat coming down on me from the higher-ups. They want new material, and they want it yesterday."

"We *just* finished our fifth album, Dix. It doesn't even fucking release for a few weeks and *already* they're pushing us. Did you conveniently forget that we are only under contract for five albums with Brighthouse? Maybe you should manage a little better and get back to them about the studio time we won't be making. We deserve some time off, and you know it. How many other artists do you know who release five fucking albums in four years?" Wes fumes.

"While doing a full tour for the majority of time each of those years," Luke adds heatedly.

"We've been doing their bidding for the long enough, Dix. Now, until we renegotiate the contract, that bidding ends. I'm tired, and I need a break." My no-nonsense tone gets his attention, and he looks at me like he's just seeing me for the first time. Hell, maybe he is. It's not as if he's paid much attention to our wants and needs in the past. I get a few manly grunts in support from the guys, but I hold my hand up before Dix can tell me—again— why we won't be getting a break. "Make them understand because it's happening. I mean it, Dix."

He sputters, but I get up from my spot on the couch and shoulder past my brother and Luke before entering the connecting bathroom without giving him a chance to speak. It's time to wash off the last three hours of performing and get ready to apparently head to the airport.

"Hey," I hear from the other side of the bathroom door.

"What, Dix!" I call back, pulling the tight crop top I had worn tonight over my head before starting the shower.

"Don't forget you have an interview and photo shoot with *Modern Rock* magazine when we get to LA."

"Seriously, Dix? Do you even look at our schedule? She did the interview last week when we arrived in New York from our hotel room," Luke snaps in an angry tone.

"Maybe we should just fucking fire you now! We've put up with a lot of your shit, but we aren't the naïve little fuckers who didn't know better four years ago," Wes snarls with so much venom in his words that even through the bathroom door I don't miss the seriousness.

Whatever else is said gets lost when I finally step under the soothing hot spray of the shower. I try some relaxing techniques to push away my stress and frustrations while I bathe, but I only seem to get rewarded by my headache intensifying despite them by the time I finish cleaning myself off.

I grab a towel from the shelving unit over the toilet, where the venue had been kind enough to stock them, when I step out of the shower. I smile to myself when I see the neatly folded pile of clothing on the closed toilet seat.

God, I love my brother.

It doesn't take me long to dress. I pull on my thong and bra before sliding my legs into some of my favorite LuLaRoe leggings and pairing that with a cozy long-sleeve shirt. One quick look in the mirror ensures me that my crotch is covered completely by the shirt—a must when you're wearing leggings. The last thing anyone wants—especially someone who has to deal with paparazzi—is a picture showing up of your camel toe trying to eat your leggings for dinner. My hair is leaving drops of water on the gray cotton of my shirt, so I start using my towel to attempt to dry it out some. Reaching out to open the door, I grasp blindly now that the towel's edges have fallen into my face.

"Thanks for putting my clothes out, Wes," I mumble, my voice muffled by the towel. When I pull it down, swiping at the hair that had fallen into my face, my smile dies. Apparently, I've stepped into a standoff that would make someone from the Wild West proud. "What the hell is going on in here?"

"I didn't put your clothes out, little sister," Wes says sharply, not looking away from the man who has all of his attention.

"Wasn't me either," Luke angrily adds in.

"Chance here forgot to tell us that he doubles as a personal assistant," Jamison all but growls.

I look over at where Chance is standing—close to the door but near Dix. However, he only has eyes for one man and that man is the only one who probably doesn't want to kill him right now. I swear the guys look like they've been possessed by a madman.

"Do you want to tell me why a man was in the shower with you, Wrenlee?" Dix questions me as if he has the right to be affronted here.

"Excuse me?"

His question confuses me, but it also gets my attention off the three men I love the most doing their best impression of someone trying to kill with their eyes alone. I was kind of enjoying the anticipation of what they would do next. Stupid Dix.

"You know the label has asked you to refrain from any

relationships. They like 'single Wrenlee,' you know that. She has more appeal than if you were in a relationship."

"Excuse me?!" I repeat, screaming this time, completely shocked at the balls on Dix.

Chance moves slightly, but when my eyes travel back to him, he stills, the muscles in his crossed arms bulging.

"You know better, Wrenlee," Dix continues to scold. His blue eyes are narrowed. "You've been so good about this, but I can assure you that the label is not going to allow you to continue."

I look around the room, realizing belatedly that the guys are focused on Dix, *not* Chance—even though the man clearly came into the bathroom while I was showering to leave me clothes. Nope, they're completely focused on the man standing close to Chance. Dix.

"I know better than what, exactly?" I narrow my eyes at Dix. "The last time I checked, the label owned our music, not *me*. If I want to have some after-show stress relief with a hot man, that's my prerogative, not yours and certainly not theirs." The pounding in my head grows stronger, and I have to pause a beat before I can continue reaming Dix a new asshole. I huff, pulling up my arms and crossing them over my chest, but before I can get another word out, I sway on my feet. The movement has Chance rushing forward and pulling me against his strong chest before I even register it.

I look up at his impassive but handsome face and frown.

"Hot man?" His words are low, just above a whisper. They vibrate against the skin on my palms—the palms that I have pressed tightly against his chest. Now that the shock of his swift movements has faded, I realize how close our bodies are. My arms are caught between us, each hand against his chest, and without shoes, his hips hit my belly.

Hard body to soft curves.

Good. God.

"You've got a lot of nerve, Dix," Wes fumes, his voice breaking whatever spell had fallen over Chance and me. "Nowhere in our contract does it prohibit personal relationships. Not for any of us. Sure, they suggested it when we signed, but that's as far as it got. We shot that shit down. A suggestion. If Wren wants to have her man with her from now on, that's her choice. As long as it isn't affecting any of our contractual obligations, then we're fine. This is what happens when you guys won't give us a break. Now you have to deal with the fact that they miss each other too much to stay apart. To be honest, Dix, if the label wanted her to stay single, then they shouldn't have dropped the subject when we objected and made sure to have put that in the bullshit contract." Wes finishes his verbal smack down before moving around to where Chance and I are standing, effectively blocking Dix from his continued narrow-eyed gaze on the two of us. "Don't even think about suggesting to add it to negotiations because that will damn fucking sure get us to walk away from Brighthouse."

"We *will* be discussing this later," Dix fumes, picking up his phone, iPad, and man-purse from the table before storming out of the room.

When the door closes, Jamison moves to lock it before

leaning back against the solid wood, wearing a lazy smile on his face. "Well, that was fun."

"My man?" I ask weakly, my voice all but a whisper. I know Chance hears me, though, because his body grows tense, reminding me of our close proximity to each other. I reluctantly take a step back, and he drops his arms. It almost felt like he was hesitant as well.

"I thought his head was going to explode when Chance came out of the bathroom. Good call on the clothes, Wes." Luke laughs, ignoring me like I hadn't spoken, even though I know for a fact he heard me.

My attention goes right back to Chance, my eyes meeting his. "My man?" I repeat. I ignore the tingle of awareness that crawls up my spine when I get a clear up-close-and-personal view of this man. Now that I'm not distracted with being in his arms, that is. Jesus, when he focuses completely on me, it feels like I'm the only woman left in the world and he's gone without sex for decades.

He takes an audible breath, and I know he feels the same thing I do zapping and zinging between us.

This feeling, whatever is happening between us, is the only thing I've ever felt that might be more powerful than the rush I had earlier before going on stage.

"I knew he would lose his shit, but I didn't think he would call her out on not having a relationship. He knows that's a bunch of shit," Jamison, I think, says, but my eyes and attention are still locked on Chance.

"Still, they've been playing that card for years now. We're

lucky that Chance caught that the other day when he was questioning us on our contract and any demands the label has on us, or we would've been shit out of luck." Weston's voice gets closer, and I reluctantly look over at him. He's not paying attention to me, though. Instead, he's grabbing some of the snack foods that the venue had left out for us, completely relaxed like he doesn't have a care in the world.

They continue to talk—Wes, Luke, and Jamison—ignoring me completely. I stand there for a few minutes, waiting for them to tell me what the fuck is going on, but they don't give an inch. Chance shifts on his feet, drawing my attention, and my eyes must give away the panic that I'm feeling with each second that the guys ignore me because he clears his throat. The sound holds my attention but also gains theirs; something I'm sure was intentional.

"There's a clause in your contract that prohibits any non-label approved security from being hired. When I noticed it, I had your brother make a formal request to hire and pay for an extra team of personal security for you during the next two months while you finish up the rest of your obligations to the current contract. However, they declined to approve Weston's request, and because of that clause, there isn't any way we can come in that capacity now." Chance's voice is calm and steady while he talks, and I feel some of the tension falling from my shoulders. He takes another breath before continuing. "Since their refusal would have kept me from being hired officially as your personal protection, we all talked it over and decided I would play the part of your boyfriend instead. Until we can get the contract renegotiated and reworked to add more details about security with your new one, this is our only option. The other men on my team are on standby for when the negotiations end with Brighthouse, but if we don't get our way with security for some reason, we agreed that you're the number one priority here, and the boyfriend ruse will work if that turns out to be the case."

"Boyfriend?" I gasp in shock.

"That's me," he rumbles, still calm as fucking can be.

"What. The. Fuck?"

I look around; meeting the eyes of the guys I love more than life before meeting the still *very* serious ones of Chance. That mask of indifference might still be locked in, but if I'm not mistaken, a flash of pure panic just crossed over his features.

Honestly, I'm not sure if that little flash thrills or terrifies me.

Well, what the fuck, indeed.

Chapter 7

Chance

This plan is going to blow up in my face.

The thought crosses my mind the second that Wren stomps out of the room, slamming the door in her anger.

"She seems … happy," Jamison comments after the echo of her anger dissipates.

To say she took the news of our new couple status well would be an understatement. I get it, I do. When I signed up for this job, the last thing I expected was to end up playing house. When they hired me, I meant what I said about my focus being solely on her safety. I also meant what I said about not taking this further, and

I know this new little twist is going to make that promise hard to keep.

With her being a celebrity, eyes will constantly be on us. In order for our relationship to be believable, I have to play the part night and day. It isn't just the concern about what this lie will mean for my attraction to her, but also the thought of letting someone get that close to me. Letting my guard down in order to be some-one who the world sees as head over heels for Wren is what makes me feel like I'm losing my control over the whole situation.

I have a pretty good feeling I'm fucked here because no mat-ter how I look at this situation, I'm not sure I can do this believ-ably and still maintain my distance. If I had been able to come in as her guard only, well, that would have been a whole lot easier. I could have done that and never fucking spoken a word to her.

"She'll get over it." Weston butts into my racing thoughts, his concerned focus still on the door his sister all but ran out of mo-ments before.

"You're sure there isn't another way?"

I look over at Luke. "If there had been we would have worked that angle instead of blindsiding her with this one. Would have been easier on her, you all, and me."

He holds his hands up. "Look, man, I didn't mean to question your call here. I just … look, I just know how Wren is. She's going to feel caged in, even more so than normal, and she's already hav-ing a hard enough time as it is."

"Hard enough time with what?"

"All of this," Jamison answers my question, waving his hand

through the air in front of him. "Let's just say, things are different than what we thought they would be when we first signed. I don't think any of us expected to have the kind of fame and notoriety that make us feel like we are fish on display. Wren has a hard time dealing with all the negatives that come with our lives now. I think it would be easier, something she could live with easier, if they would stop refusing to give us some vacation break time."

I make a mental note to look into that more but don't ask Jamison to elaborate.

"Plus, *she* doesn't think it's a big deal enough to have beefed up security at all, but we all agreed that it needed to happen. You haven't seen how crazy it can get sometimes. Men want her, and women are jealous of her. She deals with a lot more of that bullshit than we do because she is, essentially, the face of Loaded Replay. This all might be for nothing, but I can't ignore my gut feeling, telling me we need to take these little incidences more seriously." Weston sighs when he finishes, and it's obvious that he hates to upset his sister.

"I agree with you. Even though the Atlanta Police handled the death threat, proving that it was nothing more than a joke by some stupid teens on a dare, I don't think you can brush off the photographs from inside the hotel rooms. Not when it was while we were staying in a large, well-known hotel. I could get someone not used to dealing with celebrities fucking up, but that hotel wouldn't have handed out access to your floor, so that is my focus. Did you say there was a note?" I look around the room, leaving my question open for any one of them to answer.

Weston's face gets red, and I know he doesn't like to think about this—the fact that, right under his nose, someone got close enough to his sister to take pictures, let alone the rest of the bullshit that followed.

"Yeah." He pauses, and his face gets harder. "Look, she doesn't know everything about that situation, though. I left out the note when I told her about the pictures. And she hasn't even seen the photographs, so she doesn't realize how much was actually seen. She isn't aware that they took her shit either. She had it hanging in the bathroom, so when she asked about it, I brushed it off to her as housekeeping must have moved it. I didn't want to freak her out. Hell, I still don't want to, but now, I'm not sure if it was wise to keep everything from her."

I make a noise but don't comment. It was stupid as fuck not to tell her, but it isn't my job to act like his fucking parent.

"While it might not be my place, I don't think that was wise. Not when it comes to her safety. It makes a lot more sense to me now, though, that she would be able to brush everything off so easily." God, what a mess. I want to say so much more, but I push down my odd sense of anger before continuing. "And? What did the note say?"

Weston's eyes flash with ire as he reaches behind his back to pull his phone out. "That next time they won't be hiding in the shadows and to leave Loaded Replay before it's too late," he answers while messing around with the screen of his phone before handing it to me.

I scroll through the album he had opened on his phone's

photo app. Having already been told about the note, I study it briefly before moving on. The photographs left beside the note of Wren sleeping in her bed catch my attention instantly, and I try my best not to notice the fact that she is naked in them. That the sheet just barely covers her body at all. However, no matter how hard I try, I don't miss the fact that only a muted shadow from where her leg is hiked up hides her pussy.

"Are there any ex-boyfriends who we should be worried about? Bad breakups from before you got famous?" I hand the phone back and meet each of the guys' eyes, willing my cock not to react to the pictures I just saw.

Jamison laughs. "She had a few somewhat serious guys back home before we signed, but seeing as they either dumped or cheated on her—not the other way around—I would say none of them are feeling scorned by her."

"Just because they cheated doesn't mean they don't feel wronged," I add. "They might see her now as the successful megastar she is and feel like they were slighted by not being a part of that life."

"Nah, man," Jamison continues confidently. "Let's see, there's Derek, currently an insurance salesman out in Utah; he's married with a bunch of kids, last I heard. Happily married and from what I understand, he still talks to Wren from time to time. They were friends before they thought it would be a good idea to date. He meets his current wife while Wren was out on the road, and the rest is history. There isn't anything with him, guarantee."

"What about Paul?" Luke asks Weston, and my eyes move

from Jamison to Weston briefly before opening the notes app on my phone and starting a list.

"Died in a motorcycle accident two years ago," he responds.

"Harry?" Luke continues to question. I add the name to my list.

"Took over his parents' gas station. Married to Tori Scott and she's pregnant with baby number one," Jamison says. "Tori is good friends with my sister," he adds when I raise a brow for him to continue.

"Okay, well, what about Sam?" I add the name after Luke asks, waiting for one of the others to elaborate before I look up.

"Sam married the *man* that he cheated on me with," a small voice comes from behind me, causing me to snap my head around to see one hell of a pissed-off Wren. "They're waiting for their adoption paperwork to get approved, last I heard from him, which was a year ago or so when they came out to the show in Atlanta. I would guess they're now proud parents, but I can call him and check on that for you since you seem very concerned about my ex-boyfriends. Any more questions or can we stop pointing out the fact that I apparently can't keep a man happy?"

"Wren," Weston starts, pushing off from the wall where he had been leaning.

"Save it. You and I"—she points between the two of them—"we don't keep secrets. I might not believe this is something worth freaking out about, but you know I would have handled all this behind my back shit a lot better had you kept me in the loop. All you had to do was tell me! But you kept that all to yourself and I would have understood—and been on board with—all this 'new security is needed' bullshit had you done that." She turns her attention to me now; the harshness in her face does nothing to diminish her beauty. "I would appreciate it if you would come to me in the future if you would like to know more about my life."

I nod but don't speak.

"You do realize that the media is going to get wind of this relationship charade, right?"

I nod again. It wouldn't do any good to patronize her by pointing out that I'm very capable of seeing the big picture in our situation. I also wouldn't have jumped into this new role without mapping out every possible direction it could take us. I learned the hard way what happens when you don't prepare for everything, and that won't happen ever again.

"They're going to dig into your life. Pull anything from your past that can be used against you. Harass your friends, your family, your second-grade teacher. They won't stop until something else gossip-worthy pops up, and even then, they won't stop for long. They never leave us alone. So, Chance, are you sure you're ready for that?"

I raise my brow. "I'm not worried about anything in my past." Even as the words leave my mouth, I recognize them for the lie they are.

I'm not worried about the people I'm close to back in Hope Town. My employment with Corps Security is the only thing attached to my name there, and just the thought of some media witch-hunt showing up is laughable. Not only will they not even get in the door, but also no one there is stupid enough to talk. They would be lucky to get an eye twitch from any of the men who work there.

Even my old apartment was never under my name, not even the last year I lived there before moving out. We never switched it over when my best friend and former roommate, Cohen, moved out to start his new married life. We kept the apartment but only for a year after he moved out. Since I'm rarely home, it's easier for me to live out of a suitcase than to buy a house I'll never see. Which helps in times like this, seeing as I have so little attached to my name. The rest of my close friends either work at Corps Security with me, are related to someone who works there, or are married to someone who is one of the two.

Even if the media were to branch off from Corps Security and question some of the surrounding businesses, the only one who would know about me is Sway's Salon next door. Everyone in there is just as untouchable as the men who make up Corps Security—some of them being wives or daughters of my colleagues. If that wasn't enough, though, the very flamboyant gay man who owns the place could easily scare them off—but even on the off chance that he welcomed them inside and promised them makeovers, the staff is so used to cameras being shoved in their faces, they wouldn't even blink. Not since they've filmed a reality show there for the last three years.

As for my family, well … nobody is left, so no problems there.

But I'm not worried about the group I left behind as fast as I could when I heard about this assignment.

Nope, not them.

I might not be worried about my past touching me, but just thinking about getting close to someone new—that is what concerns me.

"You sure about that?" Wren asks, one hand going to her slim hip, her attitude coming off in waves.

I nod, pushing back the bitterness that always fills me when I think about the last person that I ever let close enough to hurt me.

She narrows her eyes. "You have no problem using your words for them," she snaps, pointing at the three men in the room with us, "but when I ask you something, you act like you're a mute."

"When I have something worth saying, you'll know it."

I should have kept that to myself. I realized that the instant the words left my mouth, but something about seeing the fire being lit inside her makes me want to push her buttons—to see what happens when she is provoked—and to watch the color rise on her skin. I instantly wonder if she would blush like that all over her body when she was aroused too.

"So …"

Her eyes flash to Jamison's when his playful tone breaks our staring contest. "Shut your mouth, Jami!" His hands go up in surrender, and he takes a step back from her.

"If you have any doubt in your mind about what those vultures might pull out of your past, you should tell us now. I might not be happy about this situation, but if it's something these guys think is necessary, I'll do it for them. That being said, I'll be damned if I'll let something from your past blindside me and end up making me look like a fool."

"Seriously, Wren, give the guy a break."

Her brother's words get the heat of her gaze off me. I briefly wonder if this would be a whole lot easier to get her on board with if she knew everything about the last hotel room incident, but her brother gave me strict orders to keep the details of the pictures and items taken to myself. I agreed, but I didn't agree without letting him know I wouldn't keep it to myself if I felt like it was pertinent for her to know.

"No, Wes! I give them everything, but they haven't gotten my pride yet. If we're going to do this, it's going to believable. If they find out this is all a ruse, then poof, there goes that pride! Let me tell you something; if he really was mine, I would know everything, and that includes who his second-grade teacher was. They wouldn't be able to hurt me if anything were to pop up because, guess what, I would already know about it and be prepared!" She takes a harsh breath. Her whole body seems to vibrate with her anger. "You forgot someone too, Wes. When you guys were having fun ticking off all the men who I have had in my life, you forgot about Garrett. Remember him? The one who used you to get to me and then used me to get his leg in the door. The one who is now enjoying his own solo music career?" I look from her over at Weston to see him flinch. "Well, I didn't forget him. He was just another person on the long list of them who doesn't see me as anything else but a way in, a paycheck, or whatever the fuck. I'm sick of being used. I'm sick of the press and their lies. And I'm sick of acting like it doesn't bother me."

With all of us silent, she doesn't even hesitate to continue, her voice still hard and unforgiving. "I'll ask you again, Chance. Is there anything in your past that can be used against *me*? If so, I want to know now."

Momentarily taken aback by her outburst, I shake my head, earning another heated look from her.

"Well … isn't that just as clear as mud, my mute boyfriend? Ready or not, it's time to head to the airport, so maybe you can use the time on the ride over there to figure out if I should know anything about you since what I currently do know is *zilch*. Aside from the fact that you apparently don't talk."

Fuck.

I should put my foot down and show her who is in charge here, but when she starts stomping around the room to collect all their personal shit, all I can think about is how hot it is to see her fired up and how screwed I am.

Keeping the divide between us—not getting too close to her—is going to be a challenge in and of itself because right now, all I want to do is bend her over, strip those tight as hell leggings off her, and fuck her until we both can't move.

Chapter 8

Wrenlee

Brighthouse sent their fucked-up security goons to meet us at the arena's underground entrance. I could tell Chance was far from impressed, but he kept his mouth shut and stuck close to my side. He played the part of adoring boyfriend to a T; I'll give him that. Even with no one around except the two guys assigned to get us back to LA, he kept my hand in his and his body language loose.

By the time we made it to the airport, my headache is full blown. It doesn't help that LaGuardia airport isn't my favorite, but due to the amount of high-profile passengers this airport gets, they've come a long way in making sure we're comfortable and left alone for the most part. LA is by far the best at making sure this happens, but New York City is proving to be a close contender.

We pull up to the private door slightly away from the other checkpoints for normal passengers, and even though it isn't well known to most, a few paparazzi are still waiting for us. I briefly wonder if they were tipped off about our travel plans since they were nowhere around the arena when we left. Chance, seeing them waiting, gives me a look that clearly means to wait before he turns and exits the back of the SUV.

Grabbing my favorite Louis Vuitton tote bag, I pull the hood on my sweatshirt over my head and make sure my sunglasses are in place. Even though I know I probably look ridiculous, wearing sunglasses at two in the morning, my headache demands them more than my need to keep the paparazzi at bay does. I watch as he moves from his side of the vehicle to my door, opening it and holding out his hand to help me down. My brother and Luke are already out and waiting for us by the door, being completely ignored by the men who had been waiting for us.

My feet hadn't even landed solidly on the ground before I hear them start in on me. *Don't they ever sleep?* I ignore them, like I always do, and start walking toward the door. My fake indifference to them slips when I feel the solid heat of a male body against my side moments before an arm curls over my shoulder, pulling me completely to his warm body.

I look up. I'm ready to rip Jamison a new asshole, assuming he's the one touching me like normal, since I didn't see him with Wes or Luke, but I gasp when I see Chance instead. His dark eyes—ones that I had assumed were just plain brown when we met last week, only realizing after I've been around him more that they're actually the most stunning mix of blue and green swirls— are no longer lacking warmth. He's looking at me with an expression of pure lust. Gone is the mask that he's had firmly in place since last week and in its place, is one I have no idea what to do with.

Well, that's a lie ... I know exactly what I would do with him given the chance.

"Smile, babe," he tells me before I watch in shock as his head drops and those thick lips of his land against my slack ones. He pulls back, giving me a smirk that could melt panties before moving his mouth to my ear. "If you keep looking at me like that, no one will believe that you can't get enough of me."

I jerk slightly, enough that I know he feels it but not enough for others around us to notice. His fingers curl around my shoulder, pulling me even closer to his rock-hard body.

I don't respond. Not because I don't want to, but because the second he stood to his full height, the questions started.

"Wrenlee, tell us about your new friend."

"Are you two an item?"

"Any comments on the rumors that you're pregnant?"

What the fuck? Really? Pregnant? Looking at the door, I see the shock on my guys' faces at the question. This is the first time I've been seen with a man other than my bandmates, and it's automatically assumed I'm pregnant? Can anyone say reaching? I barely fight the urge to look down and see if I *look* pregnant.

"Is there any truth to rumors that you're leaving Brighthouse?"

"Are you guys excited for the next leg of your tour?"

The questions keep coming, but Chance continues to steer me toward the VIP door. We're inside seconds later with the door shutting out their screaming questions.

"Pregnant, already? You move quick, Chance! Congratulations, Mom and Dad," Jamison jokes, and I silently vow to get him back for that when I hear a muffled gasp from the employees behind the check-in desk.

"Would you shut the hell up, asshole?" I hiss through my clenched teeth.

Even though the VIP check-in is supposed to guarantee an air of confidentiality and security, I know these employees don't have to live up to that. It's either keep your mouth shut, get paid, and keep being graced with celebrities day in and day out, or be a fly on the wall in order to sell stories to the tabloids.

My guess is that tomorrow that stupid fucking rumor will be front page *with* the pictures of Chance and I entering the airport tonight. Hell, I wouldn't even be shocked if a few of them snap some camera phone pictures while we're in here.

Chance, clearly thinking the same thing, only eases his hold on me once. It didn't waver when we checked in quickly. Instead, it grew more friendly. His touches got more intimate and I got another six kisses against my temple before we make it through security. The only reason he actually let me out of his hold was when the TSA people made him in order for us to walk through the scanner. The second we were through, his arm was back around my shoulders, and I was walking through the back tunnel of LaGuardia in Chance Cloud Nine, trying not to give in to how his touch or just the very smell of him was making me feel.

No, that's a lie.

I didn't give in to what he was making my body feel at all.

Aroused.

I was completely, purely, and deliciously aroused.

To the point a feather could touch my overheated skin and I would probably have an orgasm on the spot. Well, maybe not that bad, but I was close.

The attitude I'd had back at the venue manages to stay with me the whole way through the private walkway. By the time we're pushing through the doorway and into the terminal, I've already hatched my revenge on Jamison. Even if there are tabloids and Google alerts going off tomorrow about my 'pregnancy,' at least I know the images that will pop up with him will be worth the annoying rumors.

"Your wheels are spinning," Chance mumbles under his breath. Well, I'm sure he could have been talking normally, but because of my height and closeness to his body, it comes out muted, his voice vibrating through our connected bodies.

"You're imagining things," I muse.

He bends slightly, not taking his eyes off our surroundings. "I don't miss anything."

Whatever. I ignore him; instead, I focus on walking through

the airport and pretending I don't notice the people who are stopping, gawking, and snapping pictures of the five of us. Even this late at night—er, early morning—a good size crowd of people is waiting for their red-eyes.

What a circus.

Thirty minutes later, our group is taking up the whole first-class section of the plane. We had given up the back row to a group of military men who had been traveling on the same flight as we were, but the rest of the sixteen seats are ours. Normally, we would never give up seats. We prefer to have the whole first-class section to ourselves in order to ensure we get the privacy that we desire, but whenever military personnel boards with us, we give out whatever seats we can. The guys and I get a kick out of refusing to let the Brighthouse security guys sit with us, always saying that it's because we can't be bothered with other people while we travel, but we never turn down the offer for our brave military men and women.

Even with the four men who joined our little private first-class bubble, six pairs of seats remained, which should have meant space out sally for the whole flight back to California. Wes and Jamison took the first row, one on each side of the aisle. Luke threw his bag down on the two seats behind Jamison but moved his body into the two seats behind Wes. That left Chance and me with the third row of four seats. I place my bag in the overhead and slide into the seat behind Luke's duffel bag.

Stupidly, I had assumed that Chance would sit in the empty two seats across the aisle from me, but I'm quickly learning that Chance doesn't ever do what is assumed of a normal person.

Fuck, he sure is committed to this couple ruse. His long legs and wide body settle in next to me before he turns to give me a devilish smile.

Goddamn, that smile is dangerous.

Who am I kidding? *He* is dangerous.

I do my best to ignore him, but it's impossible. The steady brush of his arm against where mine is resting on our shared armrest constantly reminds me how much my body wants his touch. The scent of his delicious cologne hits my senses, making me want to climb in his lap and rub my face over his chest to get a potent lungful of it.

I can't even remember the last time I was this horny, which is pathetically sad, since it was probably around the same time I actually got laid. Years. I think. Close to three. Maybe that's why I'm a hot mess lately. I turn my head to study the side of his face and wonder if I can use this situation to my advantage. I mean, after all, we are in a 'relationship' now.

He turns and gives me a questioning arch of his dark brows, but I brush it off in favor of playing Disney Emoji Blitz on my phone.

By the time we had hit cruising altitude, I could hear the other men around me snoring away but not Chance. He's fiddling with his phone, completely ignorant of the fact I'm about to start humping his leg.

"Excuse me," I breathily say, unbuckling my belt and standing to move around him. I stand there, my head bent slightly because of the overhead, and wait. He doesn't move, though. Instead, he drops his phone to his lap and gives me his complete attention; his eyes even dance a little like he's finding this whole damn thing funny. "Excuse me," I repeat, no longer breathy, and seconds away from coming.

No, that's a lie. I'm still breathy and very much seconds away from soaking my panties even more than they already are.

His large hands grab my hips, and he guides me down on his lap with no resistance from my treacherous body.

"Not what I meant," I say through clenched teeth, trying to sound harsh and offended, but I just sound dazed and turned on. I wiggle in his hold, trying to get free, but he's too strong for me.

He leans up in his seat, his chest hitting my back and buries his face in my neck. I'm sure anyone who saw us would see a loving couple who just can't keep their hands to themselves. He's playing a dangerous game, though, because the second the solid, hard length of him presses against my backside, I forget this is supposed to be a game and squirm a little more. His teeth nip at my shoulder at the same time his groan hits my ears.

"Stop moving, Wren," he demands, tightening his fingers on my hips.

"You're the one who put me on your lap." I curl my fingers over the empty seat in front of me and squeeze my eyes shut when I feel him growing harder under me.

"Yeah, because the flight attendant who just walked by had

her phone out and pointed right at us. She's doing a shit job of making it look like she's doing something with her paperwork." His hand comes off my hip, and he cups my jaw, turning my head to the side just when I was about to look up at where I last saw the attendant, forcing me to shift until all it would take is me throwing one leg over his body to be face-to-face. "Do not look at her," he stresses; the sudden movement of twisting my body makes me bounce slightly in his lap, rubbing my legging-clad ass against his erection. His eyes drop to my mouth where I pull my bottom lip between my teeth and groan.

"Give me a reason not to look," I dare him.

"You don't want to go down that road, Wren. I'll protect *you* from the world, but you need to protect yourself from *me*."

"No one is asking you to."

Not even knowing if we're still being watched, I twist my torso the rest of the way, pulling my legs up until they're bent at his stomach between us. Now that I'm facing him completely, I bring my hands up to curl them both around his shoulders before dragging them up to wrap around the corded muscles at the sides of his neck. His nostrils flare, but he doesn't stop me. I give him the chance, but it never comes. Dropping my head, I press my lips to his. I explore his lips with small pecks and little licks of my tongue, learning his mouth before pressing more firmly. He sucks in a breath when I open my mouth and slowly drag the tip of my tongue over his bottom lip.

And then his control snaps.

His hands—still at my hips—lift me effortlessly until my legs are no longer folded between us, but now digging into the hard armrests with my knees pushing into his thighs, my back hitting the seat in front of me. His mouth opens, and his tongue meets mine, no hesitation whatsoever, as he deepens the kiss.

Our breathing echoes around us, making it sound like everyone on this plane could hear us, but I know it's just because our faces are so close. I let out a moan, one that he swallows, that turns into a whine when he pulls back.

"That can't happen again," he softly scolds, just as breathless as I am.

What the hell? I might not have been into this whole fake-boyfriend-slash-bodyguard thing before, but I'll be damned if I'm not going to take advantage of the situation. Especially now that I know how alive he makes me feel. Three years since I had pleasure from anything other than my own hand, and if that kiss is anything to go by, what Chance could make me feel is ten times more powerful than anything I've ever felt in my whole life.

I'm not passing that up.

Nope.

No fucking way.

"We'll see about that." His eyes narrow when I don't agree, but I just smirk.

I glance over his shoulder at the men in the row behind us. Because of my position on his lap, I can clearly see that all four men are watching us with rapt attention. Okay, so in hindsight, it probably wasn't wise to do this when four men we didn't know were within close proximity, but I guess if they left this flight talking about what they saw, it would only further paint a light of truth to our relationship.

Nothing much I can do about it now, not that I would take that kiss back.

I give them a smile, one they return, before looking back at Chance with a shrug of my shoulders.

"You're in so much trouble for that." He sighs, leaning back and helping me stand, this time on the other side of his body in the aisle.

I ignore him and reach up to the overhead to pull my bag out. I can feel his eyes on me, but he's back to silent and broody Chance. Not willing to lose the high his kiss brought me, I gently place my bag on his lap before pulling out a small pouch.

"Hold that, will you?" I ask him after the fact, loving that catching him off guard makes his lips twitch slightly. He might not want to admit it, but he's enjoying himself, I just know it. I unzip the pouch and pull out the two tubes I need from inside it before tossing the small pouch back into the bag.

"What are you up to?"

"A little revenge against the loud mouth up there," I tell Chance, my smile growing as I point over my shoulder in Jamison's direction. He looks from my face to my hands, his eyes squinting in the low light of our cabin before realizing what I'm holding *and* who it is I'm talking about. His lips twitch even more than before once, twice, and a third time before he gives in to it and I'm almost knocked on my ass at the rugged handsomeness that takes over his face.

Holy shit.

If Grumpy Chance is sinfully hot, Smiley Chance is devilishly molten.

My jaw drops.

Hands fall to the side.

And I just look at him, struggling not to climb back on his lap and demand he take me. His smile hitches up a little wider at the sides, and I fear the strength of my legs even more.

"Get to it," he says, still smiling.

"You can't do that," I lamely tell him, not moving toward my target.

"Do what?" His eyes crinkle as that smile widens until his teeth, the perfectly straight row, are showing.

White teeth. His teeth are so white. It's not normal to be turned on by teeth.

"If you keep smiling like that, I won't be able to control myself. You should know that by now, Chance. Go back to broody and grumpy. We can revisit this when we don't have these nice men behind us as an audience."

The men in question don't even bother holding back their manly chuckles.

"Go on, Wren." My eyes don't leave Chance's mouth as he speaks, his smile *still* in place.

"You *have* to stop," I beg. My God, he's ruining my brain's ability to think rationally. "Seriously, it should be illegal to be that handsome."

With a shake of his head, he places my bag down in my

vacated seat, and he stands up, turns my body, and gives me a little shove toward the front of the plane. I look over my shoulder, hoping to level him with my nasty bitch glare, but when I see him wink, I know I'm done for when it comes to Chance Nash.

One way or the other, I will have that man.

Chapter 9

Wrenlee

The bump and jolt of our landing wake me with a start. My hands fly out blindly, one hand hitting the hard, unforgiving side of the plane to my right, the other hitting a solid warmth—but equally hard surface to my left—and earning a grunt from the man beside me.

Serves him right.

It takes me a while to wake up, always has, but red-eye flights are always more of a struggle for me than when I wake up in a nice cozy bed. Something about them makes me want to just curl up in bed and sleep for a week straight. I'm sure it has something to do with actually getting a little time to sleep, but also a large part in the sleep I actually got being fretful at best. It takes me almost the whole taxi time off the runway and to the gate to wake up.

I hear the guys moving around us. The nice gentlemen who sat behind Chance and me are quiet and efficient in their movements. I thank them, again, for their service before they leave. I smile to myself when I think about how shy the manly men seemed when they had all asked me to autograph the barf bags that Delta provides at each seat. Hey, when in Rome.

Chance stands, stretching his arms above his head, and I'm knocked stupid when his shirt rises, revealing one hell of a defined V at his hips. He reaches into the overhead and pulls my bag out, placing it in his seat while I stand and go to move from our row. It isn't until I hear Wes bust out laughing that I remember my master plan of revenge on Jamison.

My head jerks up, and I smile brightly at Chance. He doesn't return the gesture but just remembering that sizzling hot smile from hours before is enough for me.

Oh, this is going to be great.

Looking over the empty row in front of me, I meet my brother's laughing eyes. Jamison hasn't gotten up from his seat yet, and judging by the way his head bends awkwardly to the side, he's not awake either. I hold my hand up, one finger over my lips, hoping Wes doesn't let the cat out of the bag. Looking around Chance's body, I catch Luke's questioning gaze and repeat my silent shushing. He rolls his eyes, unused to whatever unknown crazy that is our normal, but nods his head nevertheless.

"He's going to kill you," Chance rumbles, his voice thick with sleep.

"Maybe, but it will be so worth it."

He shakes his head while we wait for the plane to continue to clear out, the curtain that separates the first-class section from coach still closed tight. Well, that is until dumb and dumber, better known as our rent-a-cops from Brighthouse, push through. Freaking idiots.

Normally, when we aren't on a plane like this where the exit is between first class and coach, we're the first ones to rush off the plane. I prefer it like this, though. We can let everyone else go and just take our time. When traveling into LAX, we usually have a car meet us at the gate, slipping out the same door that takes employees from the bridge to the tarmac, but we were told a month ago that any time we traveled via flight, we were expected to walk through the airport into the heavily armed paparazzi. This was free PR for them, and with our newest record coming out in mere weeks, they were milking that free PR for all it was worth.

Today, I'm not even slightly bothered that I have to jump off a red-eye and straight into cameras flashing and questions being screamed at us. Nope, not today. Today, I'm going to do all of that with a shit-eating grin on my face.

"Let's go, fuckers. I'm ready to get home," Jamison grumbles, standing and rubbing his eyes.

Wes snorts, filing out of his seat and almost losing his shit when he gets a better view of Jamison. Luke grabs his bag before

Chance gently nudges me forward. I follow the idiots, who are not even pretending to give a shit about the people they're supposed to be guarding, and Chance grabs my hand before we even get past the open plane door. We smile at the flight attendants, thanking them for their discreet service, before walking up the bridge and into the always-busy hustle and bustle of LAX.

Not once in the whole walk through the airport does my smirk slip. I feel almost giddy with anticipation.

"Is the car already out front?" Chance questions the guard who I think is named Dave.

"I think," he mumbles in return.

"You *think*, or you know? Because when it comes to my girl either standing out there waiting with the fucking reporters or getting straight in a car to take us home, that's a big fucking difference."

The man's eyes narrow at Chance's attitude. "It's not really your place to question us on our job, so why don't you let us be the ones who worry about it."

My gaze flies back to Chance's face. I'm starting to feel like I resemble someone watching a tennis match at this point. I can hear some snickers from the people around us, but because of the hot testosterone show that Chance is giving me, I can't even enjoy the fruits of my labor.

"When you have a girl like mine on your arm just waiting for you to get her home safe before giving you a morning of the best fucking you've ever had, then you can tell me it isn't my place to worry. Nothing is going to stand in the way of what's promised to me when we get there, so you can bet your fat fucking ass that it's my place to question you."

Oh. Holy. Shit.

I almost feel like yelling out check please, even though that makes no fucking sense.

There's no response when Chance stops talking—not that I thought there would be. There is nothing that man could say, not after being so thoroughly put in his place.

We continue to walk for a couple of minutes, silence stretching out among our group. The whole time I feel like I'm about to come out of my skin, until I finally can't take it any longer.

"So about that promise?" I question huskily, looking up at Chance.

He glances around us, alert. His emotionless mask is back in place, but instead of finding it annoying like I did before, now it just turns me on even more. Seeing him in action is *hot*.

"Chance," I whine, craving his eyes on me.

"Stop it, Wren."

"Yeah, right," I hiss passionately. "Not after that."

He bends down, not taking his eyes off the business around us nor letting his grip on my hand loosen, his words low and steady. "Don't read into my words when I'm just playing a part."

"You can't fake chemistry like ours."

"You've known me a week," he hisses.

"So? I knew you a day and felt it. Get over your bullshit, Chance. It's gonna happen."

He doesn't respond, standing to his full height.

"Mommy, Mommy! Why is dat man wearing whipsick?"

At the young child's scream, my attention on Chance, as well as my determination to win this fight right now, ends. I almost trip trying to find the little kid who spoke, but Chance's hold on my hand keeps me upright. Wes has completely lost his battle with his own hilarity. I hear him behind me barking out a deep rumbled belly laugh. Luke isn't far behind him. I look over my shoulder and see Jamison's confused gaze on the kid who's pointing to him. I snort out a laugh but turn before he can see my eyes. It would do me no good to have him figure it out before we got to the paparazzi that I know are waiting for us.

"He's going to kill you," Chance says, again reiterating what he said before we left the plane.

I look up, my already bright smile turning up a notch when his eyes drop to my mouth. "Then I guess you'd better protect me, baby."

Those hazel swirls shoot back up to my eyes, and I watch with satisfaction as a fire of awareness lights behind them, heating up from the inside to burn bright and making each different shade of blue and green in his eyes come to life. It's hypnotizing. I could get lost inside eyes like that. Well, that is until he has to break our connection before one of the men in front of us gave the warning that reporters were just ahead.

I hadn't even realized we had made it to the security checkpoint for arriving passengers to get into the baggage claim area yet. I was once again on Chance Cloud Nine, and I quickly realized I would be happy to stay on that cloud for a long fucking time to come.

"Incoming," Chance says under his breath. I look up just in time to get a flash to the retina.

"Wrenlee! Wrenlee! Over here!" *Flash. Snap.*

"Wrenlee, are you planning on anything special when you guys head off to Vegas?" *Flash. Snap.*

"Weston, how are things going with Shelly Knight?" *Flash. Snap.*

I turn to give Weston a smile. I warned him when he agreed to go with that vapid woman to a movie premier that it would bite him in the ass. We're mutual friends with her booking agent, so to Wes, that meant favors were harder to deny, a feeling the two of us didn't share.

"Luke, any news on that movie role you're in the running for?" *Flash. Snap.*

Yeah, right. We don't even get time to sleep. There is no fucking way Brighthouse is going to let him off the hook for months at a time to film.

"Wrenlee, any comment about your pregnancy?" *Flash. Snap.* "Our sources in New York said you had confirmed your pregnancy while checking into the airport last night." *Flash. Snap.*

I'm shocked *that* question took so long. And I would put money on that source being one of those employees who checked us in. Thank you, Jamison. The jerk.

Then there is silence. The cameras' shutters still click away and the flashes still blind us. But not a single question is being thrown at us.

Ah, the taste of revenge is oh, so satisfying. How perfect for it to come right after that last question.

"What?" Jamison asks in confusion when it becomes clear that all the focus is on him.

"Jamison, uh … can you explain your new look?" *Flash. Snap.* Silence.

"What new look, man?"

I drop Chance's hand, to his displeasure, and walk between Luke and Wes, digging into my bag until I find my mirror. "Here you go." I smile sweetly at Jamison.

"Motherfuck," he mutters, reaching out to snag the compact out of my hand.

Chance pulls my back to his front, one muscled forearm crossing over my chest to hold me close. The instant I relax into his embrace, the flashes and snaps intensify until all I can see are bursts of light. Too excited for Jamison's reaction, I don't even care that my plan to make Jamison the focus of our arrival back in LA has failed … well, slightly.

Jamison's eyebrows shoot up, and his bright red lips part. I snicker, waiting for the next part. His hand predictably comes up to try to scrub the perfectly applied lip color from his lips. It took me forever last night to make sure I had applied it flawlessly. It was hard as hell to get all three layers of my favorite budge-proof lip color on Jamison's full lips, but I'm damn proud of the results. Also, I'm a little jealous of his Kylie Kardashian plump lips.

"What the motherfuck?" He bellows out his confusion, narrowing his eyes at me as I laugh so hard Chance has to literally hold me up. Jamison's still rubbing his lips furiously against the back of his hand, but the color doesn't move. My laughter becomes manic, and Wes and Luke join in.

The paparazzi around us continue to snap pictures, but I let this moment play out, knowing it's going to be worth more to them than any questions we would ignore.

Jamison looks up when it becomes clear he isn't getting the lip color off, and I see the acceptance settle in. His back straightens, and he squares his shoulders, handing my mirror back to me without a word.

Then.

Well, then Jamison proves to everyone why life will never be dull when he's around. He steps forward, grabs one of our rent-a-cop guards, and presses his bright red lips against the shocked ones of the man he's holding with an unyielding grasp on his shoulders. When he steps back, making a loud smacking sound, he turns that red painted smile on the cameras.

"It was my turn to wear the skirt," he tells them with a wink as he walks around the stunned guard and climbs into the SUV that had been idling at the curb, waiting for us.

This time, there isn't a single person around us who doesn't laugh. Well, except for the man who will be plastered all over every gossip news outlet in a matter of hours as the boyfriend of Loaded Replay's Jamison Clark.

Chance gives me a squeeze, and with tears of laughter in my eyes, I turn in his hold. His arm wraps around my shoulders, pulling me close, and I bend my arms with my bag hanging to the side of our bodies from the crook of my elbow. My hands press against his sides as the rest of the world around us just falls away. My laughing stops, but my smile doesn't drop.

"Remind me not to get on your bad side," he says with a deep whisper that makes me shiver in his hold. Something he doesn't miss.

"Duly noted."

His attention drops from my eyes to my mouth, and I lick my lips. He drops his head slightly, and I roll onto my toes. My eyes close half-mast for the briefest of seconds before the anticipation of his kiss fills my every desire.

"Wrenlee, is this the baby's father?"

I jolt out of the fog I was trapped in, and my eyes snap open, looking into Chance's. I do my best not to react, used to the bullshit they make up.

"When are you due?" *Flash. Snap.*

"Will you be getting married while you're in Vegas?" *Flash. Snap.*

Chance turns at that one, pulling me with him and adjusting me to curl into his side.

"Who says we aren't already?" he answers.

I gasp at the same time they go insane. The questions start coming so quickly now, I can't even understand what anyone is yelling at us. The camera flashes are never ending as Chance starts walking, all but pulling me into the open door of the SUV.

Well, my plan backfired.

The most shocking of all is I'm not even mad at the man for

starting the mother lode of all rumors.

Most concerning, though, is the spark of excitement that shoots straight into my chest from Chance's words alone, settling deep and creating an opening in the floodgates of hope that I thought had sealed up a long time ago.

Chapter 10

Chance

Wren is silent the whole time we're in the SUV. The guys talk around us, but they don't even try to engage conversation with her. Not once. I know they didn't miss that shit I pulled back at LAX. No way these guys could have missed it, not when they started screaming more questions at us and almost burning my eyes out of my head with their fucking camera flashes.

I shouldn't have said it, but after the words had left my mouth, I didn't regret them. The thought of being legally bound to a woman like Wrenlee Davenport isn't the worst image to have floating through my mind. Even though I knew there wasn't a grain of truth to be found, it didn't stop my thoughts from veering off the path of rationality and envisioning a future I have no right imagining. Thoughts that I haven't allowed myself to even come close to thinking since I felt the burning, searing ache of betrayal so painful I vowed I would never welcome anything close to a relationship again, not even in my thoughts—fake or otherwise.

I think it's because it's been so long since I've had the pleasure of entertaining such a pure thought that I can't find the care to stop picturing it. Between the nightmares I had when I left the Marines and the ones I had after my big fuck-up back home, I had only just recently started sleeping without those nighttime demons of the past visiting. If I'm honest with myself, I'm not ready to push this thought—however untrue—away if this is how oddly peaceful it makes me feel.

I hear a phone ring, pulling my mind from a darkness I don't like to think about envelope me.

"What?" Weston's sharpness has the conversation with Luke and Jamison halting and Wren turning in her seat to look in the back row at her brother.

I use the time to study her face. She doesn't look mad. Instead, she appears a little sad.

"Fuck you, Dix. I told you that you had no control over that."

I twist and hold my hand for the phone. I created this mess so I might as well handle it for him. Weston shakes his head and ignores me. Pulling my arm back, I wait to see what's said next.

"So what if she is? There isn't shit you or Brighthouse can do about it."

Wren shifts, and her movement makes the most delicate scent waft into my nose. I know she doesn't wear perfume, having scanned the bathroom back at the concert venue before I left her clothes in there, and I've been with her every second since, so whatever the aroma is all her and the most mouthwatering thing I've ever smelled.

"No. No fucking way. Wren isn't going to make a public statement denying anything." He holds his finger up, requesting silence before pulling his phone away from his ear and pressing the speaker button to fill the space with one irate voice.

"… run this shit. There will be no relationships, for any of you, but especially not her. Brighthouse still owns you, and when they say you'll stay single, you'd better fucking do it. Issue the statement and then make an appointment somewhere discreet to take care of that problem."

The fury that fills the air when Dix finishes speaking is almost tangible.

"Did you seriously just demand that my sister abort her child?"

"I did, and she will. You will not have a child fucking this up."

"Fucking this up?" Wes echoes.

"It's my job to make sure you four do what Brighthouse wants, and what they want is that baby gone, the marriage taken care of, and all traces of it disappearing. Get that motherfucker away from my band and clean up this mess, Weston. Or else."

Silence.

It doesn't even matter that the child he's demanding be 'taken care of' isn't a reality. It doesn't matter there is no marriage to end—hell, not even a relationship. None of that matters right now because this man has just made it very fucking clear that no one in charge of Loaded Replay's career even gives a fuck about them besides what their music can do for their bank accounts.

"You've got a lot of nerve," Luke bitterly says.

"No, I have all the nerve. I'm the one who is going to make sure that you continue to stay on top. It damn sure won't be you fuck-ups if this latest news is any indication. You're still under contract with them to finish this tour. Just because you've finished the album requirements doesn't mean you can do what you want. I've already talked to Howard, and he's going to bring this back up as an add-in with your renegotiations."

"Hey Dix," Wren says softly.

"What do you want?"

"Do me a favor, will ya?" she continues, ignoring his attitude.

"I'm not doing shit for you until you fix this problem that you've created."

She looks from the phone, meeting the eyes of all three men sitting in the back of the SUV and silently communicating her thoughts before the deep blue orbs hit my face. She gives me a smile, one that goes a long way in unraveling the tangle of unpleasantness in my gut.

"Okay, Dix. How about this then. You can let Howard know that I don't give a shit if he's the president of Brighthouse because right now, you've just screwed them out of even the chance of us re-signing. How about you let Howard know that our lawyer will be in touch. As for you, well … you can consider yourself fired. You might be employed as our manager, but that was only because we didn't know any better when we signed and picked you up through our contract with Brighthouse—one that ended when we finished *Black Lace*. We have no need for you to see us through the rest of our obligations because after the tour, we're gone. Consider our relationship severed. Problem solved. Also— and hear this clearly, please—myself, Loaded Replay—*our* band, not your band—my husband, and our child are no longer some-thing you need to concern yourself with. Have a nice life, asshole."

She reaches over the seat and jabs her tiny finger against her brother's phone, the silence only lasting a second before Weston's phone rings again. He ends the call before powering off his phone, looking at his sister like he can't decide if he should be proud or shocked.

"You do know that we aren't married, right?" I ask in an at-tempt to ease some of the tension.

She whips her head around, her red hair swishing over her shoulder. "Yeah, and you haven't knocked me up yet."

"That won't be happening," I remind her.

"Well, not the knocking me up part. We can practice for that, though."

"Uh, Wren," Jamison butts in, ending our weird-as-fuck ver-bal foreplay.

"Yup?" she answers him, but her attention stays on me.

"Did you just fire our manager?"

The twinkle in her eyes sparks. "Well, yeah," she answers, looking back at him. "I think I did. Would you rather have me break up my marriage and lose my love child?"

"Both of which aren't even a reality," Weston reminds her.

"Po-tay-toes, po-tah-toes." She sighs dramatically.

"Oh, nope … not even the same thing there."

"What is Brighthouse going to say about what just happened?" When I ask the question, I notice all of them look uneasy.

"They own us through this tour, but even if they didn't, we would finish our commitments. When we signed on almost five years ago, our contract stated that we would provide Brighthouse with two albums. We did that and re-upped with them for three more when those first two albums were such a huge success. We didn't know what we know now about the business then. It had only been eighteen months after signing the first contract when we signed the current one." Wes looks at Luke before continuing. "We've been lucky. Most artists end up in the negatives once advances and everything else they take out of our cut from the profits is said and done, but we've never been like that. We don't need them, and most importantly, because of how well our albums have always sold, we don't owe them. They have nothing to hold over our head when we tell them we won't be re-signing with them. I guess we can thank you, bro-in-law, for making us realize what it was past time to do," Weston jokes, but I have a feeling that they are more concerned about losing their representation than they're letting on.

"Why were they so eager to get you back in the studio if you don't even have a contract for further albums yet?"

Wren makes a noise that sounds like some weird laugh turned snort, drawing my attention. "That, hubby, is because they know time is money and they assumed us re-signing was a done deal."

"Okay." I rub the back of my neck, ignoring her new nickname for me. "Look, I know next to nothing about this industry, but can you really continue without being signed to a major label?"

"Brighthouse wasn't a major label until they signed us. Could we continue to produce albums, sure … but it would be a whole fucking lot easier if we had the backing of a label. They handled everything from studio time to tour details. Dix, someone we picked up because we knew we needed a manager when we signed, was with Brighthouse. He worked as our booking agent as well, so losing the label and him means we have a whole lot of nothing but ourselves and our music," Weston explains.

"So what do we do now?" Jamison chimes in, sounding just as overwhelmed as I feel.

"Now, we decide if we want to do this alone or start looking for new representation. We have the funds to do it ourselves, but that would mean our focus is taken from what we want to be doing, which is making music," Wes clarifies, not breaking eye contact with his sister. "The good news is we don't have to decide right now. We get two weeks before Vegas, so I say we spend that time enjoying the break we've needed for a long time. We pick things back up in Vegas, finish the last few weeks of shows, and then sit down and decide how we want our future to go. Wren and

I will call Don and get him on the legal end of breaking our ties to Brighthouse. In the meantime, let's try to remember what it feels like to relax."

"Don?" I ponder out loud.

"Our lawyer," Wren responds with a wink.

I nod and turn back around in my seat. There isn't much to see; traffic is already ridiculous here even in the early morning hours. The driver ignores us; his eyes focused on the road ahead of us. I take a few seconds to study my surroundings, making sure to test the air around me for any unease I might feel. Shockingly, even with the future of Loaded Replay very much unknown, all four members seem almost relieved.

All I can do is follow their lead when it comes to their label—or I guess former label—and do what I'm here to do, which is to protect the woman beside me. The one who is doing one hell of a job at burrowing herself under my skin, whether I want her there or not.

Chapter 11

Wrenlee

When the driver pulls off Sunset Boulevard, and we officially enter the Bird Streets area, I try to see things through the eyes of someone who has never been a part of our crazy little world. We pass a few of the famously named bird-themed streets on our way to our own, and I smile, thinking about how much fun I used to have just walking around and listing the street names. It's been so long since I did that, and I had forgotten how much I loved that downtime activity, no matter how bizarre it might have been.

The 'elite' area of the Bird Streets neighborhoods was the first place our realtor took us when we decided we wanted to make LA our forever home. We had been living in a tiny piece-of-shit apartment when we first came to town, but a year after our second album blew up, we knew it was time for something more permanent. Even if we were rarely home to enjoy it.

"You all live together, right?" Chance muses; his head turned while he takes in the landscape around us.

"Yeah. We have for the past eight years, ever since we left home and hit the road. We're probably one big contradiction to the rule that says you shouldn't work and live with your family without killing them," I quip.

"I've done the roommate thing, and it wasn't a hardship." My eyes widen, momentarily taken aback that he's actually speaking, let alone telling me something about himself.

He looks over when my silence ticks on. "What?"

"That's the most personal thing you've told me since you showed up in New York last week."

He shrugs, turning to look back out his window.

I turn, seeing the driveway that I know leads to the home of one of the most famous actresses around. "Why did you stop doing the roommate thing?" I feel stupid, but with an opening like that, I figure I might as well see if I can find out more about this man.

"He got married and moved into a house with his wife."

"Oh." I rack my brain to think of another way to keep this conversation going, but his body language isn't exactly screaming that he's open to continuing.

"You guys still good friends?"

"I served with him overseas, lived with him back home for a few years, and I still talk to him on the phone more often than should be normal for two dudes."

I can sense the smile in his words, betraying his annoyance.

"You should see if he and his wife want to come out to one of our shows before the tour ends." I sound needy. Like a teenage girl trying to get her first crush to talk to her. I should shut up. I really should. But fuck … he's actually talking.

"I doubt that's going to happen. Cohen and Dani have two small boys, so getting time to fly across the country isn't the easiest. Plus, I think filming picked back up for Dani."

"Filming?" I probe.

He turns and looks at me with a sigh. "She works at a salon in town, and they film a reality show there."

My eyes widen. "Holy shit! The Dani from *Sway's All the Way*?" He jerks his head back when I all but scream my excitement at him. "I watch every episode of that show. I remember a few seasons back when they made a huge fuss about her relationship and pregnancy. Wait a minute. You're best friend is him?" I gasp, reaching out to grab his arm and shake it rapidly.

"Shit, you've done it now," my brother mumbles from his seat in the back.

"Oh, my God! I love them. I had really hoped that their story wasn't just something made up for viewers. It isn't, right?"

He shakes his head.

"You have no idea how cool this is! Dyllan is going to shit herself. We usually watch the show together, and it's going to be so much better knowing that they're really in a relationship."

"Do you want to ease up on my arm?"

It takes me a second to register his meaning, but when I look at my hands and see them still shaking his arm, I feel my cheeks heat in embarrassment. "Sorry about that. I got a little excited."

"*That* was a little excited?"

I give him a heated look, but it only lasts for a second when I see him looking at me with a smile. It isn't as big as it was last night on the plane, but those white teeth are peeking out, and just like the first time I saw him smile, I resort to brain-dead status.

"You look fucking weird, Wren," Jamison exclaims, his hand reaching over from the back to poke at my shoulder.

Chance's smile cranks up a few notches, his eyes crinkling at the sides. It makes me wonder if he actually smiles often when he's around his friends. Or maybe he used to smile a lot.

"Is she drooling?" Luke butts in; he sounds like he shifted in his seat to get closer.

"Stop doing that," I hiss at Chance.

"I'm not doing anything."

"It's just not right for you to have that much power," I inform him.

"What is she talking about?" Jamison questions.

"Still not doing anything," Chance tells me, ignoring Jami.

"Yoo-hoo," Jamison yells, his hand coming into view as he waves it in front of my face.

Blinking a few times, I twist my neck to look at Jamison with a scowl. "What?"

"Phew." He sighs, falling back against his seat. "For a second there, I thought we had lost you. I figured you wouldn't want everyone to know what your O face looks like. You looked like you were about to eat Chance here for breakfast."

"I was not about to O face anyone," I sputter.

"You so were," Luke confirms, siding with Jamison.

"Can we not talk about this?" Wes complains.

"Yes, we *can* not talk about this. Great idea, Wes. Oh look, there's our street." I turn toward my window so fast that I almost crack my forehead against the tinted window. I thrust my hand out, pointing at the road sign to announce our turn on Swallow Drive.

"You live on a street called Swallow Drive?" I can hear the teasing in Chance's question, and I swear that's the only reason I open my mouth and further embarrass myself.

"Yup. It called to me when we were house hunting. You know, because I love to swallow."

That stupid, brain-killing smile is back; only this time, a deep and manly laugh accompanies it. And let me tell you—if his smile was enough to kill my ability to think, the sound of his laughter is enough to turn that dead brain into a pile of mush.

Holy. Shit.

Two minutes later, the driver parks in front of our house, and I rush out and around the SUV in seconds. My goal had been to get inside and lock myself in my room, but Chance hooks me with a hand to my elbow, stopping my movement.

"Let me check the house," he demands.

My brow furrows. "Seriously? Is that necessary?"

His eyes are still smiling when his very serious tone answers me. "When it comes to keeping you safe, yeah. I'm finding I like you, Wren. Let me do my job so I can keep on liking you."

"You like me?"

His hand comes up, and one long finger brushes the skin between my eyes, all the way down to the tip of my nose, before disappearing from my line of sight with a soft tap. Then he turns, and I watch him walk up to the huge black door. With quick and efficient movements that betray the fact he's never once set foot on our property, he unlocks and disarms the keypad, and before I can blink, he's inside.

"What happened back there between you two?" Weston quietly questions, stepping in front of me and blocking my view of our house, giving a lift of his chin in the direction of the SUV.

I let out a dramatic rush of air. "Oh, big brother." I sigh. "That man has no idea what he does to me."

Weston's quiet for a beat while he ponders what I mean. "And that is?" he continues his questioning, albeit hesitantly now. It's almost as if he doesn't really want to know, but being the protective big brother that is he, he feels like he has to ask.

"Makes me deliriously stupid with need."

"I knew this would happen!" Jamison yells, his fist going up in the air before pointing at Wes. "You owe me five hundred bucks, fucker."

"Shit," Wes hisses, his eyes looking from me, to Jamison, to the house, and then back at me. "Shit!"

Chapter 12

Wrenlee

"Let me get this straight," Dyllan slurs. With her wine glass pointing at me, I wonder if she's about to slosh some of the delicious red we've been drinking for the last two hours all over my brand-new white loungers. "The man who you've known for a week is your *not* husband is now the featured story with every entertainment show, tabloid, and Internet celebrity blogger for getting you *not* pregnant with your *not* firstborn. You may or may not be renewing your nonexistent vows when you show up in Vegas. Oh, you also fired your manager this morning and told your label to fuck off at the same time … all of this in one day?"

I take a heavy sip, enjoying the way the wine's flavors burst over my taste buds. "That about sums it up. Wait, you forgot the fact that I almost dry humped him in front of four strangers on the flight. And that his kisses could make a dead person orgasm. Annnnd that his smile alone is probably all it would take for me."

Dyllan gasps, lifting her body off the lounger and placing her wine glass down on the table between us. "Shut up. His smile alone?"

I nod, completely serious. "You have no idea, Dyll. There aren't enough adjectives in the world that would help me describe to you what that man looks like when he lets one free or what it does to me. Totally should be classified as a deadly weapon, I'm sure of it."

"Oh, wow." She falls back and looks over the pool in front of us while her eyes focus on the brightly lit lights of LA shining up at us from my lanai. "Wow," she breathes dreamily again.

"How am I supposed to play the part of the in-love girl-friend—" I stop when I'm cut off by a hand waving in front of my face sloppily.

"Wife." Dyllan giggles into her wine glass, her eyes bright with mirth.

"Whatever, Dyll. Just tell me how to make this work without going insane in the process. I want that man more than I've wanted anything in a long damn time, if ever. I don't even remember wanting to be discovered this badly!"

Her face gets serious, despite the fact that I know she's

probably as drunk as I am. The soft light coming from the pool area is making her look almost crazy. "Where is the rule that says you can't enjoy him while this whole thing is going on?"

"He's here to be my security guard, not my live-in sex toy."

"I just don't see why you can't have the best of both worlds. There are times that he doesn't need to keep a constant guard on you. Like when you're alone here, on the bus, or in a hotel. Who says you can't both get something out of this. Lord knows you should be able to now that the media is going nuts speculating and not likely to stop anytime soon."

Her words ping around in my head, and try as I might, I can't stop them from taking root in my mind. "That would make things ... complicated."

She tosses her head back, her short blond hair dancing around her. "Wrenny, I think it's safe to say that it's already com-plicated. The whole world right now thinks you're expecting his love child and that you're either secretly married or will be soon. It doesn't get much more complicated than that. Plus, you guys can think of it as studying for your roles as love-struck newly-weds. I always did say that you could tell with one glance which couples know what it feels like to stick their naughty bits together. You can just tell when a couple has that knowledge of each other."

"I highly doubt that you can tell that just by looking at two people."

"It's true, I'm telling you. Watch." She gets up from her seat and grabs my hand, pulling me up and out of the back lanai area and through the open glass panels that lead into our living room area.

We move through the house, walking by the kitchen and down a short narrow hallway that leads to the stairs to the bottom floor. I almost trip trying to keep up with her pulling against my arm. When we hit the bottom level, she looks down the long hallway that leads to the five bedrooms down here briefly before turning her attention toward the other hallway—shorter than the other—that leads to the movie theater and our in-house recording studio when the sounds of the guys messing with their instruments echoes around us.

She doesn't drop my arm, pulling me farther until we stumble into the room. I see Luke and my brother sitting in front of each other, their fingers rapidly strumming their guitars for a second before they stop and discuss something. Wes makes a note on the paper next to them before they repeat the process. Since the sound in the control room is muted, we can't hear what they're saying, but I smile at the image of them writing new material.

"Watch this," Dyllan commands and presses the button that will fill the room with our voices. "Hey guys," she says into the mic. Both of them look up and roll their eyes but give us a wave. "Carry on," she jokes with a smile.

"What was that?" I question her odd behavior.

"That is me proving a point. How did they look at us?"

I feel my face contort. "Like they always do. Annoyed with how much they love us."

"Exactly. Like great friends and brothers would look at another woman."

"Uh, okay?" I input, not knowing what else to say. Maybe she's more drunk than I realized.

"Follow me." She claps her hands and bounces slightly on her feet.

With a roll of my eyes, I follow her back the way we just came; only this time, she walks down the opposite hallway and stops in front of Jamison's doorway. Not liking where I think this is going, I stand aside and wait for her to do whatever she is going to do.

Her hand comes up, looking over her shoulder at me before knocking.

"Yo!"

At Jamison's bellow, she turns the knob and opens the door wide, giving me a clear view of the man himself as he sits on the edge of his bed with his game controller in his hand. He doesn't move his eyes from the TV in front of him. My lips twitch when I see the faint red stain on his lips—left over from the LipSense color he couldn't scrub off. I could have made it a little easier and given him some of my remover, but seriously, where is the fun in that?

"Hey, Jamison," Dyllan calls into his room, talking a little louder than normal to be heard over the noise of machine guns and war sounds.

Jamison blinks then ever so slowly turns his head and looks right through me before his gaze settles on Dyllan. I watch as recognition sparks—his pupils dilate and his breathing speeds up ever so slightly. If I hadn't been watching for something, I never would have noticed anything different in his demeanor, but fuck me, there is no way that could be mistaken.

Before he even has a chance to reply, I push off the wall and into the doorway, blocking his view of Dyllan. "You've had your naughty bit inside my best friend, you sicko!" I scream the accusation at him.

Chapter 13

Wrenlee

I can't remember the last time I was able to lie in bed for hours
and just gaze outside at the beautiful blue sky. I didn't even
close the shades last night before bed. Instead, I bypassed the
button that would silently lower the dark panels over the huge ex-
panse of glass that makes up a whole wall of my bedroom in favor
of the second night of bliss promised by sleeping in my own bed
after way too long. I should have taken the time, though, because
the sun always hits the pool at this time of the morning, reflecting
a bright beam of light right into my room. Even with that annoying wake-up call, I can't be bothered to move, so I stretch out and

decide I deserve just to lie here.

It's boring.

It's lazy.

So unproductive.

It's the perfect beginning to the day. The smile that was already present on my face before my mind had even completely woke to full consciousness widens at the thought.

How long have I wanted, no … how long have I craved this right here? I'm almost afraid to move, for fear that this will all be a dream and I'll wake up to find that I'm really on the tour bus in some city in the United States that I have to have someone remind me to get right before I go on stage.

"Morning, sleepyhead," my brother sings, coming into the lounge area that is set up right by the doorway of my room. He doesn't wait for a response before walking fully into my room.

"I think it's more like afternoon, Wes, but I'll take it."

"Just checking to see if you need anything. Jamison, Luke, and I are headed out to meet Dyllan for some new clothes and shit. I never thought I would look forward to the day I could go shopping on my own."

I laugh. "How did she take you asking to actually go shopping instead of her picking up a bunch of shit to bring here for you to choose from?"

"I'm pretty sure she thinks we've lost our minds. Maybe we have, but we've been home for a week, and I already feel like a new man."

"You aren't wrong," I agree with a bubble of laughter. "God,

Wes. All it took was a week, and I already feel like the constant struggle to breathe is gone." I pause. "I was starting to resent the music, you know," I finish, my voice small and sad.

"I know, I know. I thought by now I would have some regret over ending things with Brighthouse, but all I feel is relief ... and excitement."

He searches my face, a small smile playing on his lips. "I'm not sure if we would be sitting here right now if it wasn't for that whole *not* marriage you've gotten yourself into."

I tag one of the pillows next to me and toss it at his head. His hand comes up, and he easily deflects the movement.

"Careful, sister. Think of my *not* niece!"

"Oh, you annoying little shit," I jabber then both of us start laughing, loudly.

"Slumber party!" Jamison yells from the end of the bed, jumping and landing hard on the bed next to me, causing my body to bounce. "I always knew I would get in bed with you." He wags his brows and makes a throaty meow noise in the back of his throat.

"You're the most annoying man in the whole world," I inform him.

He shrugs.

"Where are Luke and Chance?" I question, not that I expected Chance to join in, but Luke usually isn't too far behind Jami.

"Gym, I think. At least, that's the last place that I saw Chance on my way upstairs. You have that man working out day and night to burn off his sexual tension. If you're not going to give in to me then, by God, put him out of his misery."

Wes makes a sound close to gagging and stands from the bed. I roll my eyes, but for once, I actually give Jamison's advice some merit. I have been avoiding Chance for pretty much the whole week—something that clearly hasn't gone unnoticed. I think I did it more out of self-preservation than anything else. I'm not sure what to do with the feelings swirling through my body, completely feverish in their insanity, when he's around.

"You know that can't happen," I confess with a slight wave to my words, making them come out more like a question than a statement.

"And why is that, Wren?" Wes pipes in, not looking grossed out anymore. His blue eyes almost look hopeful. I guess the question would be whether he's hopeful that I believe that, or hopeful that I'm questioning it.

"He works for us, Wes. He's supposed to keep me safe, not sated."

Jamison sits up, crossing his legs in front of him. His blond hair falls into his eyes, and he brushes it back with a lazy run of his fingers through the thickness. "Yeah, but who are we to say he can't do both?"

"I think he's the one who's saying that actually," I embarrassingly admit.

"Has he actually said you two can't be together?"

I think back to the times we have been together. He warned me not to start something with him. He advised me to protect myself from him. But he's never said no. He's never sounded like he didn't want me either. "Not that I can recall."

"Then I guess it's up to you now," Jamison says, his normally joking jabs absent as complete seriousness falls over him. "He makes you laugh, Wren. He makes those shadows dancing in your eyes vanish. For the first time in too long, you aren't acting like a dark cloud is hanging over your head. I'm not the smartest bastard around, but it doesn't take a fucking genius to figure out that all of that started almost two weeks ago. The same time Chance Nash walked into our lives in New York."

"Whoa, Jamison. Getting deep, bro." Wes slaps his shoulder. He might have wanted his words to come across as lighthearted and joking, but the way he's looking at me speaks a different story. He breaks our connection and gives Jamison a small nod. Then we're alone again, and the door shuts softly behind Jamison as he exits.

"Do you like this guy?"

"Straight to the point, Weston," I grumble.

"Do you," he reiterates.

My shoulders drop with a sigh. "Yeah, Wes. I do."

"You don't even know him, Wren. He's been around for two weeks, and aside from when we were in New York and the trip home, you've gone out of your way to avoid him. How can you like someone you don't know?"

"I avoid him because he scares the shit out of me."

He startles at my response. "How so?"

"The way he makes me feel, Wes. Never have I felt anything like that … except when we're on stage. Like I'm completely high and out of my mind with the way my nerves dance in my body.

Everything comes alive. My skin feels hypersensitive. My ears amplify the sounds around me. My vision is clear and crisp with a brightness that looks fake. It's absolutely terrifying."

"Jesus Christ," Wes sputters.

"Tell me what happens when I give in to what I feel for this man? What happens when I give in to those feelings and then … then he turns out to be just like the rest?"

Wes frowns. "Just like the rest?"

"The rest of the people who only wanted what being with us could bring to their lives. What if I do get a chance with him, and he ends up hating me because of the fame?"

Understanding dawns on his face. "Fuck, Wren," he whispers, coming to sit next to me on the bed and pulling me into his comforting arms. He waits for me to rest my head on his shoulder before he speaks again. "Not everyone is like that, baby sister. We've kept to ourselves, the four of us, since we left home. The boys you dated before then, they were just that … boys. I'm not saying that your fears aren't justified, but we agreed to leave our past behind us a long time ago. You need to let go of those fears. Not everyone is out to use us."

"Garrett did."

"Garrett was a twenty-one-year-old punk. It's been five years, Wren. Chance is a man, not some kid desperate to make his dreams come true."

"People still become greedy, no matter the age," I grunt.

"Don't let our fucking parents do that. Don't let them influence your life all these years later. Not after we've won by succeeding when they vowed we would fail."

"Wes …" I exhale. "Our own parents tried to use us. How can you believe that others should be trusted not to do it when the people who gave us life did?"

His head drops to rest against mine. His free hand comes up into my line of sight, and he holds it palm up, waiting. My eyes water, thinking about all the years we used to sit just like this when we were upset. The second my palm touches his, just like every time before, my brother gives me strength with a simple touch of our hands.

"Not everyone is like that. I won't insult you by trying to justify why they neglected us. Honestly, Wren, nothing *could* justify that, but for me, I have to believe they are the worst things we will ever have in our lives, and something better is waiting for us to find it. Someone who will show us that all the shit we put up with as kids was worth it because they're the reward waiting for us. You have to give someone a chance to discover if they're the reward."

I pull my hand from his and wipe at my eyes. "And if I fall for this man, the allure of a reward, only to find him not there to catch me?"

My brother's arm tightens around me. "Then you still won't hit the ground, little sister, because I will always be here to make sure you never fall far."

"Love you, bub," I sniffle, using the nickname I had for him when we were small children.

"Love you right back, sissy."

The guys left an hour ago. I feel vulnerable after the heaviness of my chat with Wes, in a sense, so like the coward I am, I've stuck to my bedroom instead of venturing out. For the first time since we moved into this huge house, I thank my lucky stars that the guys let me have the master bedroom suite. Not only is it huge, but there's a bar next to the fireplace that sits across from my bed, a smaller room attached to the large bedroom that holds a couch and some chairs, a TV, and some bookshelves, and a bathroom that could double as a private spa.

Seriously, it's like a small heaven.

The guys all took rooms on the lower level of our house, leaving me not only with the huge master but also making the main level of our home feel more like I live alone.

The floor plan of our house is like a large U shape; the lanai and pool area are in the middle of that U, outdoors and overlooking the city below, mountains in the distance, and houses around the hills that surround us.

My bedroom area, two of the guest rooms, and an office make up one tip of the letter's shape. The formal living room and formal dining room are on the curve with the front door, along with the staircase that leads below. The kitchen, laundry, massive pantry, complete with a wine storage room, and a second more relaxed living room make up the other tip of the letter.

The guys' rooms and two other guest rooms are all under the kitchen's side, leaving the movie theater under mine—with the studio and gym under the center.

It's huge—unnecessarily so—but I've never regretted the huge chunk of change that we put down on it. I don't even think a small army would be enough to fill the ridiculous amount of space we have in our home.

Which is perfect when you're trying to avoid someone.

I open my door and stick my head out, looking down the hallway to see if I can sense any movement further in the house. I know he's here … I can feel him. His very presence is a tangible tingle that dances across my skin, making goose bumps pop up in its wake.

"What are you doing?"

I jump, scream, and whirl around to face the man of the house, standing in the middle of the hallway, opposite of the direction where I had been looking.

"Uh," I stutter.

"You were trying to find out where I was, weren't you?"

My face heats, and his eyes drop lower. I can just imagine that my face is flaming red, probably my neck, and most likely, the parts of my chest that are exposed from the low neckline of my tank top.

"Why are you avoiding me, Wrenlee?" he jibes.

"Dammit," I hiss. It's now or never. I can continue to be a little coward, or I can hike up my pants—er, leggings—and stop being afraid. "Shit." I look around, not meeting his eyes, but then as if lightning had struck right where I stood, I know what I need to do. My spine straightens and my shoulders go back as confidence fills my body with every breath. I meet his gaze and shrug. "Because it was easier to avoid you than get turned down when you—again—deny the chemistry between us."

"Wren." He steps forward, bringing our bodies just a few feet away from touching.

"No, Chance. No more bullshit. Give me one good reason why we can't explore this, and don't you dare use being my security as one."

"It's not that simple. I ..." He cups the back of his neck, looking down as the silence grows between us.

"You know what," I quietly fuss, getting him to look up. "I lied. I avoided you because I'm absolutely scared out of my mind of the way you make me feel. It's insane. I haven't known you long enough to feel this strongly about you. I know next to nothing about you personally, but it doesn't matter. I feel my body being pulled to yours, and it scares the *shit* out of me."

"You are scared of me?" He emits an incredulous, sarcastic-like laugh with his words.

"Out of my mind with fear." I continue to hold my body, giving an appearance of confidence that I don't think I feel completely.

"You have no idea what it's like to feel fear over what someone could do to you if you let them get close, Wren. You are ... *you*, Wren. And me ... I'm just some nobody with nothing to show for his thirty-one years but a handful of friends and a whole lot of empty. I can't let you in, Wren. I'll do what I need to do for the public, but you hold far more power over me than I ever could over you. I warned you, Wren. You have to protect yourself from me."

The pain in his voice makes me falter on my feet before I move forward two steps and cup his cheeks with my hands. "I don't want to protect myself from you. I want to give myself to you."

Awareness and lust sparks in his eyes, those swirls of blues and greens turning into a kaleidoscope of magic as he holds my gaze. "I can't. I can't handle what happens when it all ends, and it always, always ends."

"Then I guess I have to prove to you that you're wrong." The truth in my words hits us both differently. My words, spoken out loud, renew my strength to let go of my past and the hang-ups that it's already soiled me with. For him, though, he looks almost nervous.

"You won't win this battle, Wren," he tells me, but he lacks the conviction needed to make me believe what he's saying.

"Oh, Chance, you won't win," I whisper, coming up on my toes to press a feather light kiss to his lips then pulling back to look into his eyes. "You might think you will, but mark my words, I will have you, and you're going to love it. Every. Single. Second. If I can put my fears aside to just take this chance and open myself up to your rejection time and time again, then you can do the same and stop letting whatever hurt you before stand in the way of your life."

I pull back and give him a small smile then turn to leave him alone to think about what I just said. One thing's for sure, though; even if he continues to deny us what we both clearly want, I'll just have to make sure he doesn't succeed.

Chapter 14

Chance

Fucking, fuck, motherfucking FUCK!

I leave the empty hallway and stomp forward, following the sounds of her puttering around in the kitchen.

"You need to stop this game, Wren." My breathing is erratic; fists balled at the sides of my hips.

"It isn't a game, Chance."

"Then what is it you want? What could possibly come of us giving in to this thing between us?"

She stops fidgeting with the cold-cut meat she had been placing on the kitchen island and faces me. Her hair falling free around her head, the patch that she had saved around her temple a little longer than it was when I first met her, making me wonder how often she has to shave it. She looks tiny, the oversized tank top falling in a baggy swoop over her chest, her torso swimming in the material. I know from watching her over the past week since arriving at their home in California that the leggings she favors cup her firm ass perfectly, and when she's walking down the stairs, the fabric molds to her pussy in a way that makes my mouth water. Even if I can't see that now, because of her shirt's length, those images have forever been burned into my brain. I've never been so thankful for such ridiculous printed leggings before until recently.

"I want to take a gamble and hope that my reward will be waiting for me. A chance for *Chance.*"

I grip the smooth surface of the quartz countertop, dropping my head with a sigh. "You're asking for the impossible."

She moves, her tiny feet taking her from the other side of the island, closer to me. She doesn't stop until she's so close that every part of her body is touching mine, her big blue eyes just looking up at me. No talking, our breathing harsh and loud as it echoes off the wall, and she shivers. I can feel it, that need my body has for hers, the power of it calling out to hers, and I feel my resolve crumbling.

"I have no way of knowing what will happen tomorrow, Chance. I can't even assume that I can predict the next hour. All I know is that even with everything I could possibly want or need in my life surrounding me, I still feel empty. Before you popped into my life, I had been struggling to find something that I even liked about that life. I sensed I was searching for something, but I didn't have a clue as to what. Then you showed up, and it was as if every lock inside me had popped open. I had no idea what to do with that until I stopped being afraid that my past would repeat itself. Now I know that, in order for me not to go back to that place I was in, I have to be able to let people in and take a chance. So, yeah … it might feel impossible, but I'm just asking for my Chance."

"You're going to destroy me," I tell her, trying to reason with her by giving her the truth of my fears.

"We're going to destroy each other and then put the pieces back together, so there aren't any more cracks." Her words, confusing to many, show me just how well Wrenlee has pegged me.

I bend my body and give in to the temptation I've felt since I met her. My hands slide around her waist, and with a tug, I eliminate any space between our bodies. She emits a shocked squeak from her lips, and a second later, her hands are around my neck. She struggles with our height difference before I give in and lift her from the ground to sit on the island, stepping between her legs. My forehead goes to hers, lightly resting there, and I don't look away from the questions in her eyes.

"It's been almost a decade since I was in a relationship, Wren. I haven't the slightest clue on how to make one work because the last one I had blew up in my face in the most painful way. You want to do this; we have to be honest with each other. I mean it. I can't move forward without complete honesty."

She studies my face, trying to read between the lines of my words. I pull in a deep breath before letting it out slowly.

"She lied to me, Wren. A lot. It's hard for me to trust people, especially women. But you weren't the only one who felt like something inside you was being snapped open when we met."

"So does this mean you're my *not* husband for real now?" she quips, trying to lighten the mood a little.

"As long as we keep the *not* babies to practice only."

"I won't lie to you, Chance."

"Then it looks like we're taking a gamble together."

Her smile is blinding. I've seen her face everywhere for the past five years, often smiling, but never like this. Something so genuine it's alight from the inside. Her legs lift, circling around my hips, and she locks her ankles behind my back in order to pull me flush against her center. I run my hands up her back and bend over slightly, holding her head in my hand when she is forced to tip it back to keep looking at me with that beautiful damn smile.

"At the risk of sounding like I only want you for your body, you have no idea how badly I want you to fuck me," she declares with a breathy voice.

"At the risk of sounding like a bastard, I want to fuck you probably more so."

"Then what are you waiting for?"

I push my hard length against her hotness. Even with my layers of clothes between us, it feels like her pussy is burning my cock.

"We need to get to know each other," I hedge, my eyes

wanting to roll back in my head when she curls her nails into my shoulders and rolls her hips against me.

"We're already *not* married, hubby. It wouldn't be right not to consummate our union by … unioning." She's almost panting, the color high on her cheeks.

"I don't think unioning is a word, babe."

"Jesus, Chance," she whines, not in an annoying way, but a needy one that is hot as fuck. "Playing twenty questions to get to know each other isn't going to change anything. You fuck me now or a week from now, it will happen. It's up to you if we have a few minutes of uncomfortable need or weeks. Because I can assure you, our bodies need this more than we could ever know. Feel that," she commands, rocking hard against my cock. "Feel that and then tell me that you don't *need* this."

"Goddamn," I hiss and then crush my mouth to hers in a kiss so brutally perfect all I can do is deepen it, drunk on the rush of her touch.

Our mouths feast on each other, hands fumbling to free each other's bodies of the clothes that stand between us. I hear myself grunt in displeasure when her mouth leaves mine, instantly wanting it back, but when she begins to pull my shirt up my torso, I calm slightly and lift my arms to help her remove it. The second her fingers drop my shirt, I pull hers up and over before putting my mouth back where I want it … on her.

Our tongues move together. Slide and twist around wet breaths of need. Her hands roam around my back, pressing in and exploring my body, while the deep whines and mewls coming from her spike my need for her, to feel the heat of her pussy without anything between us.

My mouth, wet from hers, pulls back and travels down her slim neck, my hands coming around to cup her tits through the lace of her bra, the weight of them in my palms heavy. For such a tiny girl, she has bigger breasts than she should. Most girls as tiny as her have nothing for a chest but not Wren. They fit perfectly in my hands. I squeeze them, smiling against the curve of her neck when she whimpers. Leaning up, I look into her hooded eyes, curl my fingers under the cups of her bra, and jerk it down until both globes are freed. She gasps and pushes her chest into my hold, begging without words for more.

"Please," she cries when my thumb rolls over the turgid tips of her nipples. As much as I want to look down and see what color her nipples are, she's holding me captive as I watch her use my body to find her release. Her hips rock as best as she can, given our positions, trying to find friction. Her mouth is hanging slack, breathing erratic, and her eyes are begging me for more.

Without looking away, I bring my hands to her back and unhook her bra, her arms rushing from my body to get the offensive material away from our bodies. I bring a hand up, placing it between her tits, palm to her smooth skin, and push her slightly backward. She follows my silent demand, lying back with a squeak of shock when the coldness of the counter hits her fevered skin. Then I give myself the pleasure of seeing her almost fully naked, laid out for me like a gift for a starved man.

"Wren," I grunt, bending to pull one of her dusty nipples

into my mouth. I bite it between my teeth while keeping my eyes locked with hers.

My tongue flicking against her nipple, quickly, back and forth until her back curls and she thrashes under my touch. My fucking cock is so hard right now, and unable to hold back, a burst of come leaves my body. I squeeze my eyes tight and hold back the rest of my orgasm. I know I won't be able to hold back much longer, not with her undulating under my touch from just my mouth on her nipple.

"Birth control, Wren?"

"Yes. Always. I do it. Fuck." She brings her hands up and starts to tweak her own nipples, repeating her mumbled words, still not making it clear if she understands what I'm asking. My eyes cross, and I feel more wetness coming from my cock.

"I'm clean," I pant, thrusting slightly while my hands caress her sides, leaving her to play with her own nipples, and curling my fingers into the waistband of her leggings. I use the leverage of that hold on her leggings to pull her harshly against my body. Her pussy grinds against my erection without delay. I look down, seeing the fabric against her center outlining her pussy lips as they widen to seek out my length. "I was tested six months ago, and even before that, it had been a while. Be sure you understand me."

"Goddamn, Chance. Take off our pants and get your big fat cock inside me now!" she screams, letting go of her tits to slap her hands against the counter and lift her head to give me a look of desperation.

"Not until you tell me what I need to know, baby."

"I'm on the pill. I'm clean. And it's been what feels like an eternity, so please stop stalling and put an end to this burning need I feel consuming me before it kills me," she gasps, panting with wild eyes.

I step back, pulling my fingers free of the band at her waist. Unbuckling my belt, I snap the buttons of my jeans open. With harsh movements, I push them down my legs, stepping out of both my jeans and briefs. My cock, erect and wet from my own come, points up in the air. When I look up from my red, angry, and very needy cock, I see Wren wiggling against the counter, trying to get her leggings off her body without much success.

"Need some help?" I ask, palming my cock to stroke it lazily. She looks up at my question, and her eyes widen when she sees that I'm standing there naked, not even bothering to hide her hungry gaze as she watches my hand fist my length.

"Get these pants off me. I don't even care that they're unicorns and a print I had to hunt down because all those eager bitches always steal the best ones first. Cut them off now. Cut them off!"

"Unicorns?" I bark out a laugh.

"God. Shit, Chance Nash, now is not the time for me to school you on the ins and outs of LuLaRoe!"

"Laluwho?"

Her eyes narrow at my teasing. I can't remember ever feeling this much heavy need for someone, yet here we are joking. Taking pity on her, I step forward and peel the tight as fuck fabric down her legs. Her bare pussy, glistening with her arousal, is the first thing I see, and my mouth waters instantly.

"No way, mister. There will be plenty of time for a taste test later—for both of us—but if you don't get that fat cock inside me right now, I swear to God I'm going to die. I really will." She throws the words at me, but her attention is solely on my cock. My hand is back to stroking it with lazy movements. "You seriously have the most beautiful penis I've ever seen."

My eyes fly back to her face. "Not sure if I like being compared to the other cocks you've seen."

"The thickest," she continues wickedly.

"Wren," I warn.

"Maybe the longest, but I would have to get a closer look to say for sure," she prods, knowing she's pushing my control over the edge.

"I should give him a name, so he knows how much I appreciate his perfection." She twists her body on the island; with my position between her spread legs, I see a small path of wetness from her cunt to the back of her, disappearing where the counter meets her skin.

"Hush."

"Make me," she slurs.

"With. Fucking. Pleasure."

With my hand still fisting my cock, I line myself up with her opening and push just the tip into her overheated flesh. My hands move up, thumbs sliding against the lips of her sex as my hands go to curl around her hips. I watch her widen around the tip of my cock, not even the thickest part of me, and I grind my teeth, a deeply animalistic grunt coming from deep within me.

Her tiny hands wrap around my wrists, not able to completely touch. I look up briefly, seeing her chin to her chest while she
looks at where our bodies join. With my paused movements, she
looks up and pleads with me silently.

"The second I feel your body ripple against my cock, you will
be mine, Wrenlee. Even if you ever decide you don't want me, I'm
not sure I'll grant you that. Especially not after I feel you hug me
tight inside your body, sucking my come from my cock. If we're
taking a gamble together, it's all in, or we fold before the call."

With her hold on my wrists, she pulls, impaling herself all the
way down my length until I feel the wetness of her cunt against
the base of my shaft. Her sharp cry echoes around the kitchen,
tangling and dancing with the grunt of satisfaction I feel from her
heat sheathing me.

We move together, her body welcoming mine with each and
every thrust. Her quivering heat sucking my cock back each time
I retreat from her. Never, it's never felt like this. My movements
falter when she lifts her body from her position on the island,
hands going to my shoulders.

"Fuck, you feel perfect," I tell her with a strain to my words.
"So fucking perfect against my cock, in my arms—mine. Never
…" I thrust deep, bottoming out and lifting her from the island.
"Felt …" I lift her up from my cock before dropping her down
and flexing my ass to attempt to get deeper into heaven. "Better." I
groan, her nails digging into my shoulders as she throws her head
back and screams, her pussy flexing in pulsing release. I continue to lift her up and pull her down on my body, riding out her

orgasm while she screams my name over and over with that sexy rasp of hers. Only when I feel her easing down from her pleasure do I give in to mine. I drop my forehead to her sweaty chest and groan out my own release deep into her body.

"I think I could get used to unioning with you, hubby," she pants, lifting one of her hands to run her fingernails against my scalp, urging me without her words to give her my eyes.

"Yeah," I breathe, looking up. "I'm pretty sure I could get used to unioning with you, too."

I ignore the nickname, again, finding that it doesn't even slightly annoy me. Stranger yet, I find I don't mind the visions that her nicknames put into my head each and every time she jokingly says it. I give her a light smack on her ass then take her lips in a slow, knee-knocking kiss. Walking through the house, I head toward her bedroom with my semi-hard cock still inside her body, and I push all my previous reservations about this woman out of my mind.

I had good intentions in trying to dissuade our attraction, but now that I've had her, I know I won't be able to give this up. She isn't the only one who felt that emptiness disappear when we met. She will never know how right she was. I might not know what I'm doing when it comes to being in a relationship, but I know one thing without a shadow of a doubt—the only thing impossible about us being together would be if we deny us each other.

Chapter 15

Wrenlee

"What's your biggest regret," I ask him. My head against his chest, I draw my finger in lazy swirls, tracing each peak and valley of his abdominal muscles.

"Kind of heavy for after-sex cuddles, isn't it?" he lightheartedly retorts as a huff of air escapes him with his silent laugh. His moving shoulders make my head bounce a little.

"Hey, now! You just asked me what my most embarrassing moment was." I gasp, playfully swatting his chest with my free hand. "Turnabout is fair play."

"A tampon string hanging out isn't that embarrassing."

I lift up to my elbow and gaze down at him with narrowed eyes. His arm that isn't currently being used as my pillow comes off the bed, and one long, oddly sexy finger pushes some of my wild hair out of my face.

"A tampon string hanging out while on the stage of a sold-out concert sure is! Seriously, you don't get the mortification level of that, being a man and all, but it was terrible."

His shoulders shake, deep rumbles of his manly chuckles escaping him. I'm momentarily struck dumb by the small smile, but I give my head a shake in an attempt to clear what I've been lovingly referring to as the 'brain-dead buzz' caused by his smile. I've been proud of my ability to adapt when it comes to what this man does to me.

His lips part, those teeth come out—teeth that I now know feel deliriously good when they're on my body—and his small smile turns broad and big. Okay, I'm clearly not *that* good at adapting because he starts laughing even harder as I zone out, just taking him in.

"We're going to have to work on that." He laughs, still smiling like the handsome devil he is.

"I'm not sure I can," I tell his mouth.

"Baby, you keep making me as happy as I feel right now, and you're going to have to. Otherwise, it's going to get fucking awkward when you just keep spacing out all the time."

"Whatever," I mumble in mock irritation, dropping back to cuddle into his side.

Maybe if I can't see the smile, I can hold a reasonably adult conversation with him.

"About two years ago, my best friend and his girl had some bad shit going on. She was about eight or so months pregnant with their first son when a man who had been stalking her was able to get through me. Because of that, they almost lost everything that they had finally found together. I will always, until the day I die, regret that I allowed that to almost happen."

I had almost forgotten I asked him a question, and his words didn't make sense at first. Unsure what to say or how to proceed without him closing me off again, I lift up and look at him. The smile is long gone from his mouth now and in its place are grim lines that prove just how much of a regret that memory is. Sensing there is more to the story than what little he's said, I proceed with caution, making sure to choose my words wisely.

"Tell me what happened, Chance."

His head turns away from me and I follow his gaze toward the bright sky beyond my windows.

"A lot of the attack I don't remember. I know what happened leading up to it, and what Dani and I were doing, but the rest is just what I've been told. We were helping them move Cohen's stuff out of our apartment. Her brother and another friend of ours were dealing with moving Cohen's monster TV outside, and I was helping Dani inside. The next thing I know, I'm waking up in the hospital with a knife wound to my shoulder and the worst fucking headache from my concussion. All I could remember was that Dani needed the packaging tape. Of all things, that's what

I focused on. Cohen's girl, though, she's a fighter, but if just the slightest second had been different, she might not be here. Cohen would have lost her and their son, and it would have been all on me."

My head ticks to the side, and I feel my brows pull in. "Tell me what you could have done differently, having been attacked yourself from behind with no chance to protect yourself." I didn't mean to sound so harsh, but knowing that he blamed himself for something I have a feeling he had no control over kills me. "Were you the only one who was in charge of keeping her safe that day? Where were your other friend and her brother? Obviously, the attacker was able to get past them too. Do the other two people who were with you—who weren't able to prevent this—blame themselves too?"

"I was the only one in the room with her, Wren. I might not have been the only one in charge of her, but I was the only one there to make sure of it. Liam and Nate couldn't have done shit since they were in the parking lot. The sick fuck came from the floor above us."

I shift, sitting up and climb on his lap to straddle his hips, one leg on each side of his hips. I ignore the feeling of his thickness against my well-loved pussy. Now is definitely not the time to get distracted.

"Let me get this straight. You were moving things in and out, right?" He nods. "Two of the other men weren't around, so my guess is they didn't make sure they locked up when they went out—something you would have expected of them—meaning they played a part in giving someone easy access. Either way, someone blindly ambushed you. Shit happens, Chance. I'm not trying to say it doesn't suck that shit happened to good friends of yours, but you can't control every aspect of your life. Is it harder when it happens to people who you care about, damn right, but no matter what, shit will always happen. You just have to focus on the positive—that being that you're alive, she's alive, and her son is alive. The other people who were with you could have been in that room too, and that person could have attacked you all—hurting you all. Don't beat yourself up over something you didn't even have a chance to prevent."

"You do realize that you're telling the man in charge of your protection that I shouldn't beat myself up over failing to protect someone." The harsh lines of his scowl ease from his face, and I let out a breath of relief.

"We are never guaranteed a second in life, Chance. In the time I've known you, I've seen you put nothing but your all into everything you do to keep us safe. You're alert to your surroundings, prepared for things in advance, and ready for the unexpected. All you can do is give yourself the best chance to succeed in all that you do. When it comes down to it, I know you'll give your all to me, and the rest will happen as it's meant to."

"You really believe that, don't you," he asks in awe, my words hopefully hitting the spot.

"I do. I really do. And I hope you can too."

"For years, they've been telling me that I wasn't to blame, but all it takes is my *not* wife to lay it out straight for me, and shockingly, I actually feel like what you said might be true. God, woman, what kind of witchcraft do you have inside that tempting little body?"

I shrug. "Everything happens for a reason. I didn't always feel that way, but I finally realized that as long as we give every situation our best, we've given ourselves the best chance to succeed in life. If you trip up on the way, then you figure out what you can learn from those stumbles or falls. No matter how painful it might be when we do falter, you have to be able to learn from your past, take something positive from it, and never let it hurt you again."

The silence ticks on as his eyes roam my face, studying my words and me at the same time. A few minutes later, one side of his mouth tips up, and shockingly, the sight doesn't kill my ability to function—thank God. "You know, I've never thought about it that way," he rasps, lifting up to curl his hand behind my neck. Curling his body up, he pulls me gently toward him—our lips meeting in the softest kiss.

"Stick with me, hubby. Told you, we're going to put all those destroyed pieces back together, one fucked-up past at a time," I whisper against his mouth.

He shifts and pulls me down with him, pressing another light kiss on my lips. I roll to the side, a little sad to lose the pressure of his cock against my center, but even that doesn't take away the high I have of being skin to skin with this man in my bed. I'll get his cock later.

"What about your past?" he hedges a little hesitantly. I don't think either of us thought a silly game of twenty questions would turn so emotionally heavy. "I know about the shit boyfriends, but I know that isn't all of it."

"How do you know?" I evade.

"You told me you felt empty. That even living the high life, you felt that way… like something was missing. You said your past had hurt you and that you had to learn to let people get close enough, even if they might hurt you. People, not men. You had to let people get close."

"You got all of that because I didn't specify the gender?"

"Who hurt you? Who made you afraid to let others close?"

I shift, settling in with my back to his chest and look out the window again. "My parents."

"And …" he adds, encouraging me to continue.

"Weston and me … we were mistakes. Accidents. Whatever you call a pregnancy that isn't wanted but kept, even though I know they don't have some grand moral clause that would have prevented them from terminating us. It's been Wes and me against the world. Our parents hated us, didn't hide that, and blamed us for them not making anything of their lives. When we moved into the trailer park we lived in growing up, Luke and Jamison were our neighbors. The second we met, the two of us became four, and the struggle growing up wasn't as bad. They had shitty parents too, so our bond solidified over our need to protect and care for each other. We ate more frequently and didn't spend the majority of our days dirty and smelling like trash. Hey, how about you ease up the hold, hulk." I come out of my memories when his lazy grip on my hip gets tight in the middle of my trip down memory lane, trying to sound carefree even when the ghosts of childhood past are thick in the room.

"Sorry," he grumbles. "Go on."

"They didn't touch us physically. They used their words instead of their fist. They didn't care for us, though, and even to this day, I have no idea how Child Protective Services didn't intervene. We were dirty more often than not, malnourished, and never had clothing that fit right. When Wes and I found music, though, it was the last straw for them. They didn't just hate us anymore; they *hated* us."

"Why because of music?" he asks befuddled.

I get his confusion. Out of everything I said, it does sound odd that our musical talent would be the tipping point for our crappy parents.

"Before we came around, they were just about to sign a recording deal. When I say just, I mean my mom puked during one of their final negotiation meetings, and it apparently slipped out that she was pregnant. The label decided they didn't want to sign them after finding out their lives were a little more complicated. We, according to them, stole their chance at their dream, and then when they realized how good we were, I think they looked at it as us stealing that dream all over again."

His breath leaves his body in a rush, tickling the hair at the top of my head. "That's fucked up."

I smile, despite the fact that I hate talking about my parents. Leave it to Chance to put it so simply. "Pretty much."

"How did you find something positive out of that, Wren? A

normal person would have let that mark them for life."

I ponder his words, thinking back to my chat with Weston. "I don't think I did completely, not until very recently, to be honest. I always looked at that time in my life as being worth it because I had my brother, Luke, and Jamison—who are as much my brothers as Wes is—and in the middle of all that, we found music. But it was pointed out to me recently that I let them and their greed for what we have—coupled with the greed of a few jerks I dated—make me jaded. God, I was even letting my love for music turn cynical. I had forgotten to look for the positive. But once I remembered what it was like to see things in a light that wasn't burned out and wary of others' motives—well, let's just say it isn't so hard to deal with those memories. Not when I look at my life now and think it might have been worth those years if they brought me to where I am now."

"Was that just us putting a destroyed piece back together for you?" he asks softly.

"Yeah, Chance. It definitely was." I smile and turn, pressing even closer as he adjusts his body to allow me to curl into his side. The heaviness of our lazy afternoon chat settles over us, the mood turning almost peaceful now that we both got something so heavy off our chests.

"I'm really happy," I say, softly and hesitantly.

"I am too, Wren. I am too."

"I know we haven't known each other long, but you know more about me than anyone outside of my guys. The people who think they love me—they love the Wrenlee of Loaded Replay.

They obsess over that girl, thinking that they know all there is to know about her—but they don't know *me*. No one besides my guys and Dyllan do. Until now. It's … well, it's just important to me that you know that."

His arm gives me a squeeze, his hand traveling from where it had been curled around my shoulder in slow movements until he touches my hip. His fingers flex, pads digging into my naked flesh. I lift my leg up to lay over his body, feeling the heat of his cock against my thigh.

"Thank you for giving me you," he hums into the silence.

"Don't hurt me." The words are out before I realize I didn't think them but spoke them, and I wish I could stuff them back in.

"The last thing I want is to hurt you."

"You have the power to do it, though. Like I said, we haven't known each other long, but regardless, I find I'm becoming addicted to the way you make me feel."

He's silent for so long, my eyes grow heavy, and I feel my body relax even more into him.

"The only other time I felt something close to this was right before my fiancée changed the way I looked at everything."

Well, I'm wide-awake now. I sit up, his hand falling from my side, and turn to look at him. Chills wash over me, and my stomach bubbles with unease.

"What the fuck did you just say?"

Chapter 16

Chance

"What the fuck did you just say?"

Wren moved so quickly. One second, she was soft and compliant in my arms, and the next, she was sitting next to me, naked as the day she was born, looking like she was about to throw up and kill me at the same time.

I think back to what I just told her, having been so lost in my head and the odd sense of happiness this woman makes me feel, that I didn't even hesitate to tell her about Jessica—someone who I've worked really hard not to tell anyone about. Ever. Having a hard time recalling my words, my silence only infuriates her more. I watch the color rise on her skin, wishing it was there again because of what I was doing to her body and not because I pissed her off.

"I was trying to agree with you about becoming addicted to how you make me feel but point out that if anyone has anything to worry about, it would be me." That is what I said, right? Fuck. I didn't think she would get pissed about it, though.

"Chance," she seethed deeply, her mouth hardly moving to say my name.

"What, Wren? It's true. This feeling I have now is nothing even close to what I thought I had with her, and I had years to build that up before I felt it with her. Years. I know you for not even two full fucking weeks, and it doesn't just surpass what I thought I knew; it blows it out of the fucking water. So yeah … I get being scared of someone hurting you."

"You said your fiancée."

I pause. I was halfway off my back, reaching for her, when she spoke. I replay the last five minutes. My eyes widen when I realize that I had been so lost in my memories of Jessica's betrayal that I referred to her in the present tense. Wren looks seconds away from running, so I move quickly to grab her and roll, so her body is under mine—trapped between the mattress and me.

"Let me go," she fumes, refusing to make eye contact with me. She's looking away and to the side, giving me her profile.

"Never," I vow, knowing that I'm not just talking about right now. No fucking way would I give this woman up—even though we're still very much getting to know each other, I doubt anything would be able to make me give her up.

"I can't believe you let me be the other woman. I'm not that person, Chance, no matter what people think of celebrities. I would never cheat or help someone cheat. Relationships should be sacred. Oh, my God."

"I'm not engaged, Wren."

I get her attention with that. Her head snaps from the side, giving me her furious blue eyes. "You said your fiancée," she reminds me.

"Yeah, I know what I said, Wren. You want to curb that attitude and let me explain myself?"

She deflates slightly but not much.

"I get your anger. I would be pissed too, but I'm not engaged. It was a slip of the tongue."

Her body relaxes more. The anger dimming slightly. Not completely, but enough that I know she's listening to me.

"If I roll off you, are you going to run?" I ask, concerned that she isn't comfortable with my weight on her like this.

"Don't you dare," she grunts and shifts her body. I had pinned her legs down with my swift movement but was balancing my weight on my elbows and feet while she adjusts her position. Her legs come out, spreading, and wait for me to settle back down.

Taking this as a good sign, I relax my body and let it cover hers once again. This time my cock hits her wet heat, growing harder. She widens her legs with a shimmy of her hips, her pussy lips spreading with her movements to welcome my cock with a hug. I feel the wetness from the tip of my cock against my belly, the warmth of her cunt on the bottom of my cock and balls making my eyes cross with need. She brings her legs up, hooking them behind my back, and digs her heels into the small of my back.

"There. Now finish what you were saying."

God, this girl is going to be my undoing.

"I don't like bringing other people into bed with us. Not like this." It feels wrong to talk about Jessica with her pussy coating my cock with wetness.

"I don't like bringing other people into anything with us, but at least I know it's my body that has you while it happens, not someone else."

Twisted as fuck logic, but I get it.

"Fine," I breathe. Dropping my forehead to hers, I refuse to look away from her searching gaze. "I met Jessica when I was a senior in high school. It was the typical head cheerleader meets the new transfer student turned quarterback, and just because it's expected, we went on a date. I went with it because I was a shithead teen who didn't care about anything. I wanted to play football and get my dick wet. The rest was fuck all to me."

I hate to think about this shit, let alone talk about it. The pain I feel remembering those years was never worth it, but for whatever reason, it doesn't sear through me like it used to. I have a feeling that has everything to do with the woman under me who's looking at me like she's hanging on every word I'm saying. Her body wrapped around me as if *she* is afraid I might leave her. Fat fucking chance.

"I had just moved the summer before school started. I tried out for the football team because I knew it would get me pussy. It did at my old school, so I went with what I knew worked. Like I said, I was a punk—an angry punk who didn't feel as out of control when I was fucking someone. It just so happened that I was one hell of a player on the field. I took over when, two practices in, the only quarterback worth a shit broke his leg."

"This is a lovely story," she gripes, narrowing her eyes.

"Told you I didn't like bringing other people into bed with us."

She rolls her eyes. "Just continue, and I'll try to remember that I don't want to hurt your fat cock."

"Right." I feel my lips twitch. She's trying to hold on to her anger, but my guess is she isn't unaffected by our position, and it's making it harder. Literally. "We dated through the school year. My coach was a big reason that I lost the chip I had on my shoulder. I owed him so much, but even he couldn't get me to accept scholarships to play ball after graduation. It didn't matter to me that he thought I was good enough to go pro. I didn't care about the potential riches he was dangling over my head. Nothing he could say or try to predict was going to change my mind. It was never a question that I would go into the Marines. Jessica wasn't exactly on board with that, but she stuck with me. I still don't know why she did."

"Why were you so set on the Marines?" she interrupts, making me pause.

"My dad was a Marine. He raised me alone, and his sister

helped him when he was overseas. Even as a single father, he never failed to show me how much he loved me. He was my hero, and when I lost him, I wanted nothing more than to make him proud and follow in his footsteps."

"Oh, Chance"—she trembles— "I'm sorry, honey." Her hands reach up, her fingers dipping into my hair, palms against my cheeks.

"It was a long time ago, Wren. I've made peace with losing him. The Marines did that. They gave me back my dad."

"You said your aunt helped raised you?"

"My mom was a one night of fun thing and had no interest in being a parent when she found out she was pregnant. My dad, though, he wanted me. He got her to sign over her rights, and she never looked back."

Wren's chin wobbles slightly, drawing my attention. "I'm not upset about that, Wren. Don't feel sorry for me."

"I'm not. What your dad did was beautiful. I can't help that it makes me all girly."

"Can I finish now?" She nods. "Aunt Tracy was my best friend. Even though she was a lot younger than my dad was, she took me without question when he died. She was twenty-five when she became my guardian. Eight years later, she was more of a friend than that, but she was, without a doubt, the most important person in my life. That was always a point of contention between Jessica and me, but being the stupid fuck I was, I thought if I put a ring on her finger, it would bring them closer while I was gone."

"Gone?"

"Overseas. Right out of boot camp and fresh out of high school."

"Oh." She nods.

"Jessica was taking classes at the local community college, so she was still living at home with her parents that first year I was gone. I came back, and I figured the next step was for us to get our own place. Tracy didn't like it, but she also didn't hold me back. Jessica was on cloud nine, though."

"And you?" Wren asks. "Were you on cloud nine too?"

"I had just come back from war. I might not have been a punk kid anymore, but I still thought with my dick more than my head. Moving in meant I got to think with my dick when I wanted to."

Wren frowns.

"Anyway, I was home for a while before we were called back. We hadn't been planning, so we still hadn't set a date for our wedding. When I left, we promised each other that when I got back, we would make sure and take care of that. This time, I was gone for eight months. I had moved to a specialized team at that point, and we handled some fucked-up shit. Communication back home was next to impossible, but still, when I got home, she opened her arms with a smile. We started planning with the hopes that we would get married in the fall of that year. Tracy kept telling me that twenty was too young to get married, but I was too stubborn to listen."

Knowing the next part would be the hardest, I take a fortifying breath before continuing. "My team was sent back before we could get married. I was gone for almost a year that time. Aunt

Tracy passed away two days before I got back—drunk driver. I was a fucking mess by the time the plane touched down. The only thing I could think of was that all my family was gone. I was on autopilot the whole way to the apartment I shared with Jessica. She didn't know I was coming home. With the news about Tracy, I didn't even tell her, so I wasn't shocked that she wasn't home. It wasn't even noon, so I dropped down on the couch and waited for her."

"Chance," she calls softly, and I look up, realizing I had zoned in on her collarbone while I talked.

"Yeah?"

"Is the rest of this story going to make me want to commit murder?"

I think I fell a little in love with her right then.

"Well, it did for me, so maybe."

"Right." Her bottom lip rolls, and she bites down on it with her teeth, nibbling for a second before releasing the plump flesh. "I'm sorry about your aunt. I bet she was amazing."

"Thanks, babe. Can I finish now?" She nods. "Jessica got home two hours later. I'm not sure who was more shocked, her or me, when she opened the door. Maybe I should have called her to tell her I was coming, but I had talked to her the week before, and she knew we would be coming home soon. She kept talking about how she was almost finished with the wedding plans, and she couldn't wait for me to get home. She forgot, however, to mention that she was a lying bitch. She screamed, but after she had realized I wasn't some stranger about to kill her, she got weird. I wasn't in the right mind because of the grief I was dealing with, on top of just waking up, so it took me a second to realize that the flat stomach she had when I left was now huge and swollen."

"What?"

"She was seven months pregnant."

"You have a kid?" Wren screams. I pull back my head slightly from the sheer volume behind it.

"Wren. She was seven months pregnant. Seven," I stress.

"And?"

"And I had been gone for three days shy of a full year."

I watch as comprehension dawns, the math adding up.

"That fucking bitch!"

"Yeah, my thoughts exactly. Turned out, since the day I left for my first deployment, she had been fucking around on me. For three years, I thought we were building our future, but she was only playing games. When I was home, she was still fucking around, just more careful. However, she didn't plan to get knock up. I lost everything that day."

"You loved her." Wren's voice is quiet, nonjudgmental, and accepting.

"I thought I did. I know now that I didn't. She might have hurt me, but I think it hurt more because of how much I had lost in one giant kick. Tracy was gone, and I had just found out the woman I was supposed to marry hadn't ever been faithful to me—lying our whole four years together. I felt so betrayed by everyone. It wasn't a good time for me, and I'll admit Jessica is a big reason why I spent the last decade refusing to let another woman get close. It wasn't until Cohen that I even let a friend get close. I was convinced, in my mind, that everyone I let near me would either betray me or be taken from me."

"And now?"

"I now know I can't control fate. I have some great friends back home, but even with them, I've held back a lot of me because of that fear. It didn't help that I held on to what happened to Dani as an excuse to keep that distance too. When I go back home, I'll make sure those friends know how much I appreciate them in my life. And, as for you, I've known you less than two full weeks, Wren. In that time, you've become an obsessive need my body craves to be near. I take you once, and I know a lifetime probably wouldn't be enough to quench the thirst I have for more. And I know I'll do whatever it takes to ensure that you aren't taken from me. I guess I can look back at my time with that bitch and be thankful that she did me a favor. Her being a massive slut means I didn't make the biggest mistake of my life."

"You know I would never do that to you, right?"

"Yeah, Wren, I do."

"Do you really? My whole life is in the spotlight, and the media loves nothing more than creating drama with their lies. You have to know I would never cheat on you, regardless of whatever they might print in the future."

I toss my head back and laugh, the heaviness pushing out of the room. "Babe, you almost went ape shit when you thought I was engaged and cheating with you. I think it's pretty clear where you stand on cheating. As for the media, they already have us married and expecting, Wren. I think I have a good idea about how crazy their lies can be."

"Are you saying that you're not really my *not* husband?" She gasps, a small smile on her lips.

"For now."

Her eyes widen, but I don't elaborate. Instead, I take advantage of our position and give us both some of the addiction we're hooked on.

Each other.

Chapter 17

Wrenlee

My toes curl at the same time my back snaps up, arching off the bed. I shake my head from side to side, a low whine escaping my lips. Unclenching the sheets that I have fisted in my hands, I move them with a slight tremble to the silky hair on Chance's head. My chest heaves as I drag my fingernails across his scalp before taking a firm hold of his thick hair. Lifting my hips off the mattress, I force him closer to my soaking wet pussy.

He makes a throaty sound of pleasure when I start to grind myself against his open mouth. His wetness mixes with my own, making slick sounds echo around us.

"I need more." I gasp, so close but wanting more than his wicked mouth and talented hands.

"You want my cock?" he asks my pussy, his hot breath hitting my swollen and oversensitive clit.

"God, yes."

He looks up, causing his chin to press my hot button. My eyes widen when he moves his jaw from side to side, applying the pressure I need to explode. He's refused to touch that spot on me since he started devouring me forever ago. "How bad do you want my cock?"

I whine pathetically and loud.

"Tell me." The dominant way in which he's talking to me only makes me more needy for him.

"So bad. So, so, so bad."

"Where do you want it?"

"Inside me." I gasp, feeling a slight tremor start to roll over my body. If he keeps chinning me, I'm going to come, and I want him inside me when I do.

"Your mouth? Your pussy?" His eyes get a mischievous glint to them. "Or maybe your ass?"

"Oh, shit." I gasp.

"Tell me where. Now, Wrenlee."

My legs shake; my orgasm so close. "In my pussy."

He doesn't move. He continues to look at me with so much rapture in his expression from just pleasuring me alone. His chin continues to work me to the brink of insanity, and just when I'm about to shoot off the bed into a million pieces, he lifts his head and leans back.

Next thing I know, he's pulling me by the hips further down the bed. My squeak of surprise from the sudden movement turns into a shrill scream when he bends down and stuffs his cock inside me in one deliciously rough thrust. I'm shocked I didn't shatter all the glass around us because my screams don't stop there. Nope. His fullness stretches me, mixing my pleasure with pain; the feeling is so intense that I'm half-convinced the sheer power of it is going to kill me.

He powers his cock into me, not holding back at all. I realize why he moved us almost to the end of the bed when his thrusts move us across the bed in seconds. He drops one side of his body to rest his weight on his elbow; the move catches me off guard, grinding the coarse hair at the base of his cock against my clit. I scream out again, louder. I realize why he shifted a moment later when he places his hand on the top of my head only seconds before he almost fucked me into the headboard of my bed—his hand protecting my head from the hard surface.

"Play with your tits, Wren," he demands, his nostrils flaring rapidly. "Palm your tits and feed them to me."

Fuck, that's hot.

I drop my hands from where I had been clawing at his back and do what he commands. My hands squeeze them briefly before holding one free, waiting for his mouth, and playing with the other breast's nipple. He dips slightly, pushing even deeper into me, the fullness overwhelming as he stretches me. Then his mouth opens, and he wraps his lips wide around my breast. He isn't gentle, sucking hard until he has more than just the pink skin around my nipple in his mouth. His wet tongue flicks and licks before he nips his teeth against the pointed tip.

My legs quiver, and I feel myself get even wetter around him.

He releases me with a pop before rolling us and falling to his back on the bed, never losing the connection of our bodies. He had shifted while his cock was powering out of my wetness, so when he landed, he used his hands at my hips to hold me there— with just the tip of his thick cock inside me.

My whimper is shameless at the loss of him. I can feel my body trying to suck him back as I thicken around him with fluttered kisses against his cock head.

"Please, God, please, Chance." I wiggle, trying to loosen his hold on me.

"Show me how I make you feel," he tells me with a hoarse voice. The veins in his neck pulse, highlighting the raw power raging inside him. "Give me what I crave."

I cry out weakly. Then he releases his hold on my hips, pulling his wrists free of my hands effortlessly despite the harsh grip I had on them. The second I'm free, I slam my body down, taking him deeper than ever before. He stretches me, fills me completely. I drop my hands to his chest, dig my nails into his firm flesh, and start to move.

My whole body moves against his, using him for my pleasure while giving him his own. His grunts and deep sounds of enjoyment get lost when I push up from my hold on his chest and start to roll my hips as the pleasure washes over me. My legs shake, and I lose the ability to move. My hips fall down, his cock being sucked and squeezed while my pussy pulses around him, and tremors of pure ecstasy wash over me. My head rolls back at the same time he gives a shout of completion. I look at the ceiling before my vision blurs as the warmth of his come splashes inside me, and my throat burns from the shrillness of my screams.

I'm vaguely aware of Chance moving me, his deep voice saying something, but I'm so lost to my pleasure that I'm helpless to do anything but ride it out. The last thought I have before I pass out from too much stimulation is that I was wrong—Chance doesn't come close to the high I get going on stage. Nope, he doesn't come close because he takes that sentiment and blows it into space.

And I have a feeling there will be no coming back from an addiction to *that* kind of high.

I roll onto my back and stretch my overused muscles. Opening my eyes, I look around the room, but I don't see Chance anywhere. A quick glance at the clock tells me that I must have been asleep for a while. I might have been catching up on my sleep since we've been home, but no matter how much rest I've gotten, you don't get fucked like that and not need to recover.

Or did I do the fucking?

Maybe it was a mutual fucking. Yeah, that sounds about right.

I can't keep the smile off my face as I move my sore body to the edge of the bed. Standing on wobbly feet, I make my way to my en suite. Avoiding the mirror, I walk into my shower and crank the hot water on. I spend more time than necessary in there, washing my hair and body before shaving all the important bits. Then I stand there and let the hot pulses pound over my sore skin. The long bench seat fills my vision, and I immediately think of how I need to get Chance in here before we leave for Vegas.

"I was starting to wonder if you would wake up at all."

I screech and whip my head around toward Chance's voice. He's standing on the other side of the glass door of my shower fully clothed in dark jeans and a black t-shirt. My eyes go straight to his crotch, and I think about how much I enjoy that part of him.

He's without a doubt the thickest and fattest that I've ever seen. He isn't crazy long, probably slightly above average, but what he lacks in length, he makes up for ten times over in girth.

He covers his crotch with his hands, and my eyes shoot to his. "Stop whatever you're thinking," he commands with a slight twitch of his mouth.

I shut off the water and reach out for a towel before turning to speak. "I can't help it, you know." Then I lower my voice and look up at him through hooded eyes. "I can still feel you. Deep inside my body, I still feel you."

"Shit," he hisses.

"I don't ever want to know what it feels like not to feel the ache of you deep inside me."

"God*damn*." His eyes close tightly, and I watch as he brings his hand up to adjust himself. "You're going to be my undoing, Wren."

"Same goes, *hubby*."

Getting control of himself, he does that manly juggle thing they do with their fingers against their crotch before straightening. I make a mental note to ask him what that actually does. Seems to me, it wouldn't be comfortable for your sensitive parts to be jiggled like that, but I don't have a dick, so I wouldn't know.

"Get dressed, babe. The guys and Dyllan got back a while ago, and I've had a hard time keeping them out for the last two hours."

Walking into my huge closet, I walk to the underwear drawer and pull on a bright red thong before grabbing the matching bra and dropping the towel. Chance groans deep in his chest, but I ignore him. I pull on some of my exercise shorts and one of our tour t-shirts before walking past him. It seemed safer to make sure I was dressed with him this close instead of answering him right away.

"Why would they be trying to get in here?"

I look in the mirror, pulling the brush through my hair, and wait for him to answer. If I'm not mistaken, he looks a little sheepish, but I shrug it off and drop the brush down.

"You aren't … quiet." Chance holds my gaze in the mirror, but I turn and frown at him, not understanding. "I think there was some concern for your well-being from a few people."

"Tell me you're kidding." I gasp in shock.

"Dead serious."

"You're telling me that they all heard us having sex?"

He nods and has the nerve to twitch those devil lips of his into a small smirk.

"This is not funny," I spit out.

He attempts to hold it in, but that small smirk grows.

"You can't kill my brain into forgetting to be embarrassed here."

"What are you talking about?" He laughs, that stupid smile already working its dark magic.

"Brain-dead buzz isn't going to make me forget that we had an audience."

He winces, and I cock my head at him. "Chance?"

"Not everyone saw, so it wasn't really an audience."

"Not everyone saw what?" I scream.

"And I turned you before they saw much," he adds.

"Tell me you're joking."

He steps closer. "Do you think I want anyone else seeing you like that?"

The seriousness of his tone ebbs some of my panic, and I focus on him. "I'm guessing no?"

He steps even closer, wrapping his arms around my body to pull me to him. "That would be a hell no. You're beautiful, Wren, but when your pussy is soaking my cock while you scream out your release, you're so stunning it makes my chest feel too small for my heart. So yeah … it's a definite hell no."

"I'll work on being quieter," I utter breathily, his words

melting me.

"That would be appreciated." He kisses the tip of my nose and turns with his hand holding mine to walk out of the sanctuary of my bedroom.

Chapter 18

Wrenlee

"**S**top looking at me like that," I snap at Wes, tossing my pizza crust at him. He snags it off the table before stuffing it into his mouth, still scowling. "Weston Davenport, seriously, I'll cut off your balls."

He opens his mouth to speak, but the loud thump of a body smacking against the hardwood floor interrupts our showdown. I jump in my seat and twist to see what caused the sound.

Jamison pulls himself off the floor, water dripping from his clothing to form a large puddle at his feet. He doesn't even give the audience he's attracted a single notice. He shakes his head, water droplets flying from his hair, and then starts peeling off his clothes.

That drained the shock out of a few of us.

"What the fuck, man!" Luke bellows, making Jamison look up while he continues to yanks his jeans down his legs.

"What the fuck, what, man?" he asks back almost like he's actually confused that we would be stunned by him standing in the middle of the kitchen, completely naked, and soaking wet. To be fair, though, I don't know why anything Jamison does shocks us anymore.

"I think what Luke here is trying to convey to you is that he would appreciate it if you would cover up your little pecker," Dyllan says in a monotone voice, not even looking up from the magazine she's been thumbing through for the last half hour.

I swing my eyes from her back to Jamison to see him looking at my best friend in horror before glancing down at his dick. Naturally, I follow his lead too. I challenge you to find a woman out there who wouldn't look when there's a man unabashed in his nudity flashing everyone his dangly bits right in front of her. It doesn't matter that Jamison and I are as close as siblings would be; bottom line, he isn't my brother, so the laws of naked penis viewing do not apply.

"My dick isn't little!" Jamison yells, turning his head to look down at himself from another angle then snapping his head up to spear her with a glare of outrage. "Take it back, Dyll! Take it back now."

"It's okay, Jami. There is no need to get upset about it now

175

that everyone knows. They make pills and pumps for that problem now." She continues to wind him up with little effort.

His face gets red. Or I should say redder. "You didn't think it was little when you were begging me to fuck you harder."

Dyllan throws her magazine down onto the table, looking up without a hint of embarrassment or shame, and gives him her full attention. She studies him for a second—head to toe—before smirking one hell of an evil little smirk. "Of course, I didn't tell you then. I was too busy begging for you to go harder so I could actually feel something."

The men around the table snicker to themselves, but I'm too interested in how this will play out. I make a mental note to make her tell me everything. I hadn't had a chance to make her talk after her whole 'they look at you different' pep talk the other night, but now, after this, you bet your ass I'm going to make time for that talk.

Chance's arms come around my body, pulling me across the bench seat to his side. My attention still bouncing back and forth between Dyllan and Jamison, I'm completely fascinated. This is better than must-see TV.

"Stop looking at him naked," Chance murmurs in my ear, slightly playful but definitely serious.

I snort. Yeah, right. Fat chance of that happening.

"Take it back," Jamison demands, apparently having enough of trying to kill her with his eyes.

"Get over yourself," Dyllan titters, and with one more look at Jamison's dick, she turns back to the magazine, her bored expression back.

Jesus, she's either one hell of an actor, Jamison sucked in bed, or he did something to earn this treatment from her. My guess is the former. It's more likely that Jamison was being a total douchebag than him sucking in bed, and I can't think of a single person who would be unaffected by seeing him naked. He's built with muscles so defined he looks like he could be made of stone, tattooed, tall as hell, and has model-perfect looks. He's cocky as hell for a reason when it comes to women, after all.

Jamison mutters under his breath, and I turn back from my silent attempt at trying to catch Dyllan's attention to look at him. I'm not sure what I expected, but seeing him pet himself—down *there*—while mumbling under his breath damn sure wasn't it. My eyes track his fingers as they lightly brush up and down the length of himself before quickly diverting my attention, not wanting to agitate Chance any more than I already have. However, I wasn't quick enough because before I could look away, I notice that Dyllan is full of shit.

Jamison has a monster between his legs.

Turning in my seat, I do my best to ignore the blond giant still mumbling behind me, and I pick up a new slice of pizza, pretending that the last five minutes didn't happen.

There have been some close calls over the years, living in such close proximity to these guys and their constant 'extracurricular activities,' but this was the first time I had ever seen his junk. I've walked in on one of them naked more time than I can count, but they were always covered up with a towel or a woman, so I was spared.

Now that I'm over the shock of seeing Jamison's junk for the first time, I'm not sure if I should high five Dyllan or go bleach my eyes.

I settle with taking a bite of my pizza instead. After all, I've worked up an appetite today.

I pick up my phone at the same time I hear Jamison move, but I don't look away from the small screen. Instead, I open my email and scroll through the last few days.

"I need a new phone," Jamison says with a huff from across the table, addressing anyone who cares to listen to him. Completely unfazed by the past fifteen minutes, he tosses his still wet and very fried phone on the table with a loud clatter before grabbing a slice of pizza.

"Are you still naked?" I hoot, unable to keep a straight face any longer.

Wes is next to him but quickly slides down on the bench, avoiding looking in his direction. Luke and Chance aren't even trying to keep their laughter to themselves. And Dyllan, the big fat liar, is still ignoring him in favor of her magazine.

"Yeah. I'm hungry." Jamison gives me a look that screams his confusion; like it's weird that I would even question him.

"Why exactly is it that you're naked again?" Luke wheezes through a laugh.

"Fell into the pool. I didn't want to eat wet. So, here I am, naked."

I toss my head back and laugh. "So you thought it would be

better to eat naked *and* wet?"

Jamison shrugs. God, Jamison logic. There really is nothing else like it.

"How did you fall into the pool?" Wes asks incredulously, still not willing to look at him.

Jamison stares at my brother, and his eyes narrow. "I didn't fall, asshole. I walked. It's not *my* fault that the pool was in the way."

Wiping the tears from my eyes, I gasp through my hilarity, trying to catch my breath. "In the way? It's always been in the same spot. What the hell are you talking about?"

Jamison looks offended that I would defend the pool and not him. "It was in the way, *Wren*, because I was trying to catch a motherfucking Pokémon, but the fucker poofed off even though I fed it those stupid berries *and* used my big balls! And then the little bastard tricked me into forgetting I was standing next to the pool with his little 'mon-man magic' until I was sucking in a lungful of chlorine."

Silence.

You could hear a pin drop, I'm sure.

Not a single person makes a peep. Hell, I'm not even sure anyone is breathing. Even Dyllan is now looking at Jamison like he's lost his mind.

"I was three Pikachu candies away from evolving that fucker, too!" he yells; as if that would make it sound a little less ludicrous.

My jaw drops.

"You're serious?" I gasp.

His narrowed eyes snap in my direction. "I would never joke about a Pikachu, Wrenlee Davenport. How dare you." He grabs the whole box of pizza, stands from the table with his cock dangling in all our faces, and stomps out of the room.

Silence ticks on until Chance clears his throat. "Did that just happen?"

It takes us all about a second before we're all laughing so hard we have tears rolling down our faces.

"Oh, my God. I swear you never know what's going to come out of that man's mouth," I wheeze through my laughter.

"I need to look on Amazon and see if I can find some Pokémon stuff," Wes mumbles with a few chuckles.

"Why on earth would you do that?" Dyllan questions him.

"I told him the last time he wouldn't cover his shit up that I was tired of him waving his dick around. Clearly, he's upset over whatever the Pokémon did to him. You know Jamison; he won't forget how they wronged him. I bet when he gets a new phone that he'll boycott that stupid app just out of spite. I'm going to make sure and pay him back for shoving his dick in our faces by shoving those fuckers down his throat."

"You're weird, big brother." At my voice, Wes turns to me and glares. "What?" I snap.

"Don't think I've forgotten about you two," he replies, pointing his half-eaten slice back and forth between Chance and me.

"Jesus, Wes. Not this again. Don't you think it's embarrassing enough for me to know … well, what I know."

"Embarrassing enough? For you?" he sputters.

Dyllan snorts, magazine forgotten. "Girlfriend, you were so loud, it sounded like you had hooked yourself up to some house-wide sound system. Even if we hadn't rushed in there to make sure you were okay and gotten an eyeful of you playing rodeo queen and bucking bull, your activities wouldn't have been missed."

"Would you shut up," I hiss, narrowing my eyes at her.

"Call it like I see it." She holds her hands up in surrender and smiles.

"We should probably look into getting some sound-canceling headphones for the bus," Luke tells my brother, making Wes gag on the bite he had just taken.

"Oh, my God." I turn to look at Chance. "Kill me, please?" He doesn't even look embarrassed at all. He's just watching the four of us with some weird contentment on his face.

"Yeah, that will never happen," he answers.

"This is mortifying. We're never having sex again. Not until you figure out how to mute me. Even then, we might not even have sex unless it's from inside an impenetrable vault or something."

Chance hardens his eyes. "*That* will definitely never happen either."

"Chance," I hiss through my teeth. "They all saw us!"

"Then they need to learn how to knock."

"Wait a minute," Luke interrupts our argument. "Are you two together for real now or something? Or are you just fucking?"

"Luke!" I shout, totally horrified.

"What? Seriously, Wren, get over it. So you were having sex. It's nothing to be ashamed of. You've walked in on us more times than I can even count. Why is it different now?"

I huff and cross my arms over my chest. Not having anything logical to answer him with aside from just because it was me and not them, I stick with my killer bitch glare instead.

"Are you still going to be in charge of her security?" Luke continues his questioning, ignoring my attitude.

"Of course, he is!"

"No, I'm not."

Chance and I speak at the same time, and I almost fall out of my seat in my rush to look at him.

"What do you mean you're not? Are you leaving?" My words are rapid fire with a slight panic in my voice.

Something flashes behind his eyes, but he takes his time answering my questions. He stands, swings one leg over the bench, and then settles back down. His hands tag my arms, and he slides me into the spot between his spread legs. His hands don't leave my biceps, making lazy sweeps of his thumbs against my skin while he searches my rattled stare.

"Are we not unioning?" His husky whisper eases some of the worry that had invaded my body.

"We did, yeah."

"Did we not agree to give this a go?"

I nod, woodenly. His lips twitch, and I feel myself starting to relax as that brain-dead buzz swirls around inside me.

"We wouldn't have made it past deciding to take that gamble together if I hadn't been sure we were doing this right. I don't do things halfway, Wrenlee, but I also do my best never to set myself up for failure. Our attraction was strong as hell before I had said one word to you. I think you know why I had tried to hold back, but I knew then that if something ever happened between us, I wouldn't ever want anything to taint that. You might have just given me you wholly, but I gave you *me* the day I met you."

I frown, pretty sure I get what he's trying to say, but I want to be clear. "What are you talking about?"

"I called my boss. I told him to refund your brother his deposit, cancel the hours logged, and to take me off the books for this job and any others indefinitely. He understood why without any issues, and I ended that call by asking him to grant me a leave of absence until further notice."

"You … so you are leaving? Wha … a refund?" I sputter, even more confused.

"No, fuck no. I'm not going anywhere." He adjusts us, framing my face, and just like that, I feel like we're the only two people in the world. "I took a leave from the company in order to stay here until we decide what comes next. As for the refund, I wouldn't feel right accepting money to keep you safe, not when I have a vested interest in your safety. Fuck, Wren, don't you get it? My happiness depends on you staying safe. Even when we had just met, I felt that way. But now, I know my mind was driving me to do what my heart hadn't realized yet. And when it did, I took care of things."

Dyllan sighs, but I only have eyes for Chance.

"When did you do this, Chance? I've been with you all day."

I don't have any trouble understanding the look on his face now. He actually looks a little uncomfortable.

"I can answer that," Wes butts in, drawing my notice.

"I would rather hear it from Chance himself," I tell him with an arch to my brow before looking away and back to Chance.

"A while ago," Chance evades.

"Meaning?" I ask, not willing to let this go. Not when I have a feeling the answer holds a whole lot of importance.

Chance exhales, and his hold on my arms tightens slightly. Not uncomfortable. His hold more to reassure I'm not going anywhere than an actual effort to hold me in place.

"The day we landed in LA and became *not* husband and wife."

I gasp. His glances across the table briefly, the smallest movement, but I catch it and look over to see Wes nod. That would mean … "You knew!" I scream, pointing my finger in Wes's face.

He shrugs. "Of course, I knew."

"Then what was all that shit this morning?"

"Me making sure my little sister finally gets over the things that kept holding her back from happiness. All you needed was a little nudge."

"You shouldn't have played me, Wes. I love you, but you could have accomplished the same thing without doing that."

"I asked him not to mention it," Chance voices softly, and when I move my eyes to his face, his expression pleads with me to understand him. "Wren, it wouldn't have made a difference if you had known—not to me—but I asked him not to mention the refund. Hell, you were already doing everything possible to avoid me, but regardless, I'd been fighting a losing battle since day one. Even if nothing would have come to fruition with the connection we share, I wasn't leaving until I knew you were safe, or you had a properly trained team on you at all times. Since the label had made that impossible, it was moot. I intended to stay strong in denying this thing between us. Probably would have killed me to walk away, but I would have, and I think you understand why that is now after everything we've talked about. That being said, I don't regret it because of where we are now, but I didn't feel right at the time being paid for something that I knew I had to do. I couldn't even be away from you without feeling a physical pain right here in my chest." He slams his open hand against his chest, right over his heart. I almost melt on the spot.

I think about our time together so far. Him telling me we couldn't do anything about our attraction, warning me to protect myself from him, and everything that had happened between us since. Now that I know the things he had held inside, allowing them to keep his distance from something we both clearly craved because of his fear that letting someone in meant they would be taken from him—I get it. That doesn't mean I wouldn't have liked to be in the know about him refusing to be paid to be here, but the Chance that he showed me—the one who no one else knows—doesn't need me to give him bullshit for doing what he felt was right.

"No more secrets," I request softly.

"Never," he agrees.

Chapter 19

Wrenlee

Closing my eyes, I hold out the note, listening to the rhythm of the music in my headphones as it guides me to the end of the song we've been working on all day. We had just added Jamison's huge drum solo to the track earlier this afternoon, making it ready for me to lay down the vocals.

"That's great, Wren. I knew you would rock this." My brother's voice cuts in to the last few beats of the song.

"Do you need me to go over the chorus again? I wasn't sure if I wobbled over that middle hook either."

I hear a click in my ears before he speaks again. "No, it was great. We'll do a playback later to be sure, though. Come on out for a second."

Pulling off the headphones, I hook them on the mic stand in front of me and nab my bottle of water off the small stool next to where I'm standing. It acts as a table of sorts when I'm in the sound booth since I usually never come out of here without my throat letting me know how hard I work.

I step out of the soundproof box built in the corner of our studio space. The guys' guitars and two of Jamison's kits are set up in the massive space. I glance through the large window that allows the people in the control room to look slightly down into our space. Usually, when we are working in the studio, we take turns putting everything down, and then Wes works his magic. Since we've always loved making our own shit, aside from what Brighthouse puts out, we've all learned how to do the technical end of mixing, recording, and putting together the final product. We have so many songs fully recorded that we could probably pull them all together and put out an album a month for the whole year.

Which, now that we're leaving Brighthouse officially, might be an option.

"What's up?" I ask, coming into the control room and moving to the couch where Chance is relaxing—the same spot he's been in since we started early this morning—completely transfixed on seeing the process of birthing a song. I settle on his lap with a kiss to his jaw.

He smiles, and I feel the familiar buzz hit me. Luckily, I've gotten better over the last three days of being on the receiving end of it constantly. He still seems to reserve them for me and me alone, but since we haven't spent a second apart since our 'unioning,' I get them *a lot*. It's hard to believe that it's been two weeks since he walked into our hotel room back in New York. It feels like I've known him for so much longer.

"I just took a call from Don," Wes tells the room, drawing my attention from dreamy Chance thoughts.

Shifting my weight in Chance's lap so that I can lean back and rest my body against his strong hold, I briefly glance at Jamison as he messes around on his new phone before I look at where Wes is sitting at the control panel, and Luke lounges in the chair next to him. "And?"

"At the end of the tour, we will officially be done with Brighthouse Records. We still have the rest of the promotional obligations as outlined in our contract for each album. That will be no issue since all that's left is radio interviews at this point, and we can do those while we're on the road. Basically, we're lucky that Don is so good at his job because he said they tried to pitch a fit, but he shot that shit down real quick. We only signed for five albums, and they got them without sucking us into a hole of debt. They didn't count on us selling so well, hoping to fall back on that normally occurred debt to saddle us into more albums to pay them back. Old trick of the recording industry that we're fucking lucky we escaped."

I feel a weight I didn't realize I had been holding on my shoulders ease up. You can almost feel the relief dissipate in the air. "So what now?"

Wes rubs the back of his neck. "That depends on us now. We can choose to sign with another label, making sure we are happy with them and what they offer us this time."

"Or run the risk that they sell a bunch of lies hidden in a contract so thick it would take years to understand how many loopholes they have in there," Jamison adds, not looking up from his phone.

"I heard that EWP was accepting new artists," Luke puts in.

"Is that the label that Shaft put together when they left theirs?" I question the boys. Everyone knows the story of how Evil Wiener Productions got its start. I'll admit I was skeptical about such a large band leaving a major label, but you can't argue with their success.

"What if we follow their lead?" I muse out loud.

"You want to jump into the independent pool?" Wes asks with a look of shock. I'm surprised we didn't think about this earlier.

I shrug. "Why not? Those guys are a huge inspiration. I've always looked up to them on the music end, but after they had branched out on their own, they proved that an artist didn't need a major label to succeed anymore. We don't have to put up with their shit, no one is taking a huge cut of our profits anymore, and most importantly, we are in charge of where we want our music to go. We answer only to ourselves."

Silence greets me when I finish talking. Even Jamison has stopped whatever was so fascinating on his phone to look at me with wide eyes.

"You know we could do it. The whole reason we learned how to run our own studio is to be in control of the music we produced outside of Brighthouse. Hell, we can put together an album better than some of the best engineers and producers out there can, but if we want to bring someone in to do it for us, we know enough people who freelance in the industry to make it happen. Either way, it's on our terms. Dyllan's been looking for a reason to leave her job and start on her own; we could hire her as our exclusive stylist but also take advantage of her degree in art to design our covers, tour merch, etcetera. We have the bones for the beginning of our own team, and you know it."

"What about the rest of it, Wren?" Wes asks, leaning forward in his seat to give me his undivided attention. I can tell he's already on board, even if he doesn't realize it fully yet.

"We keep Tabby on as our agent since she wasn't affiliated with Brighthouse and, to be honest, probably hates them as much, if not more, than we do. She has a PR team in place with her agency, so we have her make that connection. We'll need to hire a booking agent and a few other key players, but we can figure those out later. And"—I smile, hooking my thumb over my shoulder to point at Chance— "we already know someone we can hire to handle security of our caliber both while we're here and while we're on the road for appearances or tours."

"We need to hire a lot more than that," Luke adds. "But you're right; we do know how to handle building our own team. We have the capital for it too. I can't believe I'm saying this, but the idea is a good one."

"I'm in," Jamison grunts, shifting in his seat. "Can I get a secretary?" he adds, almost as an afterthought.

"What the hell do you need a secretary for? To hand you fresh sticks when you let the ones you have go flying in the back of Wren's head again?" Wes jokes.

"No. And that only happened twice anyway. For roleplay, fucker. Do you even watch any of the links I sent you?" Jamison leans forward in his seat and waves his phone in the air between him and Wes.

"I can find my own porn, asshole. I swear something isn't right in your head."

"Hey! I would expect the same porn love from you. If you were to find a kickass video of the sexiest chick ever doing a human taco begging for uno mas, I would want to see it. What if you find one we haven't seen yet with that one chick who could bend herself in all those fucking crazy positions? Would you really keep that from me? Keep bendy girl all to yourself?!" Jamison looks seconds away from making a PowerPoint on why porn sharing means your friend loves you when he stops talking, spearing my brother with a look that just dares for him to disagree.

I stifle a giggle, leaning back into Chance's embrace.

"The last link you sent me was for a porn called *Umpa-Loving*," Wes complains. "The last thing I want when watching porn is for someone to ruin Willy Wonka for me. That film is a classic, man."

Jamison throws his head back and bellows a deep belly

laugh.

"Can we be serious?" Luke interjects before they can continue their argument.

"I say we do it. Even if you guys won't let me have a secretary," Jamison expresses with complete seriousness. I think he might actually have been serious about that secretary too, freaking weirdo.

"I'm in," Luke agrees instantly.

"Wes?" I question, the excitement of a new beginning taking over my system.

He looks beyond me, and I have a feeling Chance is meeting his gaze since I feel him tense up slightly. "What about you?"

I hold my breath. He's made it clear that he doesn't want payment but refuses to let us look into hiring someone else to handle security who we *can* pay. It doesn't feel right to let him do all the work and not actually be paid for it. I'm not sure why he's holding firm on his adamant desire of not being compensated, especially since he won't let anyone else do it—but I'm beginning to think there's more to it than him not wanting to start something with me while being paid to be here. In the three days since I learned about him refusing our money, I've been trying to get him to agree to a wage, with no luck.

Knowing he isn't going to give in without me speaking up, I turn in his lap and look into his beautiful eyes. "You know I don't agree with you doing all this work to keep us safe without being paid. I get what you think is right, but no one is going to think differently of you because we're employing you as security. Hell, no one would even have to know."

"I would know, Wrenlee."

"Oh, the full name! That means someone's gonna get a spanking later, you defiant little girl," Jamison jabs.

Ignoring him, I do my best 'I mean business' face and try to reason with my hardheaded man. "You need to give this a break, Chance? You've said that you don't trust anyone more than yourself. Other than these three boneheads, I don't trust anyone else more than I trust you. So please say yes. We aren't asking you to be paid to keep us safe yourself anymore. It isn't the same thing as what originally brought you to us. We're asking you to be in charge of hiring a security team and organizing our travel and tour security. Like it or not, you're part of Loaded Replay because you're part of *me*. It's not like I'm asking you to accept paying for being fantastic in bed."

His lips twitch.

"Seriously, Chance. As my *not* husband, I want you by my side at all times, but I don't want you there because you're protecting that side. I want you there because I'm the happiest I've ever been since you took that position."

"For argument's sake, I should point out that as your *not* husband, it's my responsibility to be at your side, protecting you—not my job."

I raise my brow. "And I'm asking you to do something that would keep you in the same spot, but also give you the responsibility of putting together a team who would be at your side *as well as* mine—keeping both of us safe, together."

His jaw clenches, and for a brief second, I wonder if he's going to say no. I mean it; I want him here by my side, but I also don't want him to resent me down the road if he regrets leaving his job. Chance isn't the type of man who would be happy being idle. He needs to feel like he's contributing; something he's proved each day that he's been here, and I need to feel like he's appreciated for doing so. I also know that he is damn good at what he does, and no one else should be in charge of hiring the people who will protect us. If he's so dead set on being the one who keeps me safe, then so be it, but I want to know a qualified team keeps all the people I love covered—him included.

Jesus, did I just lump Chance into that category? It's too early for all of that, right? I know our relationship is unconventional and moving at a quicker speed than normal. Even if he hadn't entered this as my fake whatever, we would never have been able to date like normal people, and it's because of that our relationship will always age at a speed others would take years to reach. Even if it seems fast, it feels *right*.

"If I say yes to this, no one else aside from me will be in charge of your protection, Wren."

"Agreed." Did he really think I would say no to that? As if.

"I think we should probably talk more about this when we're … alone." He pauses, and I frown, wondering why we need to talk about this alone. It involves all of us. Unless he's having second thoughts about us. "Get those doubts out of your head, Wren. We need to talk so you can make sure this is really what you want. You're asking me to sign on to something that would mean you would have me in your face, at your side, constantly. I would always be here, and we would be taking our relationship from the early stages straight to moved in and picking out china patterns. I want you to think about this before it's offered again."

"How many times do I need to remind you that you're already my *not* husband? Maybe I should be more upset that you haven't taken me to pick out china."

"Think about it. Really think about it." He continues, ignoring my attempt to lighten the mood.

My shoulders drop, feeling oddly upset. "We can talk tonight," I concede.

"Do you mean talk to him with your south mouth?" Jamison butts in.

"Shut up, Jami!" everyone in the room yells at the same time.

Chapter 20

Chance

It's been a long as fuck day.

Everyone's been gearing up to hit the road in the morning, so the mood in the house is almost manic. These guys have been on the road for so long with no break, they almost don't know how to reorganize their thoughts and prepare to head back out. They've also been unsure about how to move forward until they knew where things with Brighthouse stood.

I think a little part of it is the bittersweet feeling they have knowing this will be their last guaranteed tour. Sure, if they decide not to go back to a major label after it's over, they can still tour—but it would be a lot easier and certain if they had the big-wigs handling all the bullshit details for them.

I've been uneasy ever since our meeting earlier today in the recording studio. I can't put a finger on exactly why I feel that way, but I know it all stems around their offer for me to leave Corps Security—officially—and let them hire me as their lead for all things security.

Would it be hard for me to accept this offer, knowing it would keep me with Wren? Of course, it fucking wouldn't be. But it's important to me that I don't give her any ammunition to doubt my desire to be here. I knew from the jump that if I were here, being paid, it wouldn't feel right to start something with her while I was being compensated by them to do a job. I almost didn't even accept the job because the attraction between us had been so strong. It had been that way since I went to one of their shows a few years prior and locked eyes with her in the middle of the concert. In the end, though, I figured I could stay strong at the same time as protecting someone I felt some sort of connection to. That all changed before we even left New York, and I knew I was fighting a losing battle. It was the easiest decision ever at that point to end their contract with Corps Security.

I will never regret that decision because now that I have her, I can move forward without her ever doubting why I'm here.

Of course, it wasn't until she revealed her fear of people being close to them for the right reasons that I realized I made the right call.

"You look deep in thought," Wren calls from the end of the

bed. I had been so lost in my thoughts that I didn't even hear her enter the bedroom.

"Rightfully so, don't you think?"

Her shoulders fall, and I feel bad for not just conceding to what they offered me, but there's no way I can without having this talk with her.

"Talk to me, Chance," she implores, moving to sit on the bed at my side and placing her hand on my chest.

"You get that I care about you, right?" Her eyes flash happiness, but other than that, she just nods, giving me the time to finish and hear me out. "I care about you a whole fucking lot more than a man should after only knowing you two weeks. I'm already close to getting lost in you, Wren, and I'm not even the least bit upset about that. But I know you have doubts about people getting close to you and the guys. I even understand why you feel that way. I don't want you to ever doubt the reason I'm here."

"I wouldn't," she argues emphatically.

"You don't know that. What happens if weeks, months, or even years down the road something happens and that doubt comes back?"

She stands, the absence of her hand leaving a burning sensation on my chest. For a second, I almost knife off the bed and bring her back, but she places a knee on the mattress and climbs up until her bottom is resting on my jeans-covered hips. Both hands hit my chest this time, rubbing softly through the cotton. Her eyes never leaving mine.

"The day I met Garrett, he asked me to introduce him to Dix.

The very day. He was the last man I had dated officially, but I had met a few who could have turned into something had they not asked the same thing of me within an hour of meeting. The day that you realized you couldn't deny the feelings we shared for each other, you did the opposite by quitting the job we hired you to be here for and then you continued as if you hadn't. You have made it clear from the very beginning that you don't want to be here for any other reason than what we've been building together, Chance. I would never, could never, doubt what we have."

"What happens when people all start saying we met because I was being paid to be here?"

She smiles coyly. "No one knows what brought us together, Chance."

"Brighthouse does. I was there when Wes made the call to formally request my presence after we found that bullshit in your contract."

"And did he ask if you, Chance Nash, could be hired? Or did he ask if we could hire someone?"

I think back to that day when Wes had made the call. "He didn't refer to me by my name."

"Then I think it's safe to say that scenario will never happen. If someone makes the connection with your background in security, then they do. If you ask me, that will make you being in charge of our security team all the more plausible with us being *not* married and all. Why would I think about hiring someone else to build the best defense team to keeping the people I love safe? After all, the only one who would do the best job of that is already in charge of the heart that does that loving."

"I don't want you to resent me, Wren. Can't you see I'm trying to give us the best start here since I know how much the past has jaded you to trust other's motives?"

"Jesus Christ, Chance. I'm not ever going to look at what we have and think that. Ever! A man who has the type of integrity that you have would never, ever do that to me. Can't you see? I'm terrified that you'll leave without a reason to stay!"

Momentarily taken aback, my jaw slacks, and I look at this beautiful woman on my lap like she's lost her damn mind. "Wren." I sigh softly. "Don't you see that you are my reason to stay?"

"I am now. What happens when you get bored of traveling with us? When you get sick of being cooped up in this house? I won't ever have a normal life, Chance, and our relationship will always be different because of that. Not to mention, when we aren't in the studio, we're always on the move. Tours keep me away for months. You aren't the kind of man who can be idle and happy not to contribute. You've proven that each day you've been here, inserting yourself in our lives to pull your weight. That hasn't gone unnoticed or unappreciated. You say I'm your reason to stay, but I can't have you resenting me later when you don't feel challenged."

It's on the tip of my tongue to remind her that she's challenge enough for me, but I know now isn't the time to joke. "I could retire tomorrow and still live a comfortable life, Wren. My dad's family came from money, lots of money, and I inherited it all from both he and Tracy when they died. I don't need the money."

"It isn't about the money, Chance! It's about you being

needed for something bigger than whatever misplaced doubts you might think I could grow into. It's about more than my fear that you'll grow bored. In five years, we have never felt safe with the security Brighthouse put on us. Not once were we confident that someone wouldn't slip through the many cracks and hurt us. You popped in two weeks ago, and in all of that time, through three sold-out shows in one of the biggest cities and travel between crazy airports, we have finally breathed a sigh of relief that we don't have to be on guard. You gave us that gift. We all trust you to ensure that feeling for a long time to come because you've earned our trust to confidently do it. So no, it isn't about the money, Chance; it's about what's right for Loaded Replay and what's right for you."

"Wren," I breathe.

"No, Chance. Let me make it perfectly clear. I will never doubt your motives for being here. We're cut from the same cloth, honey. Both of us wear the scars of our jaded past, but if you feel even a little bit like I do for you, then you've felt the healing touch of them disappearing since the moment our bodies first touched. I need what you give me more than my next breath. That isn't something anyone would be able to give up. People fight a lifetime to find this, and I had almost lost faith that I would ever have this."

Goddamn, her words hit me, and I feel the sweet sense of being whole for the first time in my life by them. She's right; some people will never find the kind of connection we have.

"I felt that two weeks ago when I met you, Chance, but each

day that we're together, it grows into something larger than I will ever understand. You say taking this offer would jump-start our relationship, but that happened the day you walked through the door and put that reporter in her place."

I clear my throat. "Actually, for me, it started almost three years ago when I stood in the front row of a Loaded Replay concert and locked eyes with the most beautiful woman I've ever seen."

"What?" She gasps.

"I took Dani and her girlfriends to your show while Cohen was overseas and all that shit was going down with her. It was the first time I had ever seen you outside of magazines and the television. I think I felt the kick of us even back then."

Her chin wobbles, and for a second, I worry that she might cry. "God, Chance. How can you say that and not get that I'll never have any doubts?"

"Because no matter how you slice it, it's still only been a few weeks."

"And in my world, honey, those two weeks might as well mean two years. Our relationship will never move at a speed measured in time. What else can I say other than when you know, you know?" Her hands move as her eyes implore me to understand.

"We sit down and come to an agreement we can all live with, and I'm on board. Even if that means you agree to donate a salary I might receive to a charity of my picking."

A smile brighter than anything I've ever seen on her face

almost steals the breath from my chest seconds before she jumps forward. Her hands push up from my chest until she's holding them on either side of my face and her mouth is moving against mine in a deep kiss.

In the end, I might have given in, but I know that after our talk tonight, there is no way that either of us could look back and regret or doubt our relationship. Not only was this something I knew I needed to do, but I also needed her to tell me that I wasn't alone in this overwhelming feeling of pure fucking bliss after such a short time. She's right; our relationship will never be measured by time, not when it feels like I've been working my whole life just to make my way to her.

Chapter 21

Chance

"So what do we say when they start asking about your marriage?" Dyllan jokes, looking at Wren before giggling.

"You don't say anything," she answers.

"Well, are you going to say anything?"

Wren glances over at me and winks. "We talked about it, and I think it's kind of fun to play the game of not confirming anything to them but also not denying it."

Dyllan lets out a boastful laugh. "That's just going to make them all rabid for more. They won't stop until they know the truth."

"I don't live my life to feed their bullshit rumor-infested magazines, Dyll."

Instantly, her hands go up in surrender, and you can tell she feels bad. "I didn't say you do, Wren. I was just pointing out that you will only make them get a little more crazy about it if you don't just say you guys are dating and call it a day."

I feel Wren slouch in her seat next to me, exhaling a long breath. She shifts in her seat, getting more comfortable. "My love life is private, Dyll. They get so much of me already that I'm allowed to decide how much of my private life is exposed."

"So you're just going to continue the marriage ruse?"

"I'm going to continue enjoying my life with Chance at my side. If they want to assume something without confirmation, that's on them."

"Got it," Dyllan says. "At least, they'll put an end to the baby rumor as soon as they realize you aren't growing a belly," she adds before turning back in her seat and looking out her window.

"Until the next time we end up ordering too much room service and all of us are rocking food babies," Jamison jokes from the backseat.

"Ha!" Wes laughs. "Wren looked like she was about to birth a real baby after that night."

I feel her shift, and then I get the full effect of her attention slamming into me when those blue eyes lock with my own. My heart picks up speed, just like it's always done, and I feel my face get soft. Something she notices when some of the irritation I had seen on her face clears.

"Why did we agree to drive to Vegas?" she questions.

"It was easier to drive since the team I would have had with us during our flight can head on out to Vegas ahead of us and make sure everything is in place before we get there. I can handle it by myself, but since news might break any day now about your split from Brighthouse, I didn't want to be the only one on you all when it hit the press."

She sags against me, and I adjust my arm behind her, pulling her more comfortably to my side. Their normal driver had arrived at the house early this morning, and I had figured after us being up all night, she would crash quickly, but the gang traveling with us made that impossible. I'm guessing since she isn't used to being so thoroughly worked over, the normal banter between them is just taking more of a toll on her.

"Why don't you take a nap?" I ask her the second she falls even further into my embrace, dropping her head until it was on my lap.

"What are you doing down there?" Jamison pipes up, and I lift my hand to flip him off.

"How much longer?" I feel her head move as I look at my wrist to check the time, willing my cock not to react to her head being so close. When I glance back down at her, she groans at whatever she sees on my face. "Tell me it's at least less than an hour?"

"About two, but we're headed right to the venue. Get some rest and it will feel like less."

She nods, the sensation on my crotch perking my cock back up. Clearly, she notices if the light patting of her hand against my thigh is anything to go by. She sits up, giggling softly, and pulls the hoodie she had put on this morning off, dropping it in my lap, and then laying back down on it.

I listen to the conversations flowing around me, now lower in volume since Wren dropped down to rest. They might play around, but the bond these guys has makes it easy for them to adjust instantly when one of them needs something. And there was no doubt my girl needed her rest. She's been snappy since about thirty minutes out of LA.

"Hey," Dyllan whispers from her seat in the front next to the driver.

I look up, dropping the piece of hair I had been playing with; I continue to run my fingers over the soft buzz of the section of hair she has shaved at her temple, running them back to the silky locks that follow until I reach the end of her length and start the process over again.

I raise one brow, the silent arch an acceptance for her to continue to speak whatever it is she needs.

"Seriously, though, you started this whole marriage ruse when you were just supposed to be the fake boyfriend, so tell me how the story is going to play out!" she whispers, excitement all over her words as they rush from her mouth.

"Who said it was a ruse, Dyllan?" I continue to hold her gaze with my stoic mask firmly in place before she looks away, turning in her seat with a frown of confusion.

I'm not sure why I even said it, but I have a feeling a lot of that is because when I hear Wren call me her hubby and joke about us being *not* married, I fucking love the way it makes me feel. I haven't been able to stop thinking about it ever since, and while it might have started out as something funny between us, I can't help myself from wanting it to be true.

How's that for lightning speed?

I know Wren likes that our relationship is private, but I wouldn't mind if everyone knew that she was mine, especially if they thought we were married. It brings out something almost caveman inside me, thinking about the world assuming I'm the lucky bastard who gets her for the rest of my life.

No, fuck that. I have no doubts that this woman is it for me. The rest of my life never felt like something I could look forward to until her. I always felt like I lacked something. I didn't have a mother then lost my father and my aunt. Everyone that I had left in my family was gone, only making that void grow.

Then Wren walked into my life, and I felt that void start to fill in. She did that. Just like she promised she would. She's taken every destroyed piece and fixed it. I know because of that, I have my future right here drooling in my lap.

Not even the betrayal of Jessica hurts anymore.

That's probably because I have a relationship now, no matter how new, to compare it to, and I can look back now and see that what I felt for Jessica was nothing but a complacent punk think-ing a warm hole for his dick meant he was in love. Hell, I should send her a thank-you note for being such a whore that I never got stuck with her.

Not once in that whole relationship did I feel like I do now. I didn't wake up in the morning pissed that I had to even sleep at all because that stupid necessity kept me from Wren.

How's that for insane?

I feel like my heart—the one thing that keeps me alive—doesn't even beat inside my own chest anymore, not when Wren has taken its place as my most vital organ. Sappy or not, it's fucking true. If that doesn't scream love, I don't know what does.

It's almost impossible to hold the thought in, not when I know it's true deep down into my marrow. Sometimes, Wren gives me a look that tells me it's on the tip of her tongue too, but she's afraid to say it first. I had been worried that it would spook her to say it too soon, but after her speech about our relationship moving on a different time scale than normal, I have no doubts that what I feel for her needs to be known.

The last thought I have before leaning my head against the window is how much of a lucky bastard I am. This might have all started as a fake relationship to keep me close, but it turned into a very real one that never keeps me away.

Chapter 22

Wrenlee

Vegas is hot.

And dry.

It feels like someone took a blow dryer, pointed it in my face, and cranked that sucker all the way up.

I forgot how much I loved being in Sin City.

The stale, over-filtered air of secondhand smoke. A hint of desperation floats heavily through the casino floor, only pausing to mix with the underlying overeager panic to win that follows behind a few poor souls. And let us not forget the enticing sounds of the slots, hypnotizing their next victim closer with the promise of winning a life-changing jackpot.

"We're spending time playing the slots," I demand, looking at Chance with an excitement that can only be compared to a puppy with a brand-new bone.

He just shakes his head with a smile, pulling me through the lobby. Dyllan had come in to get us checked in so that we could make a quick rush through, but I had made the guys go first so that I could rubberneck right into the casino, needing to see the machines I love playing.

"We're doing it." His smile grows when I don't give in. "You're my good luck, Chance. Get it? Good luck Chance?"

"Ha-ha," he deadpans, not fooling me in the least.

"No one has a Chance to win like me," I continue, not even the slightest bit embarrassed that I'm being so corny.

I was still congratulating myself on being so witty when he pulled us into the elevator, backed me into the glass wall, and pressed his body close. My head spins with the tingles of excitement I feel at his domination, his thickness pressing into my belly with a thrust of his hips.

"You want a Chance to fuck?"

My eyes snap up to him at his words, and it takes me a second to clear the arousal from my brain, but when I see the hilarity dancing in his eyes, I toss my head back and laugh.

"We should have gotten our own room," he mumbles against the skin on my neck, pressing a kiss there before his wet tongue gives a swipe, making me shiver.

"It's a big suite," I weakly respond.

"Not big enough to do what I want to do to you."

"Oh, God." I shiver, clenching my thighs together.

"When we get to Denver, we're getting our own room."

I nod, but who am I kidding? At this point, I would have said yes to anything he wanted.

He steps away so quickly in the next breath, I would have fallen to the floor had he not wrapped his arm around my body. I sagged into him the second I realized the elevator had stopped.

I glanced at the number panel—noting that we were only a few floors up from the casino, on the floor that the pool is also on, and nowhere near where our suite is—just as the doors slide open and a group of college-age kids started filing in, laughing to each other. Chance got stiff the same second that one of them glanced at us. You could tell the second a courtesy glance at a stranger in an elevator turned into recognition.

"Holy shit," the guy grunted, jabbing his elbow into the person next to him without looking away.

"What the hell, Dale!" another one exclaims.

"Dude," Dale, I'm assuming, wheezes. Seriously, he wheezes like an asthmatic person during one of their attacks.

"What's wrong with him?" One of the girls giggles.

"Probably feeling the effects of drinking his weight in those stupid yard long drinks earlier," jokes someone I can't see in the front of their group.

"You're Wrenlee Davenport," the wheezer asks, still looking at me like he's not sure if he really is drunk or I'm standing there.

"I am," I answer, putting a smile on my face. It's not this kid's fault that he's keeping me from a promised Chance to get fucked.

The others, having realized their friend isn't drunk but only freaking out because they unknowingly just got in the elevator with me, turn instantly. Chance's arm gets tighter again, and I put myself in his position. He's only had to deal with fans from afar during our shows in New York. Even the paparazzi situation at the airport was mild because they know the boundaries ... well, for the most part. Having six other people in a small elevator with us and no way to exit if things get a little crazy has to be freaking him out.

"How are you guys today?" I ask them as a whole, trying to keep things friendly and open so he can see there is no need to get alarmed.

"Holy shit! I saw you guys once in Salt Lake. I was there for my eighteenth birthday, and you guys rocked!"

I smile at the girl.

"We like totally tried to get tickets to the show tonight when we found out we would be here at the same time, but they sold out like so quick!"

I wonder if I used the word 'like' as nauseatingly much as this girl did when I was her age. My guess is no since I'm pretty sure she is, at the most, four years younger than I am.

"Uh," one of the other guys pipes up. "Actually Kammie, we did get tickets. We just didn't tell you because it was supposed to be a birthday surprise, but I mean this is Wrenlee Davenport. Totally a better surprise."

The girl's eyes get crazy just when the elevator dings again, this time on the fifteenth floor. Since it isn't ours, I give them a smile and point at the open door. "Is that you guys?"

A few turn, but the majority of them don't take their eyes off me. I watch as one of the guys in the front of the group step out slightly to block the door from shutting.

"Is that your new husband? O.M.G!" I hold back my cringe when she literally spells out the letters. "Carrie, do you believe it?"

"Congratulations on your wedding and the baby stuff."

I look at the girl who just spoke, and she blushes, looking away. I take pity on her since she looks like her heart is about to stop. "Thank you. He's insanely handsome, right?" I smile, pointing at Chance with a wink.

She makes a sound like a high-pitch wheeze and sags into the boy behind her. He catches her with a roll of his eyes.

I point at one of the girls' purses with a smile. "If you have anything you want me to sign real quick, I don't mind, but hubby and I need to get going so we aren't late for my sound check."

They all jump into motion at that, pulling open their huge purses and digging for something. I sign everything from an old receipt to an unused pad, giving them all a little attention while I do and making sure they all have something with my signature scribbled on it. Reluctantly, after that, they leave the elevator and start screaming to themselves before the door had even completely closed back.

"Add calling Denver to talk about a secure elevator to get to and from our room to the list of things I need to make sure we have for the next stop," Chance says, finally relaxing his hold slightly on my body. "They might have been harmless kids, but I will never allow you to be in that position again."

"Yes, honey." I don't even attempt to dissuade him because he's right; that could have been bad.

We go another couple of floors before he speaks again, and when he does, he knocks so much shock into me that I lose all ability to speak.

"You keep confirming our marriage, and I'm going to make sure we don't leave Vegas without you calling me hubby next time because it's true."

Oh. My. God.

Chapter 23

Wrenlee

"Take it again from the top," I say through my mic, my voice echoing around the empty venue. "Something sounded off to me."

"Left side of the stage isn't pulling power to the speakers," Luke calls from behind me, and I turn to see him wipe some sweat off his forehead.

I hate doing sound check when they don't turn the stage fans on. The house lights always make us so fucking hot, which is why I end up having to take another shower when we finish.

"Working on it," one of the roadies calls out from the left side of the stage.

"I want to run through 'Drunk Before Dawn' one more time to make sure they have everything clear for us, and then that's it," I tell the guys, getting nods and grunts from behind me.

Sound checks usually don't last that long for us, but for whatever reason, this venue always gives us trouble. We've already run through a few of our key songs, and everything was fine until the last run through of one of our new songs, "Drunk Before Dawn," when we lost the whole left side of our stage speakers. It's annoying when this shit happens, but this is why we do this in the first place. As annoying as sound checks are, I would never go on stage for a show without making sure we're producing the clearest sound possible.

Forty-five minutes later, I'm rushing into our dressing room and into the shower, leaving my hair dry so the hair and makeup girls don't have to waste time blowing it dry. We only have about two hours before show time as it is, and I want to enjoy some pre-show downtime.

"I set out something new for you to try for tonight's show, Wrenny," Dyllan calls into the bathroom.

"Got it!"

I quickly rinse, enjoy one more blast of the hot water on the base of my neck, and then shut off the water and rip open the curtain, promptly screaming. "Jesus Christ, Chance! You're going to give me a heart attack." I take the towel he offers, and roll my eyes when he licks his lips, not even bothering to hide his appreciation of my naked body.

"Dix is here," he says, talking to my chest instead of me.

"Are you kidding?"

"Wish I could say I was. Your brother looked like he was two seconds away from losing his shit, but I reminded him that we have until the end of the tour before he can do that since Dix is technically within his rights to be here."

I hiss, dragging the towel over my body to dry off quickly, wanting to get out there before Wes really did lose his shit.

"Let me guess? Brighthouse sent him in as a representative?"

"Yeah. You fired him as your manager, but since he was the booking agent on file for the tour, he's here for the rest of your shows to, and I quote, 'keep an eye on you.'"

"I can't wait until this tour is over."

"I know, but until it is, keep your distance from him. I don't like his attitude, and if I'm not around you, do your best to make sure he isn't alone with you."

I toss the towel onto the floor and grab the boy shorts on top of the pile of clothes that Dyllan left for me. Chance makes a sound of protest when I snap the waistband in place, but I ignore him and quickly pull on the red lace bra.

"Don't worry, hubby, I'll keep my distance," I agree, picking up the next item in the pile with a frown. "That little turd." I laugh.

"Is that a skirt or a top thing for your tits?" Chance asks, one long finger flicking the black fabric.

"I'm going to guess a skirt." With a shrug, I step into it and pull it up.

The second I have the skirt on, I know exactly why Dyllan

picked it out. The tiny micro skirt flares slightly right under my ass, but the rest hugs me well, hitting me about three inches under my pussy. Even when I move around the stage, they won't see anything though because my boy shorts will keep all my bits covered. Still, Dyllan did promise when I got my bows tattooed that she would make sure I had a whole new wardrobe to show them off.

Grabbing the tiny tank, I pull it over my head. The black tank is completely transparent, hugging me close and stopping just above my belly button. My red bra shining just as brightly as the diamond balls in my belly ring.

"God*damn*," Chance pants.

"Like?" I ask, spinning on my bare feet.

"I'm going to fuck you so hard tonight," he vows with a thick voice and eyes burning with need.

"Promises, promises," I tease, stepping forward and cupping his thickness through his jeans. He hisses out a breath, his eyes closing to slits as his jaw flexes wildly. "Let's go, hubby." I torment him a little more with a few strokes through the denim before turning and reaching for the doorknob.

I don't even get it turned before he's covering me with his body and pressing that delicious hardness into my back. "I'm going to tie you up and make you pay for teasing me, baby," he hisses darkly, biting my exposed shoulder hard enough that I'm pretty sure I'm going to have a mark.

I shiver, my legs getting wobbly. Holy shit, that's hot.

His arms come around me. One hand going to the knob— covering my hand with his—and the other flattening against my stomach. His pinkie presses past the waistband and lands against my mound. He uses his other to twist the knob under our hold, pushing the door open at the same time he pulls us back. The door swings in, us moving to the side to allow it to completely open, and he drops his free hand to turn my head with a light touch to my jaw, his mouth crashing down to mine for a quick but deep kiss.

"Kids these days," Jamison jokes. "Can't seem to keep their hands off each other."

"Must be the whole newlywed thing," Dyllan adds, giggling when Chance breaks the kiss. My knees buckle, but before I know it, he's sweeping me off my feet and carrying me into the dressing room. "I keep telling him he only had to carry her over the threshold once, but he still can't seem to stop."

I snap my head around, ready to put her in her place, but stop when I see Dix so red, he's about to bust a vein.

"Dix," I deadpan. "What a displeasure."

"Likewise, Wrenlee."

Chance makes a low noise deep in his throat, and I reach up to rub his chest. Dix's eyes track my movement, not looking away, and he looks even more pissed than before—something I didn't think was possible.

"Wren is here now, Dix. Tell us what you need since you apparently couldn't do it before." Wes sounds more pissed than I can ever remember him sounding.

"Brighthouse wanted me to remind you all that until the next six weeks is up, you still have a responsibility to them, and

I'm here on behalf of them to make sure you hold up each and every commitment." He turns to me. "It has been requested by Howard himself that you please stop talking about that problem of yours. Brighthouse doesn't want to be painted in the same light as someone who behaved in such a manner that would allow herself to become vulnerable to such a problem. No matter if the engagement has now turned into a marriage, everyone already knows what you created in sin."

"The fuck did he just say?" Wes bellows, trying to rush from his spot, only for a mammoth body to stop him when Jamison steps in front of him. His arms crossed and a lethal look painting his features.

I have just a second to notice that Luke is standing behind Wes, ready to hold him back if he tries to get past Jami. I should have worried less about my brother because my distraction meant that Chance left my side completely. By the time I'm looking back at Dix, Chance is backing him into a wall. He never touches him, just moves Dix back with the fury vibrating off him.

"If you *ever* talk about Wrenlee like that again, you will find out what it's like to be vulnerable to a fucking problem. No matter what you or that piece of shit label you work for thinks about her, me, or anything that's come from our love for each other, I suggest you keep those thoughts to yourself unless it's to wish us congratulations, motherfucker. Now, get the hell out of here before I forget that I'm a gentleman."

Dix, still pushing his own body as close to the wall as possible to avoid Chance's rage, penguin walks the wall length until he's blindly grabbing for the door and rushing out. Silence roars in my ears as I watch Chance's shoulders heave in anger. I can't look away, the raw power of his body holding me captive, much like Dix just was. Only mine is being held in awe and Dix was about to piss himself in fear.

"Did he just say love?" Dyllan gasps in a squeal, not fazed by the heaviness around her. She jumps from the stool, claps her hands, and does a tiny victory dance.

Oh, wow. I think back to what he told Dix, and even though he had been defending me and our very real relationship—it had been in reaction to Dix insulting our nonexistent child and the marriage rumor that we've just been playing along with for laughs. Never once did he say anything about it being fabricated; he only threatened with the parts of our relationship that were true.

When he turns, his breathing still erratic with his anger, I can see it in his eyes—the truth. He wasn't just saying that for Dix's benefit.

Nope, he sure wasn't.

Chance Nash, my *not* husband, has just proclaimed his love for me in a way that leaves no room for argument from anyone.

And I can't wait to let him tie me up and show me just how much love he has for me.

Chapter 24

Wrenlee

The first hour of our show went off without a hitch, but only because the crowd doesn't know my guys like I do. The mood that Dix had put them in was something they couldn't shake until they realized it didn't affect me. Once they saw how much fun I was having with the sold-out Vegas crowd, they lightened up and enjoyed themselves as much as I was.

Everything that I had started to hate about this life in the last few years started to drain away from me with each song that I performed on stage. I felt every last ounce of disquiet still clinging to me vanish completely. We still have things that we're figuring out for our future, but when it comes down to it, we'll get to that together.

I rocked that stage like I hadn't rocked one in a long time. Playing up the sexy image that Brighthouse had always exploited, I danced with seductive rolls of my hips, flashed my bows while I belted out the lyrics over my shoulder, and had more fun than I've had in years. It's funny how now that I see things in a new light, how I always thought this part of me wasn't real—an act that had been created by the demands of Brighthouse to give the fans a part of me. Now, I finally see that the Wrenlee the public has always craved is really married to the Wren I've always been. I know now that I'm the one who holds the power to my life. I'm the one who decides the person I am in the public eye. I get to pick how much and how little they get from me—no one else has that authority.

I have no doubt in my mind that feeling has everything to do with the man standing to the left of the stage, just out of view, with a primal hunger on his face the whole time I put my all into the music. He's made no secret that Wren's—me—his, but that he still wants the Wrenlee put on display for the world. He is fiercely protective of the person I am when I'm not performing, but he opens his arms and lets me fly when it's time to rock. He doesn't discriminate when it comes to his desire for me. He wants me with no makeup and leggings. He wants me with a face a drag queen would love and my body on display. He holds me close when I'm not performing—a shield to guard my privacy—yet he lets me go long enough to be a fantasy for others—standing back to shield and guard me from the shadows. To him, I'm just me, and that me belongs to him.

His lips start to twitch when I blow him a kiss, something the crowd doesn't miss, and their screams grow in volume at my move. I toss my head back when he lifts his hand and returns the gesture, something so unlike the stoic man he becomes when he's 'working.'

The song ends, and Wes continues a few heavy riffs from his bass guitar, while I give the masses a sassy smile. "I gotta say, Vegas, you sure do look hot tonight! What do you say we cool off and get a little … 'Drunk Before Dawn'?" When I finish speaking, I hold my arm out with the mic pointed out toward them and wait for the crowd to go nuts at the mention of one of our biggest hits.

They don't disappoint, and I'm thankful I pulled out my earplugs a while ago, so I'm able to feel the full power of their unadulterated excitement slap me in the face. "Well, then! I think you guys are thirsty! Let's go, boys! Let's show the good people of Las Vegas how to get Loaded!"

Jamison starts to pound out a voracious beat, each one vibrating through my body with pure and beautiful power. The complex time signatures of one of my favorite songs of all time rolls through me until I feel like I'm alive with the power of it. I glance over my shoulder while the boys create their magic, waiting for my intro, and see Jamison. The playful enthusiasm on his face is like a virus to your soul. I smile over my shoulder at Luke and Wes, my excitement buzzing even more intensely as their hands move quickly and their eyes smile back at me.

Then it's my turn. That magic spot in the music that marks

'go time.' I toss my hair back, look up high into the rafters of the arena, and give this song everything I feel. As soon as I start rasping out the lyrics to one of my favorite songs, the crowd is already screaming the words along with me, high on the same feeling I am.

At this moment, we're one.

I continue to sway my hips, singing with a smile, as I glance at where I last saw Chance standing. He's stepped forward only minutely, but enough that his face is no longer completely masked by the shadows around him. The new position no longer mutes his handsome face but leaves him illuminated by the stage lights, showing me just how much he's enjoying watching me perform. His plump lips—lips I know can turn me into a puddle of goo—are silently mouthing the words along with me. I knew he was no stranger to us, but I had no idea he was this familiar with our music. I don't know how to explain it, but knowing that he clearly enjoys our music enough to know the words makes me feel like a superwoman. The normal rush I get from being on stage turns into a powerful intoxication coupled with his affections.

It hits me in the middle of the chorus, and if I wasn't such a seasoned vet to holding my cool on stage, I would have stumbled terribly. Outside, you would never know that I'm on the cusp of a life-altering discovery. But inside, I'm a mess of feelings. I know, in this second, that the *something* I had been searching blindly for has finally been found.

I had been so lost that I couldn't even see that I could find most of those answers inside myself. Chance taught me, in such a small amount of time, to see the good in people. When he gave me the gift of his affection, he made sure to leave no room for arguments and that I understood why he wanted me to have his. He has helped me to stop thinking there was no hope. I no longer see people and jump to the conclusion that they are automatically going to use me.

Standing here, I no longer see the rabidly hungry fans as I once would. I see people who feel the music we're creating for them. Music that I thought had been dying in its power to make others disconnect from their worries and just … *be*. Memories are being made with each heart-pounding second that they stomp their feet and belt out the words with me. They crave the feelings that we as artists pray they'll sense within our music. And it's because of all that, in the sixteen acres of the sold-out T-Mobile Arena, twenty thousand people unify, becoming one and proving that as long as you have the dominance of music, you are never alone.

My eyes grow wet when I realize just how far I've come since we left New York. Nothing was different, in hindsight, except the contentment that I now feel within myself—allowing me to see the beauty in my life without the jade-covered lens of my fears.

This right here is what makes every one of the seconds my jaded little heart felt a disconnect in my life worth it.

The crowd before me, my guys at my back, the music that makes us all one, and most importantly—the man at my side. Because without him, I'm not sure I would have ever been able to find this again.

Chapter 25

Chance

I recognize the change inside Wren the moment that it happens. I have no idea what brought it on, but one second, she was just performing, and in the next, she was *living* that performance like it was an extension of her. I felt something shift inside me at that moment, something I hoped I never lost. It was almost as if she was seeing the world around her with new eyes. It was a change that I don't think anyone else would have even noticed, but because of our connection, it's a change that I feel snap within me as well.

Even the way in which she's holding that tight, sinful body on stage is oozing with a newfound air of confidence. She's never had trouble with working the stage in my opinion. Their fans love her because she's a master at owning the stage during their shows, but at this moment, she is no longer playing an act created to drive them nuts with pleasure; she's figuratively jumping right off the stage and joining the insanity right along with them.

Every male instinct wants to steal her away and never let her outside again until every single person alive knows she's off-limits. I want her body, the petite beauty that is on display in next to nothing, under my own so I can remind her who she belongs to. I think a little part of me worried that I wouldn't be able to handle this part of her world. That the struggle to share her would become a challenge that even my feelings for her couldn't soothe.

But seeing this side of her is what solidifies my knowledge that I can not only handle her world, but I'm also honored to be at her side while I live in it. Witnessing the wonderment of her coming into her full potential and finding herself again, while in front of thousands, makes it easy to push all those natural-born instincts aside and support her with unwavering devotion. This is who she is, who she was born to be, and it would be an injustice to deny the world the beautiful insanity she and the guys create.

Fuck me.

I wasn't kidding earlier when I put that asshole Dix in his place—anything that comes out of the love I feel for this woman is something I will protect with my last breath. It didn't even matter to my rational brain that I was about to kill a man over a media-made pregnancy lie and the rumored engagement and marriage seed I planted while I was playing the fake boyfriend. It might have started out as a lie—our relationship—but I will never allow someone to take what we have and try to make it wrong.

Coming out of my thoughts, I hear the shift in the music that begins Jamison's solo time to go nuts. Wren gives the crowd her back, arms stretched out beside her body, and she undulates to the rhythm he is masterfully creating. Her skirt, already doing a shitty job of actually covering her sweetness, pops up wickedly each time she shifts her hips. I can just see the side loop and end piece of one of her tattooed bows on the back of her thigh, inked so lifelike with a delicate lace pattern that my fingers twitch to reach out and touch them.

I feel a need for her, which I haven't felt before as I watch her, and that's saying a whole hell of a lot since I already crave her to the point of insanity. I've memorized their set list, so I know "Drunk Before Dawn" is the song before they come off, faking the end of their show before going back out to give them the final rush. I know from the shows in New York that they have a habit of deviating from the plan—adding in some surprise songs on top of the three they always end their shows with. With how they're feeling right now, I have a feeling it will be one of those nights, even though I'm hoping it isn't for my own selfish reasons.

The song ends, and right on cue, the lights go completely dark on the stage, leaving them just enough illumination to come off the stage safely. Wren's body hits mine a second later, making me step back in order to support her, and her legs wrap around my waist. I place my hands on her naked thighs and hold her close—pressing my cock against the heat of her.

"Hi," she breathes through her smile.

"Hi, back." I feel my own happiness growing, taking over the mask that I held in place for the last two-and-a-half hours while I watched her out there.

The bright red lipstick, dark eye makeup, and shine across her skin from her exertion only add to the intensive drive growing inside me to claim her as mine for all to see.

"I like knowing you're watching me," she says honestly, her eyes bright even in the darkness.

"I can tell, baby."

Her face gets soft, but before she can speak, I hear Jamison bang out a steady rhythm. The thumps slow and even but nonetheless powerful.

The signal.

Just like clockwork.

I tag Wes and Luke moving back onto the stage without looking away from Wren. I know she has forty-six seconds from that moment to get back out there, mic in hand, ready to sing a voice of raspy sex.

"You wearing that magic lipstick that doesn't come off for fuck all?" I ask, Wes' bass mixing with Jamison as the tempo picking up speed.

"Yeah." She nods, squirming in my hold.

"Then give me a deep one. Make it hard and rough, so when you get back out there, everyone knows exactly what you just did with that wicked mouth. I want you puffy and swollen in more places than one for me."

She presses closer, and I have no doubt that if I pushed those panties to the side, I would indeed find her puffy, swollen, and soaking fucking wet with her need. Her kiss is just as I demanded, our tongues picking up the same cadence of Luke's guitar as he enters into the tune crafted by the three men. Knowing her time is up, she breaks away with a heaving chest, and I drop her gently to her feet. She looks like she wants to say something, but with no time left, she spins and is singing the lyrics before she's even left the shadows.

I don't even bother hiding the thickness growing behind my jean zipper. There's no use, not when she's standing out there in front of thousands looking just fucked from a kiss alone.

Soon.

The silent promise doesn't do much to douse my desire. I try to get a hold of my body, but it's a losing battle. I hope she's feeling it as badly as I am because there will be nothing slow and soft when I finally get her to myself. It's going to be raw, hard, and animalistic. It's also going to love her so fucking good that she will know mind, body, and fucking soul who she belongs to.

"You look like you're about to go apeshit," Dyllan contemplates out loud as she saddles up to my side when they start playing the fifth song of their encore. I knew she was there. I felt her move an hour ago, coming out from her spot further down on the side closer to Jamison.

I don't speak. I'm not even sure if I could. Not to be rude—especially not to Wren's best friend—but it's taking everything I have in me to just be able to stay alert to my surroundings while the vixen on stage makes me insane with desire.

"You're good for her, you know," she continues, not even fazed by my silence. "And I hope you know how lucky you are to have earned her heart."

I turn, my gaze leaving Wren for the first time in over three hours. "I know *exactly* how lucky I am to have been given that gift."

"Don't hurt her," she unnecessarily warns.

I harden my expression, showing her without words how much her words piss me off, but I don't speak my frustration because I know she's coming from a good place.

"It's my job to warn you, so … consider it a warning that I'll do all sorts of painful things to you if you make her feel pain from even a paper cut."

"If the day ever comes that I allow that to happen, you have my permission to do just that. I'll even provide you with the tools for the job."

Her eyes widen. "Well … okay then."

I nod, hold her gaze for a second, and then look back at the woman I would rather die for than hurt.

"You've been amazing, Las Vegas! Thank you for coming out. Have a kickass night and go make Sin City your bitch! We love you all!"

With a wave, not even waiting for the three musketeers' normal after-show antics, she rushes off the stage. Dix is standing in the same spot he had been scowling from all night, but he steps to the side when the crew starts moving around. Wren hands her mic off to one of the male technicians, Curtis, before stepping over to the woman named Kellie, who helps her remove her earpieces. Both of them are efficient and quick, something I'm thankful for a second later when she is back in my arms.

"I don't think I'm going to make it all the way down the corridor to your dressing room," I say against the salty skin of her neck.

"Me either. At this point, I wouldn't care if you took me in the middle of everyone backstage."

"That won't happen," I grunt, biting at the smooth skin. "They already get to see you looking like a pure fucking wet dream; I won't give them more than that."

"Hurry," she pants, fingers digging into my hair with a bite.

"My cock is so hard for you."

She whimpers, and I look over her shoulder. No one is paying us any attention, so I open the first door I find—a storage closet—and push her inside.

The second the door closes, she shoves out of my hold and drops to her knees. If I live to be a hundred, I will never forget the vision that Wrenlee Davenport makes when she looks up at me, body flush with desire, and vibrating with the rush of performing. Her red hair, damp from her exertion, shines under the single bulb burning above her, making her look like the naughtiest angel.

"Fuck, you undo me." I rub my thumb against her bottom lip's soft flesh as I speak, trying to convey just how far gone I am for her.

"Let me love you," she whispers, and whatever control I thought I held at that moment vanishes the second her tiny, black tipped fingers slowly start to unfasten my pants. She slips her hand inside and, with a slowness that makes my every nerve ending aware of her movements, pulls my cock out. "Every second I was out there and felt your eyes on me, I wanted this cock even more."

With her eyes still connected to mine, she looks up my body while one hand wraps as far around my shaft as she can. She brings her other hand up to cup my balls at the same time she opens her mouth as wide as she can to wrap those red stained lips around me.

"God-fucking-damn," I hiss through my teeth.

If I make it through her sucking my cock like it's a treat she can't get enough of, it will be a shock.

I feel like I might die from the pleasure alone.

That's the last thought I'm capable of because Wren stops holding back. She owns every part of me at this moment. My mind succumbs to her, willing to do anything she wants. My body owned by hers. And my heart beating so hard in my chest, I feel like it's trying to reach out and never let her go.

Yeah, I'm one lucky son of a bitch.

Chapter 26

Wrenlee

My body is about to explode. Each slow drag of my tongue on his velvety hot flesh makes him jerk and twitch. His tight black shirt hides the full magnitude of his muscles, but he's holding it up so I can see each ripple that dances up from where I'm working him.

I'm doing this to him. Me. With just my mouth and hands. If it feels even half as good as when his mouth and hands are feasting on me, I know he's going out of his mind. I don't take my eyes off his face, needing to see his expression. I know he's so used to keeping himself closed off from others, even with something as simple as his appearance, that the rush of him learning to let go is intoxicating.

His eyes flash, and I have a feeling he's close. But unlike the other times I've tried to get him to finish in my mouth, he lets me continue. I hum around his thickness, making sure he understands that I'm happy he's giving me this. He jolts in my hold, his cock jutting into the back of my throat. I gag and my eyes water, but I just pick up speed. My tongue swirls around the tip before I swallow as much of him as I can, caressing his balls at the same time the hand around him flexes. He's so wide around that it strains my jaw even to take him in my mouth, my fingers not even close to touching him.

"I'm going to come," he says, voice low and gritty.

If I didn't have a mouth full of cock, I would tell him he doesn't need to warn me since I can feel the evidence of his impending release in my hands. His balls draw up, and his shaft hardens even more before getting almost impossible to keep in my mouth. I hollow out my cheeks and suck, holding just the tip of him in my mouth while I work him with my hands, eyes still on his.

"Motherfucker," he hisses, clenching his jaw seconds before I lose his gaze, and his head falls back on the door with a heavy thud. He swells, his hips shake, and then his come starts to spurt from his cock in thick streams that I swallow instantly. I don't let go until I'm sure every drop has left his body, not wanting to give any of it up.

Leaning back, I rest my ass on the heels of my boots, watching his chest heave with his heavy breaths. My hands continue to caress his spent, but still hard, shaft.

"Stand up," he demands with such force that his words literally vibrate in the air around us.

I do what he wants, naturally, and wait with anticipation for his next move. The second my feet are solidly back on the ground, he lunges, twisting us so that I'm now facing the door with him behind me.

"Hands on the door, Wren. No matter what I do to this body, you do not let go. Do you understand me?"

I nod, the lingering essence of him on my tongue driving my already fevered need higher with his words.

"Give me your words, Wren. Tell me you understand."

"I understand, Chance," I slur, gasping loudly when he pulls my panties to the side and shoves two fingers deep into my soaked core.

"Tell me you want me to fuck you so hard that you feel me in the back of your throat again."

"Oh, God. Yes. Yes, I want that."

"Words."

My eyes roll in the back of my head when he hits a spot inside me that I've only recently discovered really exists, a new rush of wetness coating his hand.

"Fuck me, Chance. Fuck me so I feel it everywhere," I strain out over the rush of need overtaking me.

"Tell me you want to feel my come deep inside you, coating your pussy like it just coated your mouth."

"I want your come. I need it. Inside me, give me it." I dig my weight into the door, flexing my fingers against the solid surface. He hooks his fingers deep inside me, and I sway, almost losing the hold I have.

"Beg me to fuck you."

My head lolls between my outstretched hands. I see his hand, pumping his fingers into my pussy, and his clothing around his ankles. In any other situation, I would think that was funny, but right now, that just reminds me that his beautiful cock is naked and waiting for me.

So I open my mouth and beg. The incoherent words leaving my mouth come out in a pitiful whine of need. I have no idea what I'm saying, but it must make sense to Chance's ears because in the next second, my feet are off the ground and the only thing keeping me from face planting is the hold I have on the door and Chance's hands on my hips.

He lifts me, effortlessly, my legs hanging uselessly in the air between us.

"Hold on, Wren. Do not let go."

That's the only warning I get before he lifts me just a little more and spears his full length deep into my needy body. Deeper than he's ever been before, his thickness stretches me to the brink, filling me up like he was made just for me. I clamp down on his flesh instantly, so beyond turned on that my orgasm hits the instant his balls swung up and slapped my wet pussy. He groans, my body rippling around his hardness, holding him captive in the tight sheath. He doesn't move until the last flutters of my release dance around his length.

Then he drags his cock out slowly, painfully so in the most delicious way, before holding himself at my entrance with just his tip. He stays like that for what feels like a lifetime but could have only been seconds, for all I know, before slamming back in. He doesn't ease up after that, pounding inside me in a toe-curling speed. A scream of pleasure burns up my throat, but I hold it in. He lets me know instantly that he isn't happy about it too because his next thrust is almost brutal in power, ripping the scream from me.

He doesn't ease up after that, making sure I'm not able to be quiet. I don't even care that I can hear people moving along the hallway outside our hideout. I wouldn't even care at this point if the door crashed down, so long as he didn't stop.

My skin starts to buzz, and I feel the tight coil of pleasure starting to twist until it has no movement left, holding me in a breathless plane of bliss until—with one more thrust deep inside me—I come. I struggle to find my breath after that; the coil having unwound in such a vicious snap that my body doesn't even feel like it's whole anymore. My throat burns before I shout his name out, begging him never to stop.

When I finally come back to my senses, I open my eyes to see my hands hanging limply at my sides, legs still dangling, the hold Chance has on my hips a bruising grip in order to keep himself buried deep and keep me from falling to the ground. I won't be shocked if I have the perfect outline of his hands on my hips when we're finished. He flexes his hips, unable to do much more, and then I feel him release inside me with low grunts leaving his body.

My feet land with care, and because of our height difference, I lose his cock the second they do. I miss the fullness instantly. His thumb hooks around my panties, moving them back in place seconds before I feel his release start to leave my body. It's an odd turn-on, feeling the combined wetness of our releases soak my underwear.

I hear him shuffling his weight behind me, the sounds of his clothes being set to right, and I turn to watch him put himself back together.

"I could get used to that kind of after-show party," I hum, dragging my hands up his chest and coming up on my toes to place a kiss to his jaw. The stubble tickling my lips.

"That's good to know. Was I too rough?" he worries.

"God, no," I reassure him. "I'm not going to break, Chance. I think you'll find that I like your rough tough just as much as I like your soft one. As long as it's always you, I want it all."

"Always," he vows, dipping down to press a kiss against my lips.

"I think we were loud," I joke with a smile that his eyes move to.

"I don't think, I know. You ready to face the music?" He nods at the door behind me.

"With you at my side, I think I can face anything."

His eyes flash right before his face softens.

When we open the door and step out into the hallway, a few members of the crew are milling around. They ignore us, not making eye contract. I see Dix looking like he's about to spit nails, but I ignore him. I look around while we move down the hallway, only seeing a few people who actually see us, as the rest are too busy with the jobs they have to complete before we can pack up and head out to the next venue.

I feel a tingle over my skin, one that tells me someone is watching, and look up to see Kellie. Instead of looking away like normal, though, she almost seems excited.

Girl power, I guess.

We reach the dressing room and push in, seeing Luke and Wes on the couch looking almost uncomfortable. They swing their heads in our direction, shock washing over them. I tip my head, trying to figure out what's going on with them. They look from where Chance and I are standing, to each other, back to us, and then over at the bathroom door—finally settling on us once again with confusion. Wes rips his headphones off, narrowing his eyes at me.

"If you two are right there …" Luke starts, stopping when a low moan echoes around us followed by a high-pitched squeak.

"Then who the hell is that?"

"Where's Jami?" I question harshly. "I can't believe you guys didn't think maybe it was him, since he isn't in here with you. Were you just planning to sit here looking ill until the door opened?"

"Hey! He disappears after shows often. It wasn't off the mark to guess you two freaks were going at it again," Luke yells.

"I just sat here listening to some bullshit Justin Bieber

song—the only thing that is apparently on Dyllan's phone—because I thought you were in there banging my sister!" Wes fumes, his attention on Chance.

"Well, dumbass, I hope you get Bieber fever because we did our banging down the hall in storage!" I snap, trying not to laugh.

"You assholes are loud as fuck," Jamison complains, coming out of the bathroom with his clothes astray and glitter all over his lips.

Luke laughs at him, pointing at his mouth. "What is all over your face?"

Jamison looks confused, standing up to walk over to the huge mirror vanity set up for hair and makeup. "Jesus Christ, I look like I just got done eating out Tinker Bell," he grumbles, wiping at his mouth with the back of his hand and making everyone laugh.

My attention moves to the bathroom door when I see Dyllan shyly move into the room unnoticed.

"You!"

She flinches but just smiles with a shrug, like she didn't mean to. I would love to see her explain this as an accident. I can just picture it now, 'I slipped and fell on his dick'!

"Seriously, Jamison!"

He looks over from his angry glitter removal. "What? We're just having some fun. No need to freak out about it."

I narrow my eyes, ready to rip him a new asshole for turning his manwhore ways on my best friend. Even though she had all but confessed to it back in LA, seeing it in person is something completely different.

Dyllan is the kind of girl you lock down and keep—heart the size of Texas just waiting for the right man. Jamison, God love him, hasn't stopped sleeping around since his last relationship failed epically. The last thing I want is for Dyllan to get attached to him if he doesn't have any intention of taking things past 'just a little fun.'

I make a mental reminder to talk to Jamison about this when I can get him alone. Dyllan heads back to LA tomorrow morning anyway, so hopefully, he can keep it in his pants between now and then.

What a mess.

Chapter 27

Wrenlee

True to his word, when we reach Denver, Chance has our own room waiting for us. It's on the same floor as the guys, but on the opposite end of a long hall. He took it a little further, though, and made sure the hotel had cordoned off the whole floor we were on, ensuring maximum privacy. He also left two of his 'men'—Hunter and Chris—to keep guard at the elevator area. It looks like the most boring job in the whole world, but they don't seem to mind.

"I'm exhausted." I sigh, dropping down in the middle of the huge king-size bed. We just spent the last ten hours on the tour bus, making our way from Vegas to Denver in good time. But as with any time I'm in Vegas, three days feels more like thirty.

"You've been working hard. You should probably take advantage of the night off and get some sleep."

I lean up, narrowing my eyes. "Does that mean I don't get your fat cock, hubby?" Even with the two nights in a row of shows and the whole day yesterday doing some press for *Black Lace*, he's never suggested sleep over sex.

He laughs silently, his shoulders moving. "How long you going to keep that nickname up?"

"Why? You don't like it?"

"Didn't say that, Wren. But you know it's just going to keep feeding the rumors." He drops down on the bed, adjusting the massive mound of pillows around him before leaning against the headboard.

"Do you care?" I ask, honestly. "We haven't really talked about it. I probably should have asked before just assuming you thought it was funny too. I mean we've been joking about being *not* husband and wife since we got to LA two weeks ago."

"Would you come here and stop panicking," he says, smiling reassuringly at me.

I shift, coming up on my knees and crawling up the mattress. When I get close enough, he pulls me down to rest against his chest. Silence thickens around us as he runs his fingers down my arm, his other hand holding ours together with our fingers linked on his hard stomach.

"You have fun with it?" he asks softly. "The paparazzi

assuming, but not knowing for sure, don't you?"

I nod my head, studying the differences in our hands. His long fingers and large palm dwarf mine. We're so different but incredibly perfect for each other.

"Yeah." I sigh. "I haven't had this much fun with their bullshit questions in years—if ever."

"Then don't stop, baby."

"But, Chance, you can't just say that because I'm having fun. If you don't want the rumors out there, we can just answer them honestly next time, and they'll stop playing it up. Your feelings matter too."

His chest moves, and I know he's doing that silent laughter thing again. "I don't give a shit about the rumor, Wren. I do, however, give a shit about you. If this is something you have fun with, then we aren't hurting anyone. So go for it."

"Oh," I breathe.

"I like it," he confesses. "Just in case it matters, when you call me that ridiculous nickname, it goes straight to my dick. So, I promise that's the only hardship I feel."

I look down at his lap, the jeans he's wearing hiding what I really want to look at, but just thinking about me calling him something silly affecting him that way makes me want to preen like a goddess.

"You know I love you, right?" he asks, his tone soft the delicious rasp of his deep voice washing over me.

I feel those words ping through every single inch of my body. He hinted to loving me back in Vegas when he was yelling at Dix, but in the days since, he hasn't said anything else about it. Hell, I think I had half-convinced myself I imagined it.

I curl into his side. "Yeah," I answer breathily. "I love you too, Chance."

"One day, those rumors won't be lies, Wrenlee. Enjoy playing your game because when that day comes, you'll be able to keep them up, always feeling that happiness you get over keeping something from them."

I lift up quickly, and he grunts a little when I put too much weight on his belly. "Did you just ask me to marry you in some weird roundabout way?"

He smiles—full-out brain-dead buzz—but his declaration has knocked me for such a big loop that I don't even get to enjoy that beautiful smile making me stupid. I gawk at him. There's no other way to describe it. My mouth hangs wide open, eyes bug out, and my breathing comes in rapid pants.

"No," he replies, still smiling even though I'm obviously dying. There's no other reason that my eyes would get even larger, my mouth gasping for breath even though I'm pulling air in and out with no problem. My body isn't equipped to deal with such up and down emotions in quick succession. Hell, my heart is still pounding wildly.

"Oh."

His smile grows, larger than I've ever seen it, and I curse him for being so damn handsome. His wicked words making me want something I didn't realize I wanted until he had put it out there. I mean, sure, I knew I loved him and never wanted to know life without him in it, but until he said that, I guess I just figured we would fall into whatever comes next naturally.

"I'm not asking because I know the answer already. Not because I don't want to." His body moves; this time, his deep guffaws echo around us.

"That's mighty presumptuous of you," I smart.

"Are you telling me that it isn't a forgone conclusion?"

He's still smiling, the beautiful jerk.

"I wouldn't go that far."

He throws his head back and laughs—loud, straight from his belly—and I feel the power of it instantly. It feels like someone just plugged me up to electricity. God, I will never get tired of seeing this side of him.

His shoulders continue to move, but he gives me his attention again. "You were right; what we have will always move at lightning speed. I've realized that now. You keep calling me hubby, making my dick hard, and one day when you have my ring on your finger, you can just roll with it. In my head, I don't need all that shit to know you're stuck with me for the next fifty plus years."

My chin wobbles, and he glances down. "I'm not going to cry," I defend, my words coming out shaky.

"You're right, you aren't. You're going to get naked, take my cock out, and show your *not* husband how much you love the idea of being stuck with him for the rest of your life."

I don't even bother trying to come up with something witty after that. Too in love and way too turned on, I jump from the bed, keeping my eyes on him while he works his cock free—stroking it with lazy movements—and I strip down to nothing.

I don't take a nap. I don't even get much sleep that night. Nor do I get a nap the next day before our show at the Pepsi Center. I did, however, wake up three days later to find a simple but the beautiful diamond band on my left ring finger. Chance never mentioned it, or how he was able to get it when he hasn't left my side once. He just continued moving around our hotel room, packing us up so we could meet the guys at the bus in thirty minutes to head out to Seattle.

The almost twenty-hour, two-day drive didn't even dull my euphoric mood. No one said a word, even if they noticed, and when we arrived at our hotel for the next two days, I made sure to show my *not* husband but very real fiancé just how much I love having his ring on my finger.

Chapter 28

Chance

Things went back to normal a few days after I slipped that band on Wren's finger back in Denver. I still haven't even said a word about it, but I don't need to. She's made no attempt to hide just how happy she is. Every time she would do something girly as fuck, like sigh in the middle of writing a song, her brother would look around until he connected with me. I'm not a stupid man; I know how important her relationship with Weston is. When I asked his permission to spend the rest of my life with his sister, he didn't hesitate. He took it a step further and arranged to have her band purchased and in my possession within the day's end. He might think she's being crazy—hence the meeting of the eyes with each sigh—but when I get an eye roll from him at his sister's antics, it's always with one hell of a smirk.

It's been a month since we left Denver, and things with their tour have been as normal as can be. Well, as normal as it gets with Loaded Replay, thousands of fans, and Douchebag Dix still trying his hardest to throw his weight around. We've all gotten damn good at ignoring him, or in my case, putting him in his place.

Dyllan hasn't come back out to meet us since she left Vegas. Wren explained it was normal for her to get stuck because her boss won't let her come out. Apparently, she's not a full-time stylist, but an intern with some big name back in LA. There's been a little strain between the two because Dyllan keeps brushing off Wren's concern. In the end, I told Wren she needs to just let it go. Whatever happens will, without her influence. She just needs to be prepared to support her friend whichever way things may fall. Of course, it took her almost until we left Seattle to stop punishing Jamison for her friend brushing her off.

In the time that we've been bussing from arena to arena, they released their last record with Brighthouse, selling over a million copies in the first week. When they got the call that *Black Lace* went platinum, it was a bittersweet excitement. Even though they know they have no future with Brighthouse, it's still hard to leave a label you've been with since the start of your career.

After a lot of consideration, they decided not to re-sign with a major label. Instead, they decided to start their own label, something so few artists have proven to pull off successfully. Loaded

Records is in its infancy stages, but they've been working to build a team they trust while on the road—not something easy to do, so that's the first order of business when we get back to LA.

In the time since I met with them back in New York, this world has become my home. It doesn't matter the location; this crazy bunch and the woman who has my band on her hand have become my home. It's funny now—looking back—but when I first told my old boss that I wanted to take this job, I never imagined that I would find all of this in the process. Hell, I never expected that I would find what I have with Wren, though, ever in my life, either. For years, I've watched as my friends fell in love and thought it was a crock of shit. Well, joke's on me because the love I have for Wren knocks me to my ass every single day I wake up to find her in my arms.

I glance over to where Wren and Wes have their heads tucked close over a pile of papers. They've been working together since we left out of San Francisco to head to LA for the final three shows of their tour a few hours ago. They've been working every chance they can on some new material. They know now that they'll be going to their own label, so time is the most valuable tool in their next solo album. The steady climb of *Black Lace* will be the momentum they need to push off of.

"Uh, guys?" Jamison addresses the room with a little unease in his voice.

"What?" Luke asks, glancing up from the guitar he had been messing with—giving Wren a melody when she would ask.

"Word got out about us leaving Brighthouse. People are going fucking nuts online wondering if this means we're splitting up."

"Shit," Wes hisses.

"Why would they announce us not renewing our contract before the tour is even over? Didn't they tell us that we couldn't say anything?" Wren asks, confused.

"Those motherfucking assholes," Wes fumes. "They didn't want *us* to say anything because they planned to use the news to drive up sales. They're going to play this up for all it's worth. Fans will be scared that's our last album—buying them with no thought. Brighthouse will play the sad label that lost a long-standing act, and because we signed a NDA not to speak about leaving Brighthouse, but specifically, not to say anything until the end of the tour, we're sitting ducks for the next five days."

"You're kidding?" I ask.

"I wish I was. I hope you and your guys have things ready because I bet we're going to be driving into a madhouse."

"I'll go call Hunter." I nod and walk from the front living room area of their tour bus to the back lounge area in the rear.

I hear them talking, low murmurs full of worry about what they're walking into, and wait for Hunter to pick up. I have a feeling calling what we will be dealing with a madhouse is like calling a gunshot wound a paper cut.

"Yeah," Hunter answers.

"You in LA yet?"

"We got here early this morning."

I sigh. "How are things looking around there?"

"Normal. The house was secure when we checked it out on

our way in a few hours ago."

"Do me a favor, Hunter. Head over there again and check on things. News got out about them not signing with the label again, so we need to be proactive with what is probably going to rain down on them. After that, meet us at the venue."

"Got it," Hunter confirms, disconnecting without pleasantries.

I've been waiting for Brighthouse to make a move. I knew they wouldn't let this go without a fight. I have to hand it to them; if what Wes says is true, they're smarter than I ever pegged them for. My gut has been telling me something is coming for a while now, but with this new bullshit, it's kicked up into overdrive. There haven't been any signs that the pictures and note that brought me here were something more nefarious. For the most part, everything points to it just being some fucked-up, isolated incident, but try as I might, I haven't been able to believe that's the case in all the time I've been here.

Making a split decision, I pick up the phone and make a call to someone who can lend a helping hand as a sounding board.

"Well, well … I was starting to think we would never hear from you again."

I smile, despite my unease. "Shut the hell up, Cohen," I gruff with fake annoyance.

"Dani won't shut the hell up about you and your girl. From how she tells it, you've been in love with her since some concert back during my last tour."

I huff out a laugh. "She's probably not wrong."

"No shit?" he asks.

"No shit. There isn't anything I wouldn't do if it meant a smile stayed on Wren's face." It feels good to tell Cohen about Wren. We've known each other for years now; we've served together, lived together—but with everything that happened with Dani before Owen was born, I pulled away. I hadn't realized how much I missed his friendship.

"I'm happy for you, man. You deserve to have that."

"Thanks," I respond, my voice thick with emotion.

"There for a while, I was worried you would push it away when you did find it, though."

"Cohen," I grunt, not wanting him to go down this road. Wren might have shown me the flaws in how I believed my role in his wife almost dying played out, but that doesn't mean I want to hash it out with him.

"Just tell me; have you finally realized you wrongly carried that burden all these years? I'll drop it, but I just need to know where your head is now that you've got what I have with Dani."

I look out the back window of the bus, seeing nothing even though the scenery flying by is far from unpleasant to look at.

"Wren helped me get there," I tell him with a deep exhale. "She's my healer, man. Anything that used to eat at me—she healed those wounds, and when she gave me her love, she eradicated any possibility that something might have lingered to come back later."

He doesn't speak right away. I hear him moving some papers around, and I picture him sitting in his office at Corps Security, knowing he's probably thinking about that day he almost lost everything while looking at the picture he always keeps on his desk of his family.

"Dani will be as happy as I am to hear that." He does a good job at hiding it, but his voice wavers slightly, and I know I'm not alone in feeling the slight burn of emotion in my throat.

"Now that we got girl talk out of the way," I jest, lightening the mood. "You got a second to let me run something by you?"

He clears his throat. "Go for it."

No-nonsense and all business. Just like my Cohen. He's a ba-dass with a heart of gold. Not only is he the type of friend who would do anything he can to help someone he cares about, but when it comes to security concerns, he's also learned from the best. Aside from his father or his father-in-law, no one else would be able to see the holes I can't.

"You know why I originally left, taking the job for security with Loaded Replay, right?"

"Yeah. Something about them dealing with a series of issues?"

"Yes … and no. A few of those issues were easy to explain or knock off the concern list. The only one left that still sits wrong with me is the pictures and note."

I explain to him what had been found, including the note, but even as fucked up as that situation was, nothing has happened since. Even the police would have brushed it off as nothing, but I just can't seem to let it go. We go over the label, them leaving, and the leak that hit the news today. And finally, I tell him what troubles me the most—that someone would go through that much trouble but then just end things without any other instances.

"Tell me, how much time passed between those pictures and when you showed up, feed the pregnancy and marriage rumor, and turned a fake relationship into the real thing?"

"Not even a full week. It happened in Tennessee, and then they were in New York for a week total. They had press set up for the beginning of that week; I showed up at the beginning of that, and then a few shows before we flew back to LA."

"So assuming that it might be someone close to her, maybe when you showed up—not knowing the relationship was a sham at the time—it changed things for them. You guys haven't denied the rumors that she's pregnant—I mean fuck, man, you play up this marriage rumor with a smile. Even I thought it was real, and I've known you for a long damn time. If they see you as taking her from the band, her pregnancy or just relationship in general, it will make sense to why the shit hasn't repeated since."

I think about what he's saying, feeling like this might be a key we had been missing. "Assuming I'm the reason it hasn't happened since, why wouldn't they make another move when it's clear she's still with the band?"

"Tour was winding down. Maybe they thought once she had that rumored baby, she wouldn't come back."

It doesn't make sense. I'm missing something here; I just know it. "And then what? Wren has a baby and leaves the group, so what does that person get out of it then?"

"Fuck," he mutters under his breath. "What's her relationship with the other guys like? Aside from her brother, I mean."

"They might as well all be her brothers, Cohen. Those four

are thick as thieves. Known each other their whole lives pretty much. They have a closeness that rivals what you and the guys have," I answer, referring to the guys he's known since birth—all of their parents being best friends.

"She's never had anything romantic with them?"

"Never, man. Jamison might flirt sometimes, but hell, he flirts with me too. That man doesn't mean anything by it when he's picking on Wren."

Cohen's silence is all I hear.

"What are you thinking, Coh?"

"Find out if someone is working that tour who might have had a relationship with Jamison. If you're right, and he's so open with his flirting, what if he had something with someone or turned them down, but flaunts his flirting with Wren in their face."

"Then it would make sense why they would want Wren gone," I finish, feeling a chill run up my spine.

"It makes sense," he adds.

"It does, unfortunately. Thanks, Cohen. I haven't been looking at things from that angle at all."

"There's nothing wrong with needing another head to see the part of the picture your blind side is facing."

Before Wren, I would have thought exactly the opposite, but I know he's right. Sometimes, things just aren't visible to you, no matter how hard you look or how trained you are to spot them.

"Hey, before I let you go, Cage or Axel around?" I ask, hoping he knows where his dad or father-in-law—also my bosses—are.

"Ax is here somewhere."

"Right, do me a favor and let me talk to him, so I don't have to make another call. And so you hear it from me, I'm about to tell him that my leave of absence will be permanent."

"What the fuck, Chance! It isn't your fault you didn't see that shit. Don't leave because you missed it."

I smile. "I'm moving out here to be with Wren, Cohen. She has my ring on her finger, and there isn't anything fabricated about that. I'm leaving so I can start my life with her."

"Oh. Right. Let me go get Ax," he responds, making my smile get bigger. "Here he is, man. And Chance?"

"Yeah?"

"I'm happy for you. Real fucking happy for you."

When I end the call ten minutes later, officially cutting all ties that I had back in Georgia, I don't feel the sadness I thought I would. It's the only place I had before Wren that even came close to feeling like home. When I made the decision to take the job Wren and the guys were offering, I knew this moment would come, but I just thought I would feel something other than ... relief. But with the blessing from two men who mean a whole hell of a lot, I know I didn't just leave good friends. They're always going to be there.

I just took the steps to start really living my life.

A life with a woman who loves me as much as I love her, free of the fear and pain I had been living with, knowing this was the last destroyed piece Wren had promised she would put back together.

And fuck, does it feel good.

Chapter 29

Wrenlee

"Sound check go okay?" Dyllan asks when I walk into the dressing room at the Staples Center.

"Yeah, always does here."

"What's up with you?" She moves to my side, looking at me with concern.

"Nothing. I'm just tired and stressed. I had hoped we would be able to go home for a while. I miss my bed. But Hunter called Chance before we even got close and said home was a no-go. Media circus there and it was easier to move us once here than have to get here, get there, and then get back. Too many moves for them to do on the fly or something."

"Things will die down. If not, just tell them you're having twins and not one baby like they assume."

I swat her, feeling some of the stress and exhaustion dissipate.

"Where is Chance?" She looks around, apparently just now figuring out he isn't with me. "God, you almost look weird without him attached to you."

"Oh, shut up. He's just outside in the hallway talking to the guys."

"About what?"

I shrug. "I'm guessing something about security. I stay out of it."

"Wouldn't that be a conversation you should be having with them?"

It did cross my mind, but I trust Chance, and if he felt the need to talk to them alone, then I wasn't going to argue with him. Instead of telling her all that, though, I just shrug. I would rather channel my inner sloth and put forth minimal effort at life until our show tonight.

Ten minutes later, the guys walk in. Wes and Luke look pissed, but Jamison almost looks dejected. I shoot my eyes to Chance, concerned, but he just holds up his hand, silently asking me to wait.

"Tell her," Chance demands, looking at Weston.

"Tell me what?"

"Fuck," Wes spits, kicking over the empty trashcan in the corner before looking at me. "I wasn't exactly truthful about why we needed to bring security in back in New York."

I look at Chance, my eyes wide. "What do you mean?" I ask when I'm finally able to look away from his steady gaze.

"I left out some shit that I didn't want to scare you with. I knew if I could just get you to agree to security, then you wouldn't need to know. I could share it with whomever we hired. You seemed so miserable, Wren. I didn't want to give you another reason to want to throw in the towel."

"I would never have thrown in the towel," I venomously defend.

"I did what I felt what right. I asked Chance to keep it from you because I knew he would protect you, even from the whole truth of what brought him there."

I narrow my eyes at Chance. He holds his hands up and points at Wes. "You can yell at me later. Let him finish."

"The pictures, they were bad, Wren. I didn't want you to know someone had violated your privacy that bad. You already looked at our lives cynical of everyone and everything. I hadn't seen you smile freely without lines of unhappiness. I didn't want to add to that. But they left a note too."

I gasp, fear crawling up my throat. "Tell me."

"You were sleeping, in bed, and there wasn't much covering you. The note basically warned you to leave Loaded Replay or there would be a next time that wasn't just pictures."

I reach behind me, searching blindly for something—any-thing—to ground me. Dyllan grabs my hand and pulls me back to the couch I had been sitting on earlier.

"What's changed?" I ask, feeling the wetness of my tears falling slowly down my face.

Chance must have had enough at the sight of them because he steps forward from his spot near the door. I hold my hand out, reaching for him even though I'm mad that he kept this from me. He's sitting next to me, gathering me up and onto his lap, before wrapping me in his protective embrace.

"Chance changed." Luke replied for Wes, and I look up to see my brother looking down. I have a feeling he's trying to get his emotions in check. One thing my big brother can't handle is knowing he's hurt me.

"I didn't change," Chance rumbles against my back. "I just talked things over with a colleague of mine. It's been bothering me that there hasn't been another attempt at contact with Wren. Nothing. I just needed to bounce things off him because I couldn't shake the feeling I was missing something. When I brought those things to the guys, Jamison gave me some information he had that confirmed Cohen was dead-on."

I glance around the room, my brother still avoiding my eyes. Luke's holding steady and strong, but Jamison is slouched in the chair, looking like he's just seen a ghost. My head spins, worried sick, and I turn to Chance—questions in my eyes.

"Cohen's theory is that it has less to do with someone wanting you, and more of them wanting you out of the way so they can have what they really want."

I shake my head, not understanding Chance's words.

His hold tightens before he continues. "When he asked me to

explain your relationship with the guys, I told him you guys were closer than siblings—aside from Jamison's flirting. I also told him Jamison flirts with everyone, but Cohen believed it was just the key I needed. He thought—and I have to say, now that I know everything, I have to agree with him—that this person had been on the receiving end of that flirting and felt like you were the reason it was either stopped or denied—depending on who it was. When Cohen came up with this, it was because of the belief that there hasn't been anything since. I showed up, and you were no longer considered a huge threat because everyone outside this room believed the rumors. However, now I know there hasn't been anything else because of that, but also because of what Jamison just told me."

My head spins, trying to figure this out with the overwhelming facts.

"What did Jamison say?" Dyllan asks, her voice quiet and scared.

"Tell them," Chance demands of Jami.

"Fuck!" Jamison explodes, knifing up to pace. He makes two quick paces before stopping, taking a huge lungful of air and looking at me. "I had a text that said now that you're married, I'm free to be theirs and they would be there every step of the way until I decided to come to them. I thought it was just some reporter who had gotten my number, trying to get confirmation about your baby rumors!"

"So it isn't me they're after but Jamison?" I ask the room, terrified.

"Essentially, yes. I believe that's the case," Chance tells my back, bending to press a kiss to my shoulder. "But that text makes me believe it's someone on the crew. They're the only ones who would be around constantly. I think they're waiting for him to come to them."

"Can you use me?"

Every head in the room jerks to Dyllan when she says those two words. Everyone except Chance, who shoots her down instantly. I look over my shoulder, seeing him study her with a practiced eye.

"Chance?" Panic bubbles up.

"Do you trust me?" he asks, his eyes colliding with mine, and I see something in them that makes me sit up a little straighter.

This is Chance in his element. The one who knows more about this than any of us ever could. But more importantly, this is *my* Chance, the man who has told me his deepest regrets and most painful secrets. This is *that* Chance asking me to trust *him*. This is *my* Chance showing me that he really did hear me almost two months ago when we lay in my bed. That he didn't just hear me, but at some point in our time together, those destroyed pieces healed completely for him—not just me.

This is him doing what he knows needs to be done and not letting the fear of losing someone who he loves in the process overwhelm him—driving him to retreat.

"Always," I say, my voice true and clear. My thoughts slam into me, making me feel the confidence in whatever he has planned because I trust him with not just me but also with the people I love.

Chapter 30

Wrenlee

"Do it," Chance whispers.

His eyes hold mine steady, trying to tell me without words that he loves me and it's okay, but I feel sick.

"I don't think I can."

My chin wobbles and fresh tears fall. They've been coming off and on since he went over his plan. He doesn't move, though. He stands there, clenching his jaw over and over—and flaring his nostrils.

"Do it, now."

"This kills me to even say the words, Chance."

"Do it so when this is all over, I can get my hands back on you and prove to you that nothing that happens next will change us."

I clench my eyes, more tears falling, and feel Dyllan take my hand—feeding me some strength through her hold.

"I love you, hubby," I sob softly.

Chance's eyes flash; he takes a step closer but doesn't touch me. We both know if he does, he won't be able to finish this. "I love you. Always. Now, do it."

Taking a deep breath, I will my tears away before squaring my shoulders and opening the dressing room door. "I'm sick of acting like I love you!" I scream, storming out of the room with him hot on my heels.

"What do you mean?" he questions, sounding confused.

I continue to rush down the hall, him keeping speed with me. "I'm sick of it!" I yell, repeating it over and over while we travel to the large area behind the stage. All of the crew is putting things together on, under, or around the stage. Those not working on that are in the space with us. Everyone who we need to hear is right here.

"It's over. I don't love you. I was just having fun. Now that Jamison is ready to be with me, you need to get the fuck away from us."

It will never be over. I love you.

"You don't mean that," Chance answers, sounding wrecked. In my head, I scream that he's right, I don't; I would never say this.

"Yes, I do. You make me sick! Now, get the fuck out of here so that I can get back to the man I love!"

Don't go. Never go!

His shoulders drop, and he makes one more attempt to reach me, but I back away. It takes everything I have not to pull him into my arms.

"Wren, we can fix this. I love you, baby."

That's when I feel Jamison, right on cue, and my stomach hurts with the pain of what's about to come.

"She said to fuck off," he cruelly hisses.

Then I feel my body being turned. Jamison looks down at me, his face not giving away anything, and I pray to God mine isn't either. Then he pulls me to him and presses his mouth to mine. It feels wrong. I feel like my heart is being shredded. The kiss isn't long, but it wasn't just a peck. When he lifts his head and gives me a wink, I know it's an act, but that wink crushes me.

"He's gone now. Come show me how much you missed me," Jamison continues his game, the roaring in my ears matching the throb of where my heart used to be.

True to his word, after the kiss, he would leave.

Even though I knew it would happen, looking up and seeing Chance gone makes it all seem like it wasn't an act at all.

I don't feel the familiar adrenaline rush hitting my body when we finish our show. I'm not even sure I was one hundred percent there tonight on stage either. We got through the show, though, and no one besides the four of us, Chance, and Dyllan were aware that our heads were not in the game. To them, we gave them a great show. Jamison and I made sure to play off each other more than we ever would. The banter between the four of us amped up not because we love being in our hometown, but because we know we have to continue to play our parts.

However, I draw the line at flirting on stage. It's one thing to put this lie on for the crew, knowing we have to, but it's another to betray my relationship to Chance with the world.

My stomach knots when we finish and walk off the stage. No one is around to take my shit this time, so I drop the mic, placing it on the table with the other backup mics. I rip my earpieces off and throw them in the same general direction as the mic.

I knew Chance wouldn't be standing here when we finished. His vacant normal spot reminds me of what his face looked like earlier—raw and real pain slicing through his features. It was fake—that's what I keep reminding myself—but he made it look so real that I can't help thinking it might have been. What if I lost him forever because of this?

Luke and Wes keep back, but as planned, Jamison saddles up to my side and kisses my temple.

"Get your sweet ass back in the dressing room, dollface. I want you naked, bent over, and just waiting for me to come get my prize."

I giggle. It's what they told me to do. Running off with a sassy wave, I head toward our dressing room.

I'm terrified, but I know Chance is here. I feel his eyes on me the second I turn the corner, headed down the hallway in a rush for our dressing room.

When I get the door open, I pace quickly to get some of the jitters out of my body. I want to call out to see if Dyllan is still inside the bathroom, waiting, just in case, ready.

I'm standing there for so long, I start to fear maybe Chance wasn't right, and it isn't someone on the crew. What if I have to do this again tomorrow? Or worse, what if I have to take this shit public? Can I go on with this if we don't end it tonight?

The door opens, and I reach up to start unzipping the zipper that runs the length of my tank top, right between my tits. "Took you long enough," I hum seductively, turning while lowering the zipper.

"You just couldn't listen."

I finish my turn quickly when I hear a voice that I know doesn't belong.

"You couldn't just stay away? He was going to be mine! You couldn't just continue being a whore with that man, could you? You had to ignore my warning and move back in on my man!"

I back up, trying to get away from her. "Kellie?" I ask, playing like I don't understand her. "What warning?"

"I should have killed you that night I broke into your hotel room. If I had killed you then, I wouldn't have to do it now. You're making me kill a baby, and I don't like that, you slut."

"Kellie, I don't understand," I rush, trying to let the fear of her words wash over me. Chance said we needed to get her on tape. We need to get as much as we can on tape—that hopefully, Dyllan is recording—so that we ensure she goes away for a long time.

"You just think you're so perfect." She takes a step away from the door, her eyes looking manic and completely out of control. "You're nothing but a whore, and there is no room on this earth for people like you."

"But my baby," I hedge, holding out my hands and begging—not even faking the terror I feel. For the first time since all this started with Chance, I'm thankful that the 'baby' in question was never real.

"You're not that far along. Your belly is still flat. But I'll make sure and stab you right through the belly so your baby dies quickly and doesn't feel the pain of its dirty, nasty mother."

Oh. My. God.

She advances, lifting up her arm to show a lethal, terrifying knife. I back up, trip, and fall to the floor just in front of the bathroom. I hear Dyllan make a cry in alarm, but thankfully, she doesn't leave the safety of the room where she's hiding.

Just when Kellie takes another step, still too far away from me to get her hands on me, the door opens, and the blessed sight of Chance with four Los Angeles police officers enter with practiced ease. I can't even focus on them because I'm sobbing so hard that my vision is blurry with tears and lack of solid air. I feel slim arms wrap around me, and I jerk in the hold.

"It's just me," Dyllan reassures, curling around the ball that I've turned myself into. "It's okay, Wren. Everything's over, and you were so brave."

Dyllan keeps holding me, rocking me softly, until long after the cops, Chance, and the crazy woman leave. When I finally look up, seeing the room empty of the one man I need more than anything right now, I lose it again.

God, what if I lost him because of this? What if, even though it was his plan, he can't get over seeing Jamison kiss me?

What have I done?

Chapter 31

Chance

Wes, Jamison, and I walked out of the LAPD hours later both mentally and physically tired. Before this all went down, we planned for Luke—along with Hunter—to stay back and be in charge of Wren and Dyllan. The plan was to get them out of the arena and back to the house, where we would hopefully be right behind them.

But that was when I had assumed we would be in and out quickly. We were handing them an open-and-shut case, along with the responsible party. But no one can ever accuse them of not being thorough.

In the end, Kellie Wallton wouldn't be a free woman for a long damn time. She was talking nonsense that no one could understand for hours. Finally, they listened to my suggestion to mention Jamison's name. After that, she sang like a fucking canary.

"God, that bitch was certifiable." Jamison drops heavily into the back of the SUV I arranged to be waiting for us.

"Whatever is beyond that. That's what she is." Wes sounds as tired as he looks when he drops his body into the front seat with a heavy slump.

I don't add my thoughts. I want to say plenty, but right now, all I can focus on is my need to get to Wren.

When I left, seeing her fallen and in a tight protective ball, sobbing into Dyllan, I felt like my heart had stopped beating. The need to get to her, show her that we're okay, is a beast inside me. I know why she didn't want to do this, but I also know she was putting her trust in me—to show me that she believes the words she changed my life with—but that she fears she lost me in the process. It was my plan. I knew Jamison would kiss her in the end. It needed to happen to be believable if, in fact, I was correct about the crew worker end. They had to see that; not so they would believe Wren and I were ending, but so they would see Jamison betraying what she believes was some sort of relationship.

It worked.

I just have to prove to Wren that this will never change us.

"How is she?" I ask Dyllan, my voice not sounding like my own.

Weak.

Worried.

But my body feeling confident.

"She cried herself to sleep." She sighs, standing from the couch that she had been sleeping on.

"Fuck." My shoulders slump, and I feel terrible for ever asking this of her. Even knowing it was the right move doesn't take away the pain of her heartache.

"You know, she loves you, Chance. She's hurting because it wasn't me she wanted here—but I think she's scared out of her mind that she finally found her happy ending only to have it tainted by this woman. She believes in you, that much is clear, but she's out of her mind that shit earlier was in the same category as her cheating."

"What?"

"I didn't say it makes sense. She's new at this. Go show her what true love feels like," Dyllan whispers, a sad smile on her face.

I walk down the hallway toward Wren's room. The lights are off when I open the door and walk through the miniature living room to stand at the end of her massive bed. She's curled up on the very edge of the bed with her red hair fanned around her. She looks even smaller than she normally does, the large bed swallowing her size.

Her breath hitches in her sleep. The sound that you hear small kids make after they've been crying uncontrollably for so long. It snaps me into action, kicking off my boots and pulling everything off except my briefs—needing to feel her against my skin.

She doesn't move when I climb onto the bed behind her. Not even when I wrap my arm around her and pull her against my body. The kisses I pepper up her bare arm aren't noticed. But when I move my mouth to her ear and whisper her name, she jolts, coming away instantly with a soul-wrenching sob.

"Hey," I coo, trying to console her. "Baby, calm down and take a deep breath. I'm here, Wren."

Her breath hitches, sounding painful as it catches in her throat, and she shifts out of my arms to sit up, pulling her legs up and wrapping her arms around them.

"Talk to me," I beg, feeling helpless. I sit up and try to reach out to her, but she pulls back, almost falling off the bed.

"I didn't want to do it," she cries, her face wet with the tears falling rapidly.

"I know, baby. I know."

"I've never felt so sick about something in my life. I hated it." She shakes her head back and forth. "It killed me to see that look on your face, knowing you were about to see me with another man."

"Wrenlee, I know it wasn't real. I know it didn't mean anything."

"I promised to fix all those destroyed pieces, and I took a hammer right to the heart of them and heaved a swing full of damage."

God, she's killing me. I reach out, placing my hand on one of her arms. Her head jerks up, eyes colliding with mine, and she lets out a cry from deep in the pit of her belly. "Wrenlee," I try again, hoping she hears me.

"I'm so sorry," she shakily cries.

"Baby, you have nothing to be sorry for. You were so brave. I should never have asked that of you, but I knew it was the only way to end it quickly. My gut has never been wrong. I took a gamble, but I did that because you taught me I had the strength to do it in the first place."

"I kissed another man, Chance. I betrayed us."

Having enough, I grab her and roll our bodies until I'm on top of her at the other edge of the bed. My hands cupping her face, my mouth just a breath away from hers, and my body holding her where I know she will be forced to hear me.

"You played the part that needed to be played to ensure that not only was that sick fuck put away for good, but you did it for us too. Maybe it would have been better weeks ago, but I've been working without the full deck this whole time. I couldn't do anything to change the timeline. And I wouldn't even if I could. It's because of that time you've healed me with your love. We used that time wisely because we built something together that will never be breakable. You told me once that everything happens for a reason, and Wren, I need you to believe those words."

"All I see when I close my eyes is your face when I told you I didn't love you," she wobbles through her mouth.

"I know you didn't mean it. I was playing my part."

"It killed me to think that you might not be able to look at me again."

"No, Wren. That would never happen."

"It's really over?" she asks with tears still in her voice.

"It's over. Now, it's time for us to begin the rest of our forever."

"I love you, so much." Her eyes are still blurry with tears, but she is smiling up at me instead of looking heartbroken.

"God, Wren. You will never know how much I love you."

"Then show me."

Chapter 32

Wrenlee

"Then show me," I whisper, my words just a breath of air between us.

He studies my face before lowering his mouth. He doesn't go to my mouth, which is what I expected. Instead, he starts to kiss the wetness on my cheeks. Moving from side to side with each soft brush of his mouth, he removes the evidence of my sadness. He doesn't stop until he's satisfied that he's removed every wet line. Lifting up to study me one more time, he presses his lips to mine—finally.

He doesn't rush our connection.

His mouth takes mine in a deep, slow, soul-consuming kiss. Each lazy swipe and tangle of his tongue against mine sends a shockwave of bliss straight down my spine, exploding in a small burst of pleasure between my legs. I'm desperate for him; the need to have him fill me the only way he can hits a fever pitch. My legs scissor, trying to get loose of the hold his body on top of mine has so I can spread them wide and feel him against me wholly.

Chance makes a noise, one that I swallow through our fused mouths, telling me he's denying me and to remind me he's in control. I whine, pathetically.

He pulls back, his mouth wet from our kisses, eyes roaming over my face and down to my chest, covered by the material of the shirt I had yanked on before falling asleep earlier—his shirt. I watch his eyes flare the second he notices whose shirt I'm wearing, but still, he doesn't speak. His weight shifts minutely on top of me so he can balance on one elbow. He brings his free hand up, long dexterous pointer finger extended as he traces the font on the front of the shirt—placed in the perfect center of my chest.

My nipples strain, begging him to do more than dance over them. He has to notice; how could he not? But still, he denies me. Slowly, repeating the process—over and over—until I'm writhing with need under him. All from the subtle brush of the tip of his finger as he traces some stupid brand name on the cotton. I'm pretty sure I'll never look at American Eagle the same again.

When he looks back up, his eyes are pure liquid. The green

and blue swirls are twisting together so vibrantly; it almost looks like they're really moving. The color on his tan cheeks tells me he is burning for me just as badly as I'm burning for him.

No words are needed.

No sweet nothings.

None of that.

Because when he gives me this completely open expression, I feel like I can see straight into his heart.

Without looking away, he moves us so that I'm on top—hands resting against his defined stomach muscles, legs spread to welcome the cotton-covered thickness, and wild hair dancing around my face. His hands rest on my bare thighs as his thumbs rub in soothing sweeps. I have only a second to sink in his unguarded handsome features before he slowly lifts his back from the bed. His abs ripple under my palms as he moves his hands up my body, dragging my shirt and arms up in the process until he has me naked except for my panties.

His head dips, eyes still connected to mine, and he opens his mouth around one of my pointed nipples. He sucks—greedily—pulling not just my nipple into his mouth, but also the meaty flesh of my breast. His suction doesn't ease as he flattens his tongue and slathers my nipple with attention. I squirm, rubbing myself against his hardness, the pleasure of it zinging through me. When he pinches my free nipple, I whine.

I'm dizzy with need. Having his hands and mouth on my sensitive breasts while my pussy soaks my panties only heightens the demand for more. I lose his hand when I start rocking, and he grabs both sides of my hips to stall the process.

I could cry with disappointment.

He switches to the other breast, and I roll my head back, unable to hold myself up anymore, trusting his hold on my hips to keep me where we both want him to be.

It isn't until I truly feel like I'm going to go into a lust-driven madness that he finally removes his mouth with a soft pop, echoing through my bedroom. He lifts me off his hips, setting me on my ass next to him before rolling off the mattress and standing next to the bed. I sit up and turn, my legs straight in front of me. If I pointed my feet, I could probably graze my toes against the bulge in his briefs. As soon as the thought hits my mind, though, he hooks his thumbs in the waistband and pulls them down his legs, kicking them behind him with no care to where they land. His thick cock springs free, pointing directly at me, a drop of come drips from the ruddy tip as I study him, telling me that he enjoys my appreciation.

I lick my lips, still eyeing the part of him where I could spend days upon days of worshipping, feeling my core tighten shamelessly in want. I see his arms move, but I'm not even registering the destination until I feel a firm grip on both ankles. My back hits the mattress a second later when he uses his hold to pull me forcefully to the edge of the mattress—spreading my legs wide right when it feels as if my ass is dangling completely off the bed. A soft scream leaves my shocked mouth when he lifts my legs, placing my ankles on each of his broad shoulders and ripping my lace panties at each hip a moment later.

His hungry gaze narrows between my legs. I don't need to see what he does to know what has him held with rapt attention. I can feel how wet my bare sex is the second the cold air hits my flesh. The slow roll of my arousal as it leaks from my center, traveling down my crack until it falls from my body. I should be slightly ashamed of just how wet I am. Instead, I eat it up—loving the expression on his face as he sees the evidence of just how badly I crave him.

Stepping forward, closer to me, he doesn't release my legs. My chin goes to my chest so I can look down my body, watching over my heaving chest as he connects the parts of us that demand attention—equally needy. His cock touches my slit, pushing up until his length is resting against my wetness, the tip pointing up between our bodies.

He rocks his hips, coating himself with my cream. Over and over, I watch as he repeats the slow movement until he has to stop because we're both shaking too badly in need. My legs almost slip from his shoulders, but he reaches up to steady them in place. I lift my body, reaching down to wrap my fingers as far around him as I can. The hot flesh, soaked from my wetness. A small burst of come escapes his control when my hand touches him, running down his cock in one long stream until it settled against my pussy. I have no idea how he was able to stop his orgasm, only allowing a small burst of come to eject from his body, but I don't dare move my hand. I know he's on the edge here, evident in how tightly restrained he's holding his whole body, literally vibrating with the effort to hold himself back.

I move his cock until the tip of him is resting against my entrance. If he's going to come again, I want to feel the burning heat of it inside my body, not on me. I clench my core muscles around his bulbous head, getting a low moan from him that I feel down my legs seconds before he steps into me, bottoming out. His hands hit the mattress, bending me in half with my legs still captive by his body. He isn't resting his weight completely on me, making sure he isn't hurting me, but with my legs held straight, it pushes my hips off the mattress to give him an angle into my body that we've never touched. He's impossibly deep, stretching me, and I swear to God, I feel like he's touching my womb.

Whimpers, cries, and moans come from me as I adjust to the thickness invading my body so quickly. I feel myself growing wetter as the evidence starts to fall down and over my asshole. I don't think I've ever been this wet.

"I love you." He groans, still not moving.

"God, Chance." I gasp, needing *something*, anything. "I love you too. I love you. Love you, so much."

His hips move, pulling out the tiniest bit before entering me again. Each time he pulls back, I lose more and more of his length, but he always comes back sinfully slow. The lazy ebb makes way for an even slower slide back into my body.

I feel him everywhere.

Not just inside me—spreading me wide and filling me full— but over every inch of me. But *everywhere* I never knew it was possible.

My skin burns with the heat of his touch. My lungs fill with

285

the tantalizing scent of his cologne mixed with the essence of our sex. My eyes visually see the adoration reflecting in his own eyes, as my heart fills with the overpowering mix of all my senses coming together with an explosion of love in its purest form.

There isn't an inch of me that doesn't feel *him ... us*, and I know this is so much more than him showing me his love.

This is *us* completing the process of repairing the pieces our destroyed pasts had left in their wake. A wall of protection forming around those memories so that they will never be able to hurt us again as we fulfill the promise that I had given him when I told him to take a gamble on us almost two months ago.

Earlier today, I went through every emotion on the gauntlet until I truly wasn't sure I would survive. My fears had come back, and I was terrified that I had lost him. Convincing myself that everything I had finally begun to love again about my life would return to a daily torture session of desperation to feel whole. I knew if he came back to me and said he regretted us or that the threat of another stalker coming into my highly publicized life was too great a risk for him given his past—I would let him go, but it would kill me.

I trust him. I mean that and will always mean that. I also knew going into that plan that if I lost him while I healed him—showing him that he had the power to heal from the fears he had about letting those he loves get hurt—it would be worth it because he would be free from that.

I should have known better and trusted not only him but our love too because right now, with his body moving above and into mine, I know that nothing will ever be able to compromise the solidity of our bond.

My knight in tarnished armor had finally found his broken princess, high in her jaded tour—changing both of our lives for eternity.

This is the evolution of two jaded hearts seeing the beauty of life again.

This is the creation of two broken souls, healing solidly, connected as one.

This is the foundation of an unbreakable love.

This is the clarity of our forever love.

Epilogue

I t's been the talk of the entertainment world since Loaded Replay left their former label, Brighthouse Records. It's no shock to the industry that since their departure, Brighthouse has been struggling to find someone to fill the large shoes that Loaded Replay left behind. Even with the overwhelming success of *Black Lace*, the last record released by their former label, Brighthouse hasn't been able to recover. It wasn't until news of the label's mistreatment to their artists started to leak that Brighthouse was forced to tuck the proverbial tail between their legs and try to contain the damage. There's no news yet on what the rumors mean for the future of Brighthouse Records, but as more artists follow in the departing footsteps of Loaded Replay, one could only guess that future is bleak.

As for Loaded Replay, they've found nothing but success in the year since forming their own label—Loaded Records. Everyone was waiting to see what would happen, but the fabulous foursome proved to fans worldwide why they're such an unstoppable force.

Their first solo album, *OURS*—aptly named to celebrate the control they were taking with their music and lives—was released merely five months after the announcement that they would be forming their own label. I don't think anyone was shocked when they took over the charts, staying in the top ten for the last thirty weeks since its release, with no signs of leaving anytime soon.

Fans around the world have been going nuts with excitement over the new album, but that excitement hit a fever pitch when Loaded Replay announced they would be going back on tour mid-year. This will mark almost a year and a half since their last worldwide tour. No doubt, the break is largely due to them building their Loaded Empire, but also because they already have plans to release a second album before that tour. *YOURS* is set to drop in just two short months.

A label representative credited *YOURS* to Loaded Replay's hidden vault, music that the group created solely on their own with songs personal to their own struggles during their first few years in the industry. It's raw, honest, and relatable to many hard issues listeners may have—*YOURS*, if you will, to use as a guide toward finding whatever you may be searching for.

There isn't a single person—aside from possibly their former label—who isn't thrilled to see Loaded Replay proving wrong the few critics and doubters out there. There is no doubt that their career shows no sign of stopping, even having many jokes that they have the Midas touch.

While their career is at an all-time high, all four of them have remained incredibly humble. Even though they are—for the most part—fiercely protective of their privacy, they seem to enjoy the sport of evasion and speculation more. Lead singer's, Wrenlee Davenport, relationship with Chance Nash—a former Marine and security specialist now head of Loaded Records' security teams— is still very much unconfirmed by the duo. The two have famously been taunting the world with just how committed they 'might' be since news of their relationship broke earlier in the year. Even without confirmation, Wrenlee has had a diamond band on her hand for almost the whole duration of that year, but it wasn't until recently that one appeared on Chance's finger. For now, they continue to answer the question of their marriage with laughter and ambiguity.

With their rising star still climbing high, Weston Davenport, Luke Madden, and Jamison Clark still seem to be linked only to their label and the success of Loaded Replay. While the singlehood of their female lead is very much over, fans everywhere are left guessing who will be next to find love while taking the music world by storm.

I don't know about you, but everyone here at *Modern Rock* can't wait to join Loaded Replay for another year that promises to be another career high for the group.

The End

Loaded Replay will be back next year with Jamison stepping into the spotlight.

Manufactured by Amazon.ca
Bolton, ON